TANGLED WEBS

T.T. Henderson

Parker Publishing, LLC
www.Parker-Publishing.com

Parker Publishing LLC

Noire Allure is an imprint of Parker Publishing LLC.

Copyright © 2008 by T. T. Henderson
Published by Parker Publishing LLC
12523 Limonite Avenue, Suite #440-438
Mira Loma, California 91752
www.parker-publishing.com

This book is a work of fiction. Characters, names, locations, events and incidents (in either a contemporary and/or historical setting) are products of the author's imagination and are being used in an imaginative manner as a part of this work of fiction. Any resemblance to actual events, locations, settings, or persons, living or dead, is entirely coincidental.

ISBN: 978-1-60043-024-4
First Edition

Manufactured in the United States of America

Cover Design by Jax Crane

DEDICATION

To Alan—for your sweet caresses, easy banter, playful tackles, insatiable desire and unwavering love. May our love affair never end.

Chapter One

Jewel St. John sat on the commode, knees pushed together, red thong underwear lying carelessly about her $400 pumps. She was a woman who had everything, but for the first time, she had something she wasn't at all certain she wanted.

The word "pregnant" seemed to grow larger in her mind as she stared at the plastic indicator stick in her hand. "I'm pregnant," she said quietly. The words, when spoken aloud, created an uncomfortable tightness in her gut. Where was joy? Happiness? Or any other positive emotion she was supposed to be feeling right now?

"What's wrong with me?" She tossed the stick into the gold filigree wastebasket near her sunken tub and tried to suppress her growing disappointment and anger.

She was exactly like Eloise; that's what was wrong with her. And this proved it, Jewel decided. She and Trevor had been waiting for five years for this pregnancy. For months, she'd taken fertility shots, tested her ovaries and fallopian tubes. Trevor had gone from wearing briefs to boxers to ensure a high sperm count. They'd had to make love at the right time, on the right day... Jewel smiled... Well, not everything had been a hardship. Still, every month they'd hoped for this news.

And here she was, taking a pregnancy test in her bathroom behind a locked door so she could carefully gauge her reaction without her husband witnessing it. Hell, she should be flipping cartwheels right now.

Irritably, she stood and tugged her panties back into place with a snap of elastic. Leaning across the cool marble counter of the sink, Jewel looked into the depths of her dark brown eyes. "Don't do it, girl." She searched the panicked eyes in the mirror. "Don't be like her."

"Jewel?" Her husband's voice sounded anxious on the other side of the bathroom door. Cool, calm Trevor never sounded anxious. "Anything yet? If you're having trouble with that pregnancy test,…" he offered.

"I'm doing fine, hon. It's okay." And it would be. So what if she was going to be a mother? If she raised her child as Granny Glen had raised her, it would be okay. Plus, Trevor was the father. She smiled. Her anxiety eased and the tightness in her stomach relaxed.

This will make Trevor happy, and Lord knows, when that man's happy, you're happy! She winked at the now calm and confident dark-chocolate face in the mirror. Collecting herself mentally, Jewel unlocked the door then threw it open. She draped herself seductively in the doorway. "Trevor St. John, do I look any different?" she asked, tossing back her long, freshly relaxed hair and running a hand down her bare chocolate midriff.

An unrestrained smile stretched across her husband's sexy, bearded face. He was gorgeous. He was dressed in a navy suit with a gold tie and had his hands tucked deep inside his pants pockets. Jewel could hear the change and keys jingling in his trousers, indicating his excitement.

"You're pregnant?" Despite the low timbre, his voice held wonder.

"Looks that way," Jewel teased, feeling a moment of envy as Trevor whooped and pumped a fist into the air, barely able to contain the happiness she seemed incapable of experiencing. "Don't I get a kiss or something?" she asked, suddenly needing to feel the strength of his embrace, the comfort of his love.

He took a step toward her but didn't reach for her. Instead, he held her in his gaze. "Have I told you how absolutely incredible you are?" he asked breathlessly.

Jewel warmed as the deepness of his voice shook loose her lust. That was better. She liked having his full attention.

Craving his touch, she arched toward him. "Don't tell. Show."

She parted her lips, inviting his kiss.

Trevor placed a warm hand on her belly and moved it in slow circles over her tiny red panties. "I've waited all my life for this."

Jewel knew he meant having a baby, and the thought messed with her groove. "Don't talk," she instructed. "Touch." She moved his hand lower until the width of his hand forced her legs apart.

Of his own accord, he brought his other hand around her hip and warmed her bare behind with massaging motions.

The subtle scent of his cologne swirled around Jewel. She trembled as his fingers fondled and teased the most sensitive parts of her body. He could still drive her wild even after five years of marriage.

"This is a miracle." Trevor kissed her neck and shoulders. "You're a miracle."

Jewel closed her eyes and sighed. She loved the way he touched her, kissed her, held her. "Trevor, if you don't make love to me right now, I swear I'll die," she said, sucking in air. She brushed the neatly trimmed coarseness of his beard with her cheek and pushed her tongue into his mouth, needing to feel closer to him.

Trevor's groan was low and long. "Don't start, Jewel." He pulled away only slightly. "You know we've got places to go," he warned, even as his hands moved beneath her thong, making her warm and wet.

"I know. But guess what?" She kissed his ear and brought her arms around his narrow waist to cup his behind in her hands.

"What?" he asked, his voice dripping in lust.

Jewel pressed her bare stomach against the magnificent erection straining the fine material of his slacks. "We're the hosts of the luncheon. They can't start without us." She pulled his shirt out of his slacks and ran her hands up the warm, hard planes of his back. He felt so good.

"That's true," he admitted between the kisses he trailed up her neck. "But you're trying to sell these people on a vision. You're asking them for their money and their time. If you waste their time by keeping them waiting, they may not give up the Benjamins. Then, where would you be, hmm?"

His hands were now moving over her bra and driving her mad.

Always the salesman, she thought, closing her eyes to better enjoy the feel of his mouth as he ravaged her face, her mouth, her breasts. "We would be right here, Trevor. Making love like we just don't care. And right now, baby, I don't care one lick about those folks." She let her head fall back and her arms open wide as if to prove it.

Trevor laughed and brought a hand between her breasts to the front clasp of the flimsy red undergarment. He released it with one deft movement and filled his hands with her flesh. "You wouldn't say that if you were in your right mind, my jewel."

Opening her eyes, Jewel met her husband's soft, sexy stare as he fingered her nipples. It was heady to see herself in his eyes, to see his love reflected back at her. "You're so fine," she breathed. "How could I ever be in my right mind around you?"

His arms were around her the next instant, his mouth soft, warm and needy as he kissed her. "I love you, Jewel. Good Lord, how I love you," he said.

"Show me," Jewel insisted breathlessly. "Show me."

He had no choice. Jewel drove him insane with desire. Always had. Trevor eased her onto the bed and filled his mouth and hands with her essence. He tasted her soft, ebony skin, licking, kissing, and suckling like a child tasting his first chocolate candy. Her moans and gasps fueled his overheated passion, making him hot and hard. Trevor loved that she wanted him and was happy to forget about the clock. Happy to forget everything except the way he felt when he pushed inside the soft, brown velvet of Jewel's thighs.

His heart and his loins joined in one focused goal, to love Jewel St. John as she'd never been loved before, to show his appreciation for the gift she had given him. A child. Trevor had wanted a baby for as long as he could remember. And after five long years, he and his gorgeous wife were going to be a real family.

"Oh, Trevor," Jewel panted and thrust up against him quicker, forcing Trevor to lose all thought and quicken his pace. He liked making love to her slow and easy, but today she wasn't having it. "I see what you want," he smiled and eased up to his knees. He draped one shapely leg after the other over his shoulders and cupped her soft bottom in the palms of his hands.

"Yes, Trevor. That's it," she urged.

Trevor felt the warmth as he disappeared inside her dark folds and cursed softly. This was too good to last long. He would need an act of God to keep his satisfaction at bay for much longer. "Sweet, Jewel," he said, feeling his control slipping away. "You'd better come on, baby," he urged.

"I'm almost there," she promised, tensing and tightening around his member, sending shock waves through Trevor's system. They moved in perfect unison for several more incredible moments. And then it came—the gloriously fleeting moment when they became one. Neither breathed. Neither spoke as they experienced the burst of pure joy that filled their bodies with light and energy before lessening to short ebbs and flows of contentment that drifted from one to the other.

Completely drained, Trevor rolled off his wife to regain his strength and his breath.

"That was incredible, Sir Trevor," Jewel panted as she called her husband by his pet name. "Absolutely incredible."

"Glad you liked it." Trevor felt smug as he enjoyed the chill of air conditioning on his overheated body. "Because we're going to be really late."

"No, we're not." Jewel jumped up from the bed and ran to the bathroom. "I'm not going to let it happen," she called out from behind the glass blocks enclosing the shower. A moment later she was pulling Trevor from the bed. "Let's go, studly."

He didn't understand how she had so much energy when all he wanted was to curl up for a nice nap. She was five years younger, he reminded himself. Still, he didn't remember being so full of spirit at the age of thirty-five. "All right, cruel woman. I'm up." He eased from the bed and made quick work of cleaning up and dressing.

They were out of the house in fifteen minutes flat. Trevor took the driver's seat of their Jaguar while Jewel put the finishing touches on her makeup. "I don't know why you bother with that stuff," he said as he steered around their circular drive.

"Camouflage," she said. "Gotta hide all the imperfections."

Trevor stopped the car and took a hard look at her. "You have none. You're perfect in every way, Jewel St. John," he said with all the love in his heart.

His wife leaned over and rewarded him with a long, slow kiss. "You're so good for me," she said. "Now drive or we'll never make it."

Because he was suddenly thinking of taking her back to bed, Trevor did as he was told.

Rae Angelique Paris pulled her wrap tightly around her shoulders to guard against the chill of the January air. There was no wind inside the parking garage, only the bitter chill of air held captive between concrete slabs. Rae hated the cold. "That's why I live here in San Antonio, Texas," she grumbled as she walked quickly toward the elevator that would take her to the hotel lobby. "If I'd wanted to be in thirty degree weather, I would've moved to Montana or something."

Of course, the weather wasn't what had put her in a foul mood. It was that dog Tyree. The nerve of him taking off in her car as if he had a right. Without looking back, Rae pointed the small remote key chain toward her new pride and joy, the Hummer H2, and chirped the security system into place. Her dream car had cost her a bundle two months ago, and worth every penny to have a car big enough to fit her long, six-foot frame into comfortably. However, she was beginning to believe it wasn't worth having Tyree around. The sex was good, but he was walking around her house, eating her food, using her phone, and making a mess as if he lived there.

"That'll be a real cold day," she said out loud just as the elevator chimed open. Rae smiled politely at the Hispanic couple as they exited. Stepping inside, she pushed the button that would take her to the lobby of the Westin Hotel. By the time she stepped out onto the lovely marble flooring, she had resolved to kick Tyree's behind to the curb the second she got home that evening.

In the meantime, she thought about the reason she was here—primarily because of Trevor St. John. They'd been best friends since junior high. Both had a passion for basketball, and both had wanted desperately to become wealthy and leave the east side of town.

Rae smiled. For the most part, they'd both done exactly as planned. They both lived on the northeast side of town, and she'd played pro ball in Europe for five years. They'd been through a lot—good times and bad. And now he was happily married, a thought that made it difficult to sustain her moment of good humor. In truth, even as she stood beside Trevor as his "best woman" at the wedding, she hadn't expected the marriage to last; both Trevor and Jewel had such strong—and opposite—personalities, Rae had been certain one of them would hurt the other.

Rae headed for the ballroom where Jewel's luncheon was being held. Even this, Trevor supported. The woman was never satisfied with the status quo. She always had some project, some idea, some scheme cooked up that Trevor just went along with. Homeboy was sooo whipped, she thought, knowing her jealousy was messing with her head. She hadn't been as lucky in love, and it was downright depressing.

Rae, feeling herself overheat, removed her overcoat and folded it over her arm. Over the years, she'd found many a male companion, but no relationship that had a chance of lasting. It was her own fault, and she knew it. She didn't seem able to do anything about it.

Falling into step behind a lively group of well-dressed black couples, Rae noted how one heavyset gentleman guided his lady with a hand placed gently at her waist. Another couple held hands as if they were still twenty and not the forty or fifty their graying hair indicated. Rae hated public displays of affection…mainly because none was being displayed toward her.

In vain, she tried to find away to get past the group, but they filled the hallway with their lively gestures and sheer numbers. She guessed she would look rude elbowing her way through them. Buying patience at the price of gnawing her lip, she followed the group at a distance until the throng of people in the ballroom finally enveloped them.

Rae stood in the doorway of the big room. It was a grand place, from its richly ornate carpeting to its fabulously opulent chandeliers. The chairs were a soft mauve and the tablecloths pure white. Gazing upon the sea of good-looking Black folk who were chatting in ever-shifting groups, Rae had never felt more alone.

Just as she decided she'd rather be home watching How Stella Got Her Groove Back for the hundredth time, Rae spotted the most spectacular-looking Black man the Lord had ever placed on the face of the earth. The man exuded sexuality and sensuality, wearing them like a tailor-made suit. Rae approached him as he talked with a group of older women who, she noted, were barely able to hold back their admiring looks and dentured grins. "Hey, handsome," she whispered in his ear, "how about you and I getting out of this place?"

Trevor laughed, turned and moved Rae forward with a gentle hand to her back to introduce her. "Ladies, this is Rae Paris, the new coach of our WNBA expansion team. What's the team's name again?" he asked as he finished the introduction.

"The San Antonio Silver Spurs," Rae offered, thrilled that Trevor thought enough about her new job to mention it.

"These lovely ladies are in an investment group," Trevor continued, acknowledging the three sixty-something ladies dressed in their Sunday finest—including fancy hats. The ladies acknowledged Rae politely but could hardly keep their eyes from Trevor.

Rae had to admit the man looked good in navy. Of course, she'd always considered Trevor to be handsome...even when he'd been a skinny, awkward fifteen-year-old.

"It's a pleasure to meet you, ladies. Jewel will be thrilled you came," Trevor offered and turned his attention to his friend. "Let's go," he said quietly, heading for a table at the front of the room. "The sweet-faced one with the glasses pinched me while the other two had my attention. I think they were preparing to pounce," he whispered conspiratorially.

"That's what you get...lookin' all fly like that," Rae said.

"You've never pounced on me," he argued.

"You ain't my type," Rae lied, giving him a matter-of-fact look.

"Speakin' of your type," Trevor offered her a chair and took one next to her at the round table, "where's Tyrone?"

"Tyree," Rae corrected, taking a sip of the tea already placed for the luncheon. "You know he doesn't have two dimes to rub together.

Besides, I'm fixin' to drop him like a bomb on Bin Laden. He's on my damn nerves."

"Still pissed about him takin' off in the Hummer, huh?"

"Pissed off about the way the man breathes, to tell you the truth, Trev. How do I end up with all the worthless ones?"

"You get what you settle for, Rae. I keep telling you that."

"I know. But there's something about a gangsta," Rae sighed. It was always nice talking with Trevor. He didn't approve of her choice of men, or a lot of the things she did, but he never judged her. He always accepted her just as she was.

Trevor leaned close enough to touch shoulder-to-shoulder. "Guess what?"

She noted the way he rolled his glass of tea between his hands. He was excited about something. "What?"

"Jewel's pregnant."

"Oh, Trevor!" Rae was genuinely happy for him. He'd wanted a child for so long. "Congratulations! You're going to be a great daddy." She hugged him tight, holding him just long enough for the flash of jealousy and disappointment to subside.

Trevor beamed as if he'd swallowed a bucket of sunshine. "I am, aren't I?"

"Damned right," she said with a nod. They had both dedicated their time to helping kids. As a high school girls' basketball coach, she'd had an opportunity to influence the lives of her kids, not simply coach them to win games. It had been tremendously fulfilling. Rae knew this aspect of her old job was what she would miss the most as she accepted her new coaching role with the WNBA. She would miss watching the girls grow and develop into young women.

Trevor had spent a great deal of his personal time and money making sure the inner city kids had a community center that supported activities that would keep them off drugs and off the street. Building the Youth First Center had been his way of giving back something positive to their old neighborhood and probably the only project he'd led, as opposed to his wife.

"How far along is Jewel?" Rae asked.

Trevor shrugged. "Don't know. She took a home pregnancy

test right before we came."

Because he looked so thrilled, Rae decided to let him talk more on the subject. "What do you want? A boy or girl?"

Shaking his head, Trevor let his hands rise and fall to the table. "I don't think I care one way or the other, Rae, honest."

"I do," Rae said, studying her reflection in the bowl of her spoon. "I always wanted to have a daughter. I want to dress her up like a doll in those cute dresses and tiny patent-leather shoes."

Trevor laughed. "You? Since when are you a fan of anything prissy? I can't remember the last time I saw you in a dress, Rae. When was it? Prom night?"

"Probably," she admitted. "But what you need to understand, Trevor, is that I'm not opposed to dresses. They're just so uncomfortable." Rae fidgeted, remembering the discomfort of her taffeta gown with tulle underskirt. The truth was, her gown had been too short. It had come to her calves instead of falling to the floor, despite her wearing flat shoes. It had been a hand-me-down from her cousin and had made her feel like a bull dressed up like a ballerina. Especially since she was a full five inches taller than her date, Jeremy, whom she'd had to beg to take her. "And pantyhose." She rolled her eyes. "They're the worst."

"So why make your child wear them?" Trevor insisted.

"I wouldn't make her…exactly," Rae faltered. "But it doesn't even matter." She moved her hands in the air as if to erase the entire conversation. "I'm not the one having a baby here."

"I guess you two are talking about me." Jewel was smiling as she moved to stand beside Trevor. She was a stunningly beautiful woman. Rae envied her flawless, dark, porcelain complexion and petite features. Jewel was as feminine as they came in a curve-hugging red and black business suit. Jewel bent down to share an intimate kiss with her husband.

As bold as she was about most things, Rae never kissed a man in public and felt very uncomfortable when it happened in front of her. "I hope you two have a room in this here hotel," she said to break up the display.

Trevor and Jewel laughed as they moved apart, but their gazes lingered for several additional heated seconds.

Not for the first time, Rae longed for a man to look at her with as much love as Trevor St. John looked upon his wife. She longed for it more and more these days.

"I've gotta go," Jewel said.

Rae looked around and was impressed at how full the ballroom had become. If anyone could pull this project off, Jewel would, she decided. The woman could sell ice to an Eskimo. "Knock 'em dead, Jewel," she said, meaning it.

"Thanks, Rae. I plan on it."

Rae watched her stride confidently toward the podium. "Your wife isn't scared of anything, is she, Trev?"

Trevor sat back in his chair with a satisfied smile planted firmly on his handsome face. "She's a helluva woman, Rae. I'm lucky to have her."

"You certainly are," said the man who had just arrived at the table. "Sterling LeRoi," he offered, extending his hand to Trevor. Standing, Trevor shook his hand and introduced himself.

Sterling's eyes shifted to Rae. "It seems you're surrounded by lovely women, Mr. St. John."

Rae noted the narrow slant of the man's eyes and the small scar beneath his jaw. His movements were fluid, almost elegant, his smile dazzling, but slightly askew. He was just this side of handsome with a demeanor Rae could only describe as slick. She wanted him instantly.

"This is my friend Rae Paris," Trevor stated.

"Nice to meet you," Sterling took her hand and kissed it.

The routine was a tired one, but Rae smiled politely. "Nice to meet you, Mr. LeRoi." She tried to sound cool. The last thing she needed was to take up with another scrub while she was trying to get rid of one.

"I hope you don't mind my joining your table." Sterling sat in the seat beside Rae, not waiting for permission. "The place is packed."

Trevor frowned but sank back into his chair.

Rae could tell her friend didn't like Sterling LeRoi, which meant it was inevitable that she would. All the more reason to keep your distance, she reminded herself. Besides, the man probably didn't have a steady job.

Of course, his designer suit said different. As did his well-manicured nails and professionally trimmed hair and goatee. He was a stunning man, all caramel-colored, trim and—familiar. Suddenly, Rae was certain that she'd seen him before.

"What is it that you do, Mr. LeRoi?" Rae couldn't contain her curiosity.

"I'm self-employed," he offered with another blazing smile. "I'm always on the lookout for new investments. This one looks promising."

"Self-employed?" Trevor now leaned forward, forearms on the table, eyes narrowed in assessment. "In what trade, Mr. LeRoi?"

Sterling leveled a gaze at Trevor. "A little of this, little of that. I just recently sold my chain of soul food restaurants out in Atlanta, The House of Soul. Have you heard of it?"

There was a hint of challenge in Sterling's tone. Rae could almost smell testosterone in the air. She crossed her legs, as if the act could stop the desire dampening her panties.

"I have," Trevor stated. "I believe Black Enterprise did an article on you a while back."

"That's right," Sterling acknowledged with a less than modest smile.

That's where Rae had seen him before. Jewel was always forcing her and Trevor to read article after article from that magazine, and Sterling LeRoi's story had been a recent one.

"What brings you to San Antonio?" Trevor asked.

"Damn, Trevor, you're grilling the man like he stole something." Rae moved in to save the man who was certain to be her next ex. "Don't mind my friend, Mr. LeRoi—"

"Sterling," he offered, turning his light-brown eyes in Rae's direction. His irises were gold with light on the edges and full of dark storms and secrets near the center. Rae liked this man. He had potential. Her last few men had been simple and predictable.

"Sterling," she said slowly, softly, as she cocked her head in a full flirt, letting her short corkscrew twists bounce a little. "You're going to think this is a line, but...have we met before?"

"I'm certain I would've remembered if we had, Rae." It was his turn to say her name, softly, sexily. "But I've only been in San Antonio for three weeks."

"You have a family, Sterling?" She hated to be obvious, but before she clubbed him over the head and dragged him home in her Hummer, she had to find out if he was married. She didn't believe in bustin' up homes.

His eyes lit with mischief. "I have a string of ex-girlfriends from Europe to Atlanta. Apparently, I'm a hard man to love." Not even a hint of an apology sounded in his voice for having all those affairs.

"I'll just bet you are." Rae ignored Trevor's hand swatting her leg beneath the table, ignored the warning sirens sounding in her own head, ignored everyone else in the room as all six-feet-two inches of her fell in lust with the intriguing Sterling LeRoi.

Chapter Two

The ballroom, though spacious, was packed with people. Men and women clad in mostly navy, black and tan business suits chatted in small clusters around the room. Other attendees were retirees, entrepreneurs, professional athletes, and executives of the most prominent companies in town. On the side of the room were a modest number of television reporters with their cameramen at the ready.

Pride filled Jewel's chest. This was her chance to hit the society pages of the Express-News, to be invited to the most prestigious parties, to be the belle of the Governor's Ball.

Representative Daniel McWilliams offered a stately nod as he held a chair for his wife at a table near the front of the room. Mrs. McWilliams had recently resigned her position as a top executive at IBM, enabling the fifty-something couple to ride the winds of retirement on her golden parachute of a retirement fund while Mr. McWilliams rode out his last term in the Texas House of Representatives.

Jewel had sold them their first home over seven years ago when she'd first started out as a realtor. This year, they'd moved into a pricey mansion in The Dominion, a neighborhood so swank they knew their gate security guards better than their neighbors. They would make great investors in this project.

Jewel looked over at Trevor. His forehead was deeply lined as he frowned at whatever Rae was saying to the man at their table. Jewel took in the man's pricey suit, his engaging smile and precise haircut.

He looked too perfect, as if he were trying hard to appear…legitimate. Rae had moved close enough to the guy to make her exposed cleavage a part of the man's salad. Jewel clucked her tongue and shook her head. When would the woman finally settle down with a man who was more substance than flash?

No doubt Trevor was thinking the same thing, she decided. His distaste for the goings on at the table was obvious, though none of his business, really. Rae was more than old enough to handle her own affairs. Still, her husband had some insane notion he was responsible for Rae and thought he could somehow influence the things she did.

For five years, Jewel had watched them play the same game: Rae picked the worst scrub she could find and ended up in trouble, and Trevor always ran to her rescue.

Jewel shook her head and frowned. They were a pair, Rae and Trevor, the oddest pair of best friends she'd ever seen.

Checking her watch, Jewel brought her thoughts back to the business at hand. It was time.

"Good afternoon future business partners," she said with a confident smile as a wave of excited jitters shot through her veins. The crowd hushed until only the clink of silverware could be heard. "For those of you who don't know me, I'm Jewel St. John, half of the partnership of St. John Realty. My husband Trevor is the other half." She extended an arm in his direction and met the warm comfort of his chocolate brown eyes. "We're still debating which of us is the better half."

Trevor smiled, gave her a wink, then stood and gave a cordial wave to the audience before re-taking his seat. Encouraged by the audience's laughter, Jewel continued, "We're glad to see you here in such large numbers. Glad you made the choice to be with us this afternoon." The majority of the attendees were Black or Hispanic, though a table here and there held a sprinkling of white faces. "I promise that by the time this luncheon ends, you'll be lining up to become partners in the project I've named the San Antonio Diversity Initiative; SADI for those of you who like acronyms.

"And most of you out there know I don't make promises I can't keep." She cast a knowing eye across the audience.

Nods, laughter and banter swept the room in appreciation for the statement.

"I don't know how many of you read Black Enterprise magazine, but I've been a reader for many years. My favorite articles are the ones on Black wealth initiatives. Well, I came up with SADI as my, make that our, way of further diversifying the business community here in San Antonio.

"So what's in it for you? The same as what's in it for me. By implementing this initiative, we can support one another in creating profitable, competitive, minority-owned businesses, renovate and strengthen our downtown community, create jobs, and increase our presence in this great city."

Enthusiasm for the subject made Jewel reach for the microphone and move around the podium and out into the room to gain more intimacy with her audience. As she spoke, she met every eye she could, touched a shoulder here, gave a nod there. They were right where she needed them, attentive and interested. All she had to do was close the deal.

"Imagine walking past the Majestic Theatre on Houston Street and passing a designer boutique owned and operated by a Black woman. You walk in and find clothing labels by Black clothing designers.

"You take a few more steps, and you're in front of a Hispanic-owned restaurant, barbershop, bookstore, or coffee shop. You go across the street, and there's a Black-owned microbrewery or a popular fast-food franchise owned and managed by Asians.

"Around the block, there's a Black-owned souvenir shop, a store of African imports, a furniture store, a shoe store, a postal center, a dry cleaners…anything you can imagine could be found in this one part of downtown San Antonio. Can you see it?" She leaned closer to a table of older ladies whose wizened eyes reminded her of her own granny's. One of the ladies nodded as if she could in fact see exactly what Jewel was describing.

Jewel dropped her tone to a near whisper. "And all that you see will be owned by you." She pointed to a table of business people. "And you." She pointed to a group of confident-looking thirty-somethings. "And all of you." She swept her arm in a wide arc around the ballroom.

As applause thundered, she continued talking, like a preacher who sparked the Holy Spirit in a congregation. Jewel knew now was the time to bring them home to the idea. "It's time we brought our collective wealth and power together to make a positive impact on the community in which we live. This is not a unique idea; we've seen successful models in every major city. New York's Chinatown is one of the best known.

"All of you have proven yourselves to be successful in your own right, but now it's time to put our collective knowledge and wealth together for the future of our children, for the future of our city."

Applause thundered through the room as if she'd just finished running a mile. Jewel's heart pumped furiously, and her head was light with joy.

The applause died down and she continued. "Making this happen will be no small feat. We all know that," she acknowledged, walking back toward the podium. "But tell me this." She turned in challenge as soon as she reached the front of the room once more. "Are you sitting where you are now because you took the easy road?"

The room grew lively with shaking heads and conversation. No indeed. Not a one of them had made their money by sitting back and inheriting it. "I want you all to look to your right and to your left. To the front of the room and to the back. This room is filled with people who are competitive, ambitious, energetic, and intelligent. This room is filled with people who didn't let the size of the challenge defeat them before they tried. This room—" Jewel stopped as a tall, elegant woman in cool white wool slid quietly inside the ballroom doors. For a moment, Jewel's tongue froze to the roof of her mouth. A cold rage filled her veins, forcing Jewel to fight to defrost her thoughts.

"This room," she continued, still rattled by her mother's unexpected and unwanted presence, "is filled with people who have given all they had to get where they are today. And I want you to know I'm not asking you to put your finances at risk for this Initiative. I want you to put them to work.

"Now, please turn your attention to the video." She gestured toward the screen dropping from the ceiling as she fought for internal control. "You'll see a virtual representation of the Diversity Initiative. Afterward, if you're interested in joining the investment group for SADI, sign up with Cara and Theresa, who'll be sitting to either side of the double doors on your way out. The first official meeting for the Initiative will be in two weeks. Thank you."

Thunderous applause accompanied her departure from the podium to her table. Jewel dropped into the chair beside her husband, unable to hide the visceral reaction caused by Eloise Jubilee-Hunt crashing her party.

Only when the lights had dimmed and she'd taken a long swallow of iced tea could she find her voice. "Can you believe her nerve?" she whispered violently to her husband.

Trevor took her hand and kissed her cheek. "Take it easy, babe. Don't let her ruin this for you." He spoke softly. "Did you see the reaction you got?"

He was trying to distract her from allowing the simmering in her veins to become an all-out boil. It wasn't working. "She's here to ruin everything. I know it, Trevor."

"You don't know that," he argued.

"What's up?" Rae was leaning over Trevor's shoulder and looking back and forth at her two friends.

Jewel just made out the wry look Trevor gave Rae in the dim light. "Nice to see you take your nose out of that man's crotch long enough to see what else is going on in the world." It was harsh, especially from Trevor, who rarely spoke a harsh word to anyone, let alone his best friend.

"Give it a rest, Trev. Mr. LeRoi had to answer a page. He stepped out of the room. Now, what's going on with you two?"

"My mother is here." Jewel was all too happy to share the nature of her ire. She stole a glance at the back of the room. She recognized the elegant silhouette dressed in white wool standing near the door. Eloise was talking conspiratorially with a portly man in an ill-fitting dark suit. "I wonder who that man is she's talking to? I can't make out his face in the dark."

Trevor and Rae turned to look. They were unable to see well enough to identify the man either.

"She doesn't even have the courtesy to take a seat," Jewel spat.

"There's not an empty seat in the room, J," Rae said.

Jewel couldn't argue that point, and it made her even angrier. "Then she should have the decency to leave and not disrupt the place. In fact, I think I'll tell her to do just that."

Trevor quickly wrapped a strong arm around her shoulders as she attempted to rise. "Not the time, Jewel."

"But Trevor—"

"Not now." His tone brooked no argument.

He was right, of course. Showing the "family business" here in front of all these people would only do harm to the Initiative and her own good name to start. Still, if they knew Eloise the way she did, they would understand. She was certain of it.

"You can talk with your mother when you're done with business," Trevor coached. "Now put on your game face, babe. The video is ending."

Jewel walked back to the podium, an artificial smile pasted on her face determined to stay focused long enough to complete her pitch and invite the attendees once again to join the Initiative. She wouldn't get the opportunity to kick Eloise out, however, because the woman walked out the doors the moment Jewel resumed speaking.

Instead of feeling relief, Jewel became even more agitated. Even as she shook hands and thanked people for coming, Jewel asked herself repeatedly what had prompted her mother to come and leave so abruptly?

All Jewel knew for sure was that she had a bad feeling about her mother's presence. She had to get to the bottom of this, even if it meant speaking to the woman and breaking the vow she'd made, and kept, to herself for the past five years.

Willful women. Trevor was surrounded by them and wondering how he managed to survive. There was Rae, his best friend since junior high. Why was she always attracted to men of questionable convictions? No. He corrected himself. Most of the men she'd fallen in love with had definite convictions: possession of drugs, assault and battery, armed robbery... Something about a thug drew the woman like flies to rotten meat.

Sterling LeRoi had been well dressed, but almost too much so in his expensive Italian suit and silk tie. He was slick. A slick dresser, a slick talker, but the man had revealed no real information about himself despite Trevor's efforts at drawing him out at the luncheon. The man made him uneasy.

Then, there was Jewel, her mother, and her grandmother. All were the most stubborn women on the face of the earth, he'd decided long ago. Jewel had insisted on driving to her mother's home in The Dominion right after the luncheon. Trevor hoped no emergency vehicles would have to make a call to the scene.

Trevor had Rae drop him off at the office. Dutifully, he had shown the two houses Jewel had scheduled for that afternoon. He had intended to knock off early and go watch Rae's high school girls in their playoff game. More and more, all he wanted was to get away from the rat race, take more time off with Jewel. And now that they were going to have a baby…A smile captured his face and his heart. A baby. He couldn't wait.

At five o'clock, Jewel pushed through the glass doors of their office. One glance told him she was still fuming.

Trevor looked up from the papers on his desk, removed his reading glasses, and sat back as his wife tossed her purse and suit jacket onto a guest chair. "Eloise give you a hard time?" he guessed.

"She wouldn't let me in." Jewel threw her arms up in exasperation. "She drives inside the gates, sits there so I can't get in, then lets the wrought–iron gates close between us. Is that the most hateful thing you've ever heard of?"

"That's pretty bad," Trevor agreed. "But what did you expect?" The last time Jewel and Eloise had been together hadn't been a cordial affair.

"I don't know, Trevor, civility maybe."

"Don't let her get to you."

"I need to know why she showed up. This is my Initiative and it's too important for her to mess it up. I've got fifty people who are interested in investing, way more than I expected."

Trevor leaned forward. "Yeah, it's a good sign. We're going to need a lot of money to pull off this project. But what makes you think she wants anything?"

Jewel gave him a shrinking look. "She doesn't speak to me for most of my life, then all of a sudden she shows up at the moment of my greatest achievement. She wants to steal the glory somehow." She put a hand to her stomach and grimaced.

Alarmed, Trevor rushed over to usher her into a chair. "What's wrong? Is it the baby?"

"No," Jewel answered irritably. "I'm hungry. I was too nervous to eat at the luncheon."

"Oh." Trevor put a hand to his chest in relief. "Well, we can take care of that. How about we get some Rudy's barbecue and take it home?"

"Fine," Jewel agreed. "I swear, Trevor, you act like I'm the only woman who's ever been pregnant. You're not going to be like this the whole nine months, are you?"

"Like what?" Trevor slid into his sports coat and held the door open as his wife exited the office.

"Like a mother hen."

Trevor chuckled. "Maybe. Gotta look after what's mine." He patted her round bottom affectionately. "By the way, I told my family. Just got through talking to Patrick before you came in."

"Oh yeah? What'd your crazy brother have to say?"

"Threatened to kick my Black behind if I had a boy before he does."

Jewel smiled. It was good to see her smile. "He's already got three girls. What's he going for...a world record?" she quipped.

"He said four's his limit. If he doesn't get a boy this time around, he's giving up."

"You mean Christa's pregnant again?" Jewel's mouth hung open as Trevor helped her into the Jag. Her skirt slid up to reveal silky, brown thighs. Trevor indulged in a look before closing the door and heading around the vehicle to the driver's side.

The view of her thighs was even more enticing from the vantage point of the driver's seat. Trevor was suddenly hungry for something other than food. He placed a hand on one smooth thigh and slid it up to her skirt, then down again.

"Trevor," his wife cautioned. "Don't start nothin'. I'm hungry."

Because she had spread her legs just a little and was wearing her sideways, sexy smile, Trevor ignored the comment. Leaning over, he placed his mouth softly on her open lips and kissed her.

Jewel's hand moved to his crotch, sending him from flaccid to rock solid instantly.

Deepening the kiss, Trevor nearly climbed over the gearshift to pull her closer. They rocked and rolled his car like two teenagers parked at Make Out Point before Trevor finally came up for air. "How 'bout a quickie before I buy you that barbecue?"

"I thought you'd never ask," Jewel answered breathlessly, sliding out of her side of the car.

Trevor tugged the keys out of the car and jumped out. Quickly, he adjusted his briefs and tucked his keys inside his jacket pocket, then took long, anxious strides to catch up with his wife.

Jewel's hands trembled slightly as she struggled to unlock their office door. Knowing how badly she wanted him made Trevor twice as anxious to get inside.

On the other side of the door, Jewel barely had time to turn the key before Trevor pressed her against the glass with another hungry kiss.

"Trevor, the keys…" Jewel protested as he pulled her away from the door and toward his office.

"They're not going anywhere," Trevor said, turning around, leading her by the hand. "I have an urgent matter that needs your attention in my office, my dear."

"I'll do what I can," she answered huskily. The moment they were inside his office with the door slammed shut, she wrapped her legs around his waist.

Trevor could feel her heat as she pushed against him. His head began to spin as aching need demanded release. Fumbling with his belt and zipper, Trevor rid himself of his pants. By now, Jewel was nearly naked, and the look of her dark skin in her sexy red underwear had him swearing under his breath. He pressed her onto the leather sofa opposite his desk and tried his best to be gentle as he removed her bra and panties.

They didn't speak as their bodies moved through the familiar steps of their lovemaking. Familiar, but never boring.

Trevor pushed inside Jewel's slick, hot folds and had to take a moment to pause as the feel of her overwhelmed him. She felt like warm chocolate melting his resolve. "Look at me, Jewel," he demanded as he started to move in and out of her.

She opened her eyes. They were dark and drunk with lust, just the way he liked them. "I'm looking at you, Sir Trevor."

To look into one another's eyes as they made love was a ritual for them. It was as if they were not only a part of each other's bodies, but of each other's souls and made Trevor feel connected to her in a way beyond explanation...beyond reason.

She was taking him deeper and deeper into her sweet ecstasy, and Trevor was getting high on the feeling. "Why is it, the more I have you, the more I want?" he asked.

"Because I put a spell on you the night I met you," she whispered with a giggle into his ear. "A love spell that bound us together forever. Every time we make love, the more in love we become. It's that simple," she let out a moan, "and...oh...that potent."

"If that's true," Trevor's entire being pulsed with desire, with need, "then how do you explain me being the one with the magic wand, huh?" He thrust into her harder and faster to emphasize his point.

Her only response was to scream out his name and tighten around him.

It was his undoing. Trevor let out a conquering cry as liquid lightning forced its way out of him to fill her. When the final spasms of delight ended, he collapsed on top of Jewel's glistening breasts. "My sweet Jewel." He kissed her gently as he adjusted himself enough to lie underneath her side and pull her into his arms. "Do you have any idea how much I love you?"

She rolled to face him. "Tell me."

Trevor smiled at how genuinely interested in his answer she seemed. "It was a rhetorical question, Jewel."

"I know," she answered, pulling herself up on an elbow. "But

I'd really like to know." Her forehead was creased with concern. "We made a deal, you know. We wouldn't get married unless—"

"Unless we thought we could love one another for a lifetime," he finished. "Jewel," he touched her face to ease her concern, "have I ever made a promise I didn't keep?"

She relaxed a little in his arms. "No."

"Have you?"

She sighed heavily and lay back against his arm. "No, I haven't." She brought a hand to her still flat stomach.

Trevor placed his hand over hers and let their fingers entwine over their unborn child. "Look at the gift you're about to give me, Jewel." He kissed her temple. "How could I help but love you?"

"Don't ever stop, okay?" she asked before relaxing back into his arms.

"I don't plan to," he answered honestly, wondering how she could ever think that he would.

Trevor was wrapped in cozy contentment. It was Sunday and they had no homes to show. If they hadn't met their sales goals for the month, he would've been worried. But the number of referrals they were receiving lately was making the realty business very easy.

Trevor adjusted the pillow beneath his head. Satisfied the Spurs had a win firmly in hand at the expense of the Seahawks, he flipped the remote to a different basketball game. As he did, the insistent buzz of the gate intercom filled the room. Grumbling, he made no effort to move from his comfortable position.

Jewel came out of her office on the second buzz. "I'll get that since you can't tear your butt off that sofa," she offered with a wicked grin.

"I deserve to sit on this sofa and watch ESPN until I die of overindulgence. I've made more than my share of sales this month," Trevor countered. " 'Specially since I took those two clients of yours last week."

His joke was met with a withering glare.

Jewel put a hand on her hip and pressed the button. "Who is

it?" she asked.

Trevor vaguely registered the response as being Rae's as he stared at his wife's slender, dark legs beneath her shorts. They were exquisite legs, shapely, smooth with a certain sheen to them that reminded Trevor of fine satin.

He set down his Coca-Cola and popcorn and crossed the room to embrace his wife.

"Oh, now you want to move." She stiffened in his arms and pressed the buzzer to let their visitor inside the gate. "I don't have time for this, Trevor." She turned her face so that his lips met the edge of her jaw instead of the lips he'd targeted. "I've got to look at these credit reports on our prospective investors, pick the ones we want on the board with us. Then I've got to schedule the meeting, get our attorneys to draw up contracts.... There's a ton of things to do."

Reluctantly, Trevor gave up on loving her into a romantic mood. Besides, Rae would arrive any moment. "You've got to calm down, Jewel. The Initiative will be fine if you just take one step at a time. Take it easy. If not for me," he placed a hand over her womb, "then for our baby."

Instead of calming her down, his words and action seemed to upset her even more.

"Is that all you're worried about, Trevor St. John? The baby? Well, in case you haven't noticed, I'm not simply here as a vessel to carry your child. I'm much more than that!" She flung the door open just as Rae walked up the steps.

"Hey, girl," Rae greeted Jewel.

"Hey, Rae. Come on in." Her tone was considerably kinder to their friend.

Trevor was still standing in stunned confusion as Jewel excused herself and enclosed herself behind the French doors of her office.

Rae's customary grin fell into concern as she regarded his face. "What's wrong?"

Shaking his head and shrugging, Trevor turned and walked back to the sofa. "Apparently, I'm some awful oaf who takes my wife simply as a vessel to carry my child."

"Oh. 'S that all?" Rae closed the front door and headed for the kitchen. She retrieved a soda and joined Trevor in the family room. She fell back onto the leather sofa and swung her long, sweat-pant-covered legs over the arm and into a comfortable lounging position without spilling a drop from her can. "Probably hormones. I hear women lose their minds when they're pregnant. I'd love to confirm that, but I haven't found myself in that condition—yet."

Trevor lifted an eyebrow at her tone. "What do you mean, 'yet'? You trying?"

Rae scrunched her face and shook her head. Her tight, nappy spirals bounced on her head. "Nah. Could you imagine Tyree as a father? I don't think so. I may not seem picky about my men, Trev, but I assure you I have standards for my baby daddy."

"Not Sterling LeRoi, I hope." He watched her reaction carefully.

Cocking her head to the side, Rae squinted as she looked at him. "Jury's still out. I'm going to Vegas with him next week. I can start to form an opinion then."

"Have you lost your ever-lovin' mind, Rae?" Trevor came to the edge of his chair and put down his popcorn. Though Rae was a grown woman; sometimes she exercised the worst judgment. "You don't know enough about that man to take a trip with him. What if he turns out to be like that a-hole Jackson Browne?"

Damn Trevor for never forgetting anything. "How was I supposed to know the man was a woman beater?"

"Maybe after the first time he blackened your eye," Trevor stressed, using the same sarcastic yet concerned tone he'd had when he'd visited her in the hospital.

"Hmph." Rae wriggled a little to adjust her position on the couch. "I've been hit worse than that on the basketball court. Women can be vicious when a championship is at stake," she chuckled.

"I can't believe you're joking about this, Rae. You let it go on for a year, and the only reason anybody knew about it was because you ended up in the hospital. I still don't understand that." Trevor shook his head and drained his can of soda.

"I was holding my own, okay?" Rae said with a shrug. "He got as good as he gave until that last time. I hadn't counted on him bringing out a baseball bat."

"He played Triple A ball, Rae Angelique." Trevor let the subject rest when he saw his friend push her fingers through the spirals at the back of her head. She still had scars where her head had been split open. "All I'm saying is you should be more careful."

"I know, Trevor." She dropped her eyes so he couldn't see how his soft tone affected her. "I am being careful this time. I'll insist on having a separate room and tell him there'll be no hanky-panky. This'll just be a getting-to-know-you trip."

Trevor's skeptical look told her he wasn't buying it.

"I am a grown woman, Trevor," Rae said matter-of-factly. "Besides, I'm not looking for love, just a sperm donor."

"So you've told me." Trevor sighed and began rolling his empty soda can between his palms. "You're not serious about bringing a child into the world all on your own, are you?"

"Serious as a heart attack," she confirmed. "In case you haven't noticed, the world's a different place these days. It's no longer a requirement for people to get married before they have kids. You and Jewel are an anomaly."

"Maybe," Trevor acknowledged. "But it's a shame. Look at how hard our mothers worked, trying to raise kids on welfare checks and food stamps because our fathers didn't think it was their responsibility to hang around past the fun part."

"My mother was a hooker and an addict. I took better care of her than she did of me."

"She was just trying to escape the hardship of her life, Rae. It's not easy to raise kids alone."

"If you're broke," Rae countered. "Which I'm not. I can afford to give a child anything she needs and most of what she wants."

She sat up and took a serious tone. "Listen, Trev. I'm not doing this on a whim. I know what I want. A man's love comes and goes, but a child will love you forever. Despite everything, I give my mom anything she needs because…because I love her. You know what I mean?"

He nodded. "Yeah. I know."

She loved that he worried about her. Hell, he was the only

person on the planet who did. She wanted to go over and hug him, give him a kiss on the cheek and tell him she was going to be just fine. But they had never crossed the "touchy-feely" line during their relationship, and it would be awkward if she acted on the impulse.

To her surprise, Trevor stood, came over to where she lay, and kissed her gently on the top of her head. "You're not as tough as you pretend to be, Rae Angelique Paris. Never were."

Overcome with emotion, Rae dropped her eyes once more. The aching lump in her throat ensured she would be unable to give a pithy reply—even if she could think of one.

Trevor left the room, taking their empty Coke cans with him as he headed for the gourmet kitchen. "Staying for dinner?" he asked casually. "I was going to make Jewel and me a couple of steaks. No problem to make a third," he offered.

"Sounds good," she said. Rae draped an arm over her eyes because they were starting to mist. "I love you, Trevor St. John," she whispered so quietly he couldn't possibly have heard.

Jewel stood in stunned silence in the doorway of her office. She hadn't intended to overhear Rae's quiet declaration, but she had. She knew Rae's feelings ran deep for Trevor, but love? Only in a buddy, buddy platonic kind of way she'd assured herself time and again. She'd seen with her own eyes how Trevor treated her more like a kid sister than a...than a lover.

Still, Jewel had half a mind to go in there and tell Rae Paris that she'd overheard her and then tell her to get the hell out of her house. But she did neither. Instead, she closed the French doors tightly, opting to say nothing. In a way, she felt sorry for Rae. It must be awful to want something you can't have.

She sat at her desk staring at her laptop screen. Was it any worse than to have something and not want it?

And then she felt it. A small fluttering...like a butterfly flitting about in her stomach. Jewel sat erect, wondering if it were a fluke. But it happened again. The stirring of the tiny life was like a small electrical charge to her system. She started to cry out for Trevor but decided against it. Letting him see the absolute terror in her eyes would be a mistake.

For the last several weeks, she'd been so wrapped up in other things that she didn't have much time to think of the life growing inside of her. But now the tiny thing was making its presence known. No longer could she pretend this wasn't going to happen. In a few short months, she would be a mother. And Trevor... Well, she was pretty certain things would never be the same between them.

It wasn't fair.

Jewel moved aside the papers on her desk she'd been reading and laid her head down on her hands. She had to get a grip on herself. She had to believe everything would be fine. Only one person who could ease her mind, Granny Glen.

Chapter Three

Jewel stared out the huge picture window of her granny's apartment. It was a gorgeous February day. The sky was a bright, pristine blue, unblemished by even a single cloud. It hardly seemed to be winter, as the cool temperatures of the previous week had turned into fifty and sixty-degree temperatures in the past few days. In fact, since Monday the sun had shone bright—as if God Himself was trying to melt the cold distress that had seized her soul since her doctor had further confirmed the existence of the tiny life with an ultrasound picture.

"You haven't answered my question, Jewel Marie." Her granny scolded her quietly from across the room. Jewel continued to stare out the window. As always, every curtain was pulled back, every shade wide open in Glendora Jubilee's cozy assisted living apartment. Sunlight beamed into every corner of every room. Exposed curio shelves sparkled as the light glinted off Granny's prized collection of music boxes. No dust was to be found here, and Jewel found that disturbing. To truly live, there had to be some messiness in a person's life. Nothing and no one could be perfect all the time. But if anyone came close, it was her grandmother.

Here was a woman who had insisted on living life on her own terms—never having to rely on anyone for a meal or a roof over her head. To this day, how Glendora had amassed a small fortune without ever holding a real job—or a man—was the source of many a speculative conversation during family gatherings. Her aunts and uncles had asked Jewel tons of questions as she'd grown up, hoping to discover the truth from her. But Jewel couldn't tell what she didn't know.

A small smile took a corner of Jewel's mouth. Many an interesting person had crossed the threshold of Glendora's homes over the years, but not a single one had stayed long enough for Jewel to get to know him. No one was ever allowed to stay long enough to gather any dust.

Not knowing what had gone on right under her young nose all those years made Jewel crazy. But she hoped that one day Granny would let down her carefully built shroud of secrecy and Jewel would be the one to hear all about her life. The story would be spectacular; she was certain of it.

Ironically, the woman who held so fast to her own life's secrets couldn't stand for a speck of dust to rest peacefully or for a shadow to exist in her home or in her granddaughter's life.

"Well?" Glendora asked from her dinette table. She took a sip of her tea and set the flowered china cup neatly back into its fragile saucer. "How are you feeling, child? I know Trevor couldn't be happier. A baby is all the man has wanted since you met him. You knew that."

Because her last words seemed accusatory, Jewel stepped away from the living room windows and walked across the French blue carpeting to set her grandmother straight. "Of course I knew that. I'm thrilled with the thought of having a baby. It's just…" Jewel stopped herself and looked away from the older woman into the amazing bouquet of fresh flowers in the center of the table. Naturally, Jewel's curiosity peaked when she noticed the bouquet wasn't grocery store flowers but professionally arranged. "These are gorgeous flowers, Granny Glen. Who sent them to you?" Jewel turned the vase looking for the card, only to find the plastic holder empty.

"You're changing the subject, Jewel."

From the corner of her eye, Jewel saw her grandmother shift uneasily in her chair. Smiling, Jewel decided she'd discover the truth sooner rather than later. "It makes me feel better to know I'm not the only one holding onto secrets," she teased.

Glendora frowned with annoyance. She was nearly eighty but

with a mind as sharp as a diamond tip.

Jewel had seen pictures of her grandmother when she had been younger. She'd been quite a looker in her day. Even now, her pale brown skin barely wrinkled, her snow-white hair closely cropped, her golden brown eyes bright with intelligence, she had an elegant beauty.

Rising slowly from her chair, Glendora took hold of her walker. Only her legs and hips had given out over the years, which was why she was in this home. The assisted living center provided meals for those who couldn't cook, transportation for those who couldn't drive and help with cleaning for those who couldn't move around as well as they used to. Glendora had settled on Greenview Estates once she realized she couldn't do for herself any longer. Jewel and Trevor had offered to let her live in their home, but Granny had refused to be a burden on them or anyone else in her family. She had a proud, stubborn streak Jewel admired and often strived to emulate.

"Wash that cup for me and then come join me in the living room," Glendora instructed. She then muttered something under her breath as she made slow but steady progress toward the sofa.

Happily, Jewel did as she was told. Anything to delay the "Great Inquisition" Granny was plotting at that very moment. As she filled the sink with hot water and dishwashing detergent, Jewel's thoughts turned back to the flowers on the table behind her. If she recalled correctly, this wasn't the first bunch of flowers that had suddenly appeared to grace her granny's table. Last January, she'd received an elaborate arrangement as well.

It had to be a man. Why else would Glendora be so secretive? Maybe that nice Mr. Boyd in the apartment four doors down? He was always finding reasons to be in Granny's apartment or at her table during dinner in Greenview's homey cafeteria. The old guy couldn't hear worth a lick, but his eyes glazed over every time he caught sight of Glendora. Jewel hadn't figured out if the look was love or lust. She shrugged. What did it matter when you were almost an octogenarian?

Jewel washed and rinsed the delicate teacup and saucer and the odd pieces of silverware she found in the sink as well. She then dried the few items and put them away in the tidy cupboard to her left. Teacups with the teacups, saucers with the saucers, she said to herself, overriding her normal tendency to just place things anywhere there was a space. Granny wouldn't tolerate having things all mixed up.

"Well, don't be all day, child. You'll be leaving me soon, and I won't have heard a single thing about what's going on in your life." Glendora was nearly begging.

"I've told you the most important thing, Granny Glen." Jewel dried her hands and turned to face her grandmother. The little bit of devil in her made her drop the dishtowel on the countertop in a heap before making her way to the living room. "What could be more exciting than learning you're going to be a great-grandmother?"

"Actually, I didn't think I'd live long enough to see the day." Jewel could tell she wasn't kidding. "Why's that?"

"Well, you're my only grandchild, and until five years ago, I didn't think you'd ever settle down to get married. Didn't think you even wanted children." Her eyebrows lifted just enough for Jewel to see she was being baited.

Jewel didn't know why she bothered to keep her feelings locked up. Granny Glen had always known how to read her, since she was a child. "Okay." She blew a long breath and kicked off her shoes as she entered the living area. "So I hadn't really thought about it. Not before meeting Trevor," she added. "You should see how happy he is, Granny. I've never seen a man so proud. In fact, he's going with me to the doctor's office on my next visit."

"What for?"

Jewel shrugged. "The doctor's going to do an amniocentesis to make sure the baby doesn't have Down Syndrome."

"Why in the world would he do such a thing?" Glendora asked, settling back against the couch cushions.

"I'm thirty-five, almost thirty-six. They say women at this age have a greater chance of having a baby with Down Syndrome."

"Hmph." Glendora scoffed. "My sister Raynetta had babies into her forties and ain't a one of them been anything but healthy. 'Course none of the ten turned out to be worth a darn either."

Jewel hadn't hit it off with her cousins. The last time she'd seen them had been over ten years ago during a strained family reunion. She recalled one of the twin boys being hauled off to jail for beating his sister's boyfriend within an inch of his life. Her boyfriend's hospitalization left cousin Krystal on her own to corral the three screaming hellions they'd brought into the world.

After seeing those bad kids, was there any wonder why she had reservations about having one of her own? Jewel settled into the peach and blue upholstered chair across the room from her granny, tucking her feet beneath her. Despite their opposing personalities, Jewel always enjoyed her time with Glendora. There was something both comforting and unsettling about talking with the one person who knew every fiber, every moment of her life. She'd shared a lot with Granny. Good times and bad. "I didn't know you and Aunt Raynetta were talking again."

"Truth is, I can't remember why I was so mad at her in the first place," Granny said.

"That's a lie," Jewel laughed. "You don't forget a thing, Granny Glen. Maybe it's just not important to you anymore that Aunt Ray called you a 'two-bit penny-pinching spinster' in front of everyone at the reunion." This time she was the one who was fishing for information.

Granny Glen chuckled. "You got me on that one, Jewel Marie. But I s'pose she was right. It wouldn't have hurt my pocketbook at all to bail her son out the jailhouse."

"I thought you said he needed to understand that his actions had consequences." Jewel was intrigued by this change of attitude.

"I've softened over the years." Her expression turned thoughtful. "I used to think everything was so doggone serious. Used to have a fit over the smallest insult. Couldn't take a joke," she said, shaking her head. "Time has a way of changing a person's heart. Sometimes for the worse, sometimes for the better."

What an awfully personal thing to say, and it touched Jewel to have Granny share it with her. "You've always had a good heart, Granny," she said before giving it a thought. "Who else would've put up with me?"

"Why on earth would you say such a thing, child?" Annoyance made Glendora frown once more.

"Come on, Granny," Jewel said a little impatiently. "My own parents kicked me out of the house when I was ten. Said I was hateful and unmanageable." Jewel had tried her best to make her parents miserable because they made her miserable with all their fighting. "Why did you even take me in?"

"Because every child is worth loving, Jewel Marie." Glendora sat up erect. "Even when they tryin' their best not to be."

Fondness for the woman squeezed at Jewel's heart. "I can't tell you how many times I wished I'd never been born when I was younger. I couldn't figure out why they had me when it was obvious they didn't want me in their lives."

"That's not true, Jewel." Granny had her hands in front of her as if trying to stop a speeding train. "Your parents were young and… and…confused," she finally managed. "They just hadn't planned on having you so soon."

"My mother told me she'd tried to give me up for adoption when I was born," Jewel argued, feeling her jaw tighten with anger. "The day I left that house she told me her only mistake was not going through with it."

"Those were hateful words from a frustrated woman, Jewel. She couldn't put you up for adoption because she loved you."

"How can you say that?" Jewel pushed to her feet. "I saw the look on her face when I left. She was smiling. Smiling with relief and joy and…and it was the same look she had on her face when she burst in on my SADI luncheon."

"She was there?" Glendora asked with interest.

"Yes," Jewel said, the irritation creeping up on her once more. Or perhaps it had never left. "You told her, didn't you?"

Granny Glen shrugged. "A mother has a right to know what's going on in her child's life. I thought she might be proud to know about this ambitious project of yours. She seemed quite interested. Said she might even participate."

Jewel glared at her grandmother. "She wouldn't dare."

Glendora shrugged. "Would it be the worst thing in the world?"

"I can't think of anything worse, Granny. You know we can't stand the sight of one another. Besides, I can see it now." Jewel began pacing the room and gesturing widely, "One second it'll be my

Initiative, and the next, Eloise'll find some way of putting her name on it. Probably try to invest more money than the rest of us. Well, I'm not having it."

"And what about that child you're carrying? She doesn't have a right to know about that either? She don't have a right to love it if she wants to?"

That thought was the root of Jewel's distress at having a baby. She realized that now. Staring out the window, Jewel crossed her arms and asked the question that had haunted her thoughts non-stop for the past two weeks. "Do you think Eloise ever loved me?"

"I know she did."

"How do you know?" Jewel insisted. "I lived with her and can't say I ever felt a drop of anything but resentment come my way. I couldn't even sit on my father's lap without her shooing me away. I have no doubt she would find a grandchild equally distasteful."

"Hush that talk, child. Your mama—"

"My mother got pregnant with me to hold on to my father," Jewel interrupted. "And after years of trying, neither one of them turned out to be parent material." Jewel was surprised the words didn't hurt anymore. It was a fact—one that she'd learned to deal with. She walked over to her grandmother and sank to her knees before her. "Isn't it wrong to bring a child into the world if you can't love it, Granny?"

"Depends."

"No it doesn't." Jewel shook her head as misery began a slow swirl in the pit of her belly. "It doesn't depend, Granny. It's not right, admit it."

"Now, child—" Glendora reached for her granddaughter's hands.

"I'm just like her, Granny Glen. I don't feel anything for the baby I'm carrying…except resentment."

And there it was. The ugly truth, hanging there like a huge overripe fruit about to fall.

"Come up here," Granny said sternly, patting the pretty patterned cushion next to her on the sofa. "Always interruptin' me."

Because the room suddenly felt huge and cold, Jewel did as instructed and sank onto the sofa and into her Granny's open arms.

Glendora was a slight woman, but her thin arms were strong and her bosom soft. She smelled of expensive perfume. Jewel held tight to her. "I don't want to be like Eloise, Granny. I don't want to resent my own child."

Glendora stroked Jewel's braided head. "You're more like your mother than you think, child, but you won't make the same mistake."

"How do you know?" Jewel insisted.

" 'Cause it ain't that hard to love a child, Jewel Marie. It just ain't." Glendora tightened her grip around her granddaughter's shoulders. "Just you wait 'til your eyes fall upon that tiny little face…" her voice turned soft and loving, "…and you touch those precious little hands and toes. You'll see. Everything'll be just fine."

"But what if I don't fall in love with it? What if everything isn't fine?" Jewel was far from convinced.

She could feel Glendora's sigh. "It ain't like you to be so pessimistic, Jewel. Here you are, cookin' up the biggest, grandest scheme this city has ever seen, and you're all negative about something simple like having a baby. I am truly surprised at you.

"Besides, you have Trevor," Granny added. "He's a good man. The finest I've seen. Think of what a great father he'll be."

Jewel had no doubts as to Trevor's capabilities as a father. She could imagine his strong arms cradling a child, his eyes full of love… and then she wondered if he'd still have room to love her. Of course, he would, she chided herself. But the selfish thought—but one of her greatest fears--wouldn't go away, which was probably why she'd snapped at him the other evening when he'd touched her tummy and tried to make her feel better. "Maybe Trevor will love it enough for the both of us."

"You'll love it, too. Just give yourself a chance." Glendora's hand stroked the sleeve of Jewel's blouse reassuringly. "This is very nice. Find it in New York?" she asked.

"No," Jewel said. "I found it in the cutest boutique. The designer there is absolutely gifted. She's investing in the project and whipping me up an original gown to wear to the mayor's ball next week."

"Do tell." Granny's voice lifted with just the right amount of awe. "Your own designer. Well, well, you are moving up in the world, aren't you?"

"You're coming to the ball with us, aren't you, Granny?" Jewel let her mind take hold of the thought. "If you want, I could bring the designer by, and she could measure you for a gown, too."

"That's awfully sweet of you, child," Granny stated as Jewel pulled out of her arms. "But I've got a few gowns of my own in the closet I bet you haven't seen."

"Really?" Jewel loved clothes. "From Europe?"

"Tuscany, to be exact," Glendora said with a tilt to her elegant honey-toned chin. "Why don't you go in there and pull out the bag labeled Florence for me."

Jewel leapt to do her Granny's bidding. She couldn't wait to see the dresses. Glendora had spent six months in Europe the previous year before her hips had gone out on her. She'd come back happier than Jewel had ever seen her. She wondered if her granny's more and more frequent lapses into quiet reverie had anything to do with what she'd done while she'd been there. She was certain a man had courted Glendora to keep her there so long—a suggestion her granny vehemently denied to this day.

A half-hour later, after Jewel had modeled the luscious gowns in tulle, lace, chiffon and taffeta for her granny, she and her grandmother decided on a nice winter white suit. The skirt fell to the ground in waves of satin; with a matching faux fur collared jacket tapering seductively at the waist. She would be the best looking seventy-plus-year-old at the gala. That was for certain.

Checking her watch, Jewel's heart jumped with small panic. "Is it really three o'clock?" she asked, realizing she had to get to the office. She had a home to show at three-thirty and then had to check on a room in the city council building for her first SADI meeting. And then she had to run to the attorney's office for the contracts and arrange for one of them to explain the finer print to her new partners.

"I've gotta go, Granny Glen." She kissed her granny on the cheek and laid a throw over her so she could nap to the throes and woes of her soap opera. "See you later."

Glendora held tight to her granddaughter's hand for a moment. Her bright eyes held Jewel's for a long moment as if looking into her soul. Finally, Glendora nodded and offered her granddaughter a soft smile before letting her go. "Don't you fret so about that baby or your mother, you hear?"

Jewel agreed because she knew no other answer would be acceptable. She pulled on her leather jacket, then slung her small purse over her shoulder before heading for the door.

"And, Jewel Marie?" Glendora said just as her granddaughter reached the edge of the carpet. "Hang up that dishtowel before you go."

Smiling, Jewel turned slowly on her heel and headed for the small kitchen. She folded the towel neatly so the little blue goose was perfectly centered, then hung it over the handle of the oven door the way Glendora liked. "Should've known I wouldn't get away with even that small bit of rebellion," she laughed. But when she turned to look at her grandmother, she was fast asleep.

On a whim, Jewel lifted the vase of flowers on the table in hope of finding the hiding place of the card that had to have come with the arrangement. Only the center of the lovely lace tablecloth was there. "Sneaky old thing," she said quietly as she lowered the vase to the table once more. "I love you." She blew a kiss at the sleeping woman before closing and locking the door of the little apartment behind her.

***

Eloise Jubilee-Hunt moved the phone from one ear to the other, adjusted her position and let out a pained sigh. Her morning power yoga class had been particularly tough and her muscles were dying for a relaxing turn in her whirlpool bath. Instead, she sat on the stone steps leading to her bathtub in her thick terry robe, running her fingers through the warm silky water as her mother told her about Jewel's reaction to her dropping in to the luncheon—as if she hadn't seen it personally.

"I could tell she wasn't happy to see me, Mother," she said. She remembered well the cold stare her daughter had sent her across the ballroom. Eloise had expected as much. Still, to see so much hatred… "What does she think I was doing there, Mother?" she asked, only slightly curious. Jewel had seemed half out of her mind—which was precisely why Eloise had thought it best to keep her at the gate instead of inviting her inside her home.

"She's got in her head that you wanted to start some kinda trouble," Glendora stated simply. "I assured her that wasn't the case." She paused. "I was right, wasn't I?"

Eloise sighed. "Of course you were. What kind of trouble would I start?" She could hardly tell her mother the truth about why she was so interested in the project.

"Hmm," Glendora hummed. "I guess nobody ever knows that until you've done the deed. Isn't that right?"

"I suppose you're referring to the reunion?"

"It wasn't right what you did to that child."

Eloise sucked in a long breath, wishing she'd never picked up the phone. "I made a mistake, Mama, I wasn't in my right mind. I was drunk."

"Still making excuses for yourself. Eloise, why don't you tell the girl you're sorry?"

"I don't need this." Eloise shoved her way to her feet, holding the phone in a death grip. "If all you called for was to tell me what a disappointment I am again—"

Glendora backed down. "That's not why I called."

"Well, then what do you want, Mama?" Eloise kneaded her forehead in exasperation.

"I received another bouquet."

Eloise felt her heart stop, then start again with renewed vigor. "When?" she asked breathlessly.

"Same day as every year."

"I see," was all Eloise could manage. She eased herself back down to the cool stone steps. "Was there…a card?" she asked hesitantly.

"Of course." Glendora seemed to shuffle something. "It says 1604."

Eloise closed her eyes and willed her heart to stop thumping so pathetically.

"Did you hear me, Eloise?"

"Yes, Mother," she acknowledged. "I heard you."

"You going?"

"I can't," Eloise answered softly. "I just can't."

"Listen, baby," Glendora's voice was suddenly soft and kind. "The least you could do is go see him and tell him to stop waiting for you. If that's what you want," she added.

"Of course it's what I want. Haven't I been saying so for years?" Eloise could hardly breathe. She opened her robe at the neck and began fanning herself, angry at her own reaction. The idea of getting all hot and bothered about a worthless, womanizing SOB.

"I can't see him, Mother. I'm…I'm hosting a party tonight… the ladies from the historical preservation guild…I've got to go."

"Eloise—"

"No, really. I've got to go, Mother." Eloise hung up before Glendora could plant any more unhealthy ideas in her head. She sank back against the stone tile and stared up at the skylight. "1604." She whispered it, afraid to say it too loudly. Every year the same thing. Flowers, an airline ticket, and a room number at the hotel in Vegas they'd stayed in the night they were married. Since she'd refused them ten years earlier, he'd begun sending them to her mother. Some mother. Always telling her to give him another chance. Whose side was Mama on anyway?

What if she went? It wasn't as if she had anything else to do. She'd lied about having a meeting with the historical restoration guild. They weren't scheduled to meet for another week.

She placed a hand over her still overexcited heart. "Charles." She whispered his name, let it slide softly from her lips. Closing her eyes she could almost see him, handsome as sin in his pilot's uniform… could almost smell his fresh, spicy cologne. Did he still look the same? Smell the same? She wondered. Opening her eyes, she forced herself out of her love-struck reverie.

"If there's any justice in the world, he's bald, fat and looks like a toad." She stood and dropped her robe to the floor. It was the least God could do after allowing him to break her heart so completely.

Eloise surveyed her plush bathroom. This room, this house, the life she led now…that's what she wanted. She'd worked hard for everything she owned, and her lifestyle had brought her happiness.

Unfortunately, a small turn in the stock market had now put everything at risk for her, and for her mother.

Stepping into her still hot bath, she turned the jets on high. She had to think. Glendora's retirement fund was nearly spent. Eloise had only a fraction of her own investments left to work with. She had to come up with a way to make big money quickly, or she'd have to confess to her mother that she'd made a huge error in handling their money. Her pride wouldn't allow that.

Jewel's project, if successful, would make her money grow the quickest with the largest return on investment, given the current market. She had enough money to keep her mother at Greenview for the moment. And, if push came to shove, she would convince her to sell her old house—that would buy more time. Her daughter's Initiative would have to be making money within a year for her to be out of the woods.

She had no choice. She had to invest the last of her savings into the Initiative and become a member of the steering committee to ensure the project's success. She was sure Jewel wasn't going to welcome her with open arms. Nor did she blame her.

Chapter Four

Glendora hung up the phone slowly. Shaking her head, she tried to push herself to standing. Her knees gave out and sent her dropping to the sofa. Getting old was hell. She hated feeling weak and unable to do for herself. She'd prided herself all her life on being independent, and now she was nearly as helpless as a child.

Accepting that she had to wait a few moments before she had enough strength to rise, she pulled a worn photo album from beneath the cushion of her couch and into her lap. Slowly, she flipped through the time-weathered pages where all the faces, including her own, were young and happy. Her friends, her lovers, and the life she'd led through her youth were all there. Her memories began in black and white...some in sepia tones. These were the ones she remembered most fondly. Turning the page, her mood turned sour. She ran a hand over the picture of herself and her baby Eloise lying in the hospital. She remembered her mother standing nearby as her brother Ronnie snapped the shot. If she could have, Glendora's mother would've thrown blankets over all of their heads when they left the hospital later that day. She'd walked with back straight, head lifted against the disapproving clucks and whispers of the nurses, her friends, until they reached the seclusion of her tiny house. Afterwards...

Glendora closed her eyes and tried to shut out the anguish of her mother's harsh, judgmental words. "You shoulda stayed your trashy behind in London. Least then you wouldn't be shamin' me so."

"I should've never come back," she said. The disapproval of her mother and aunts had worn on her; along with the horrible heartbreak she'd had to endure. "My dearest Arthur," she whispered, lying back against the couch cushion, "maybe I should've listened to you. Maybe we could've made it."

She'd been a chorus line dancer for some of the most famous plays in most of the European theatres in Belgium, France, Milan, and London. Glendora remembered wishing to be famous enough one day to have her face plastered on playbills and posters. She had wished to be stopped on the street with requests for her autograph just once.

A smile filled her face as she remembered how happy she'd been…always happy…until she'd had to come home.

Slowly, Glendora opened her eyes and let them rest on the pictures on top of her fireplace mantel. Her precious girls, Eloise and Jewel. Sighing, she wondered what she could've done differently. Her daughter and granddaughter were both fiercely independent, a fact that delighted Glendora. They were both intelligent, successful women. But they hated each other, and neither of them trusted in love.

The fault was hers, Glendora realized. Some sort of family curse had been brought down upon her girls because of her. One thing about the Jubilees—when they fell in love, it was completely.

She'd loved one man her entire life. She'd wanted to fight for him, but the price had seemed too high at the time. It was too late for her now. But not too late for her girls. Eloise had been miserable for over a decade because of Charles. And, if she weren't careful, Jewel's insecurity would put a riff in her relationship with Trevor.

Not acceptable, Glendora thought. Not at all.

She had to do something before time ran out. She flipped to the last page of her photo album and opened the two envelopes she'd placed there. The smaller one held a number to reach Charles Hunt. The other, an invitation to attend an awards ceremony in London.

Time to get up. Glendora pushed against the couch cushions with renewed purpose. Reluctantly, her legs held her weight as she rose to a standing position. Breathing heavily, Glendora chuckled with her small victory. Grabbing her walker, she moved across the room to the telephone. She had things to do.

What in the world was she doing? Rae poked her head out of the posh six-seat jet and looked past the airport to the lights of Vegas in the near distance. She loved Vegas, loved its energy, its flash and sexiness. Time meant nothing here. She could eat, sleep, do anything… or nothing, at whatever time of the day or night she pleased.

"You coming?" Sterling stood on the pavement below her, offering a hand to help her down the short series of steps.

But she didn't love him. She waved off his assistance, suddenly irritated at having agreed to accompany a complete stranger on a weekend vacation. Trevor was right; it was trifling and low.

She imagined Sterling wouldn't care about that small detail. Rae sank into the air-conditioned interior of a waiting limousine and crossed her arms and legs. "Why did you bring me here?" she asked abruptly, as if it were completely his fault she was miffed.

Sterling removed his designer sunglasses that were unnecessary since it was dark, and leaned closer to Rae. "For the same reason you agreed to come," he said in a conspiratorial whisper.

"See, that's the problem right there." Rae shifted in the seat as the limo headed out of the airport. "I have no earthly idea what made me say yes to such a spontaneous offer. In fact, I've been doing and not thinking for so long, it's more reflex to agree than it is to ask myself if I really want to do something or not."

"Mmm," came Sterling's reply. "I'm not sure how to take that comment."

Rae shrugged. "Don't try to read anything into it, sugar. I don't mean anything personal against you. I tend to say whatever I think, whenever I think it. It gets me into trouble sometimes."

"Sometimes?" Sterling lifted an eyebrow as a smile caught the corner of his mouth.

Rae laughed. "Okay. My mouth gets my behind in trouble all the time."

Sterling nodded, replaced his sunglasses on his long, angular face and sank back comfortably against the leather interior. "Well, that's why I asked you to come along. I find you refreshingly direct. I'd like to get to know you better."

"Yeah, well, that's the other thing." Rae sank further back against the car seat, mimicking his pose. "You don't get to know anyone while you're in the sack with them."

Again Sterling's eyebrow lifted. "You sure about that?"

The way he asked made Rae smile. Maybe he wasn't so bad. At least he had a sense of humor. "It's been my experience, Mr. LeRoi, that you don't find out 'til you're at dinner with a man that his wife frequents the same restaurant when she thinks her husband's away on business. You don't find out 'til you're at a Spurs game, listening to the whispers of those around you, you're the fifth woman that season to join your man in his box seats. You don't find out 'til he's incarcerated and begging you for bail that your honey is the local drug dealer. And you never realize 'til the morning after what the stranger lying beside you provided wasn't love or happiness."

Sterling nodded. "Is that what you want? Love and happiness?"

Rae turned to stare out the window. "Doesn't everyone?"

"I suppose they do," he answered. "But I can't promise you that. No man can."

"I know," Rae sighed. "I don't expect you to."

They rode the rest of the way to the Mirage in silence. Rae was unsure if she should go inside after her limousine confession but decided to follow Sterling's lead. At the counter he requested a suite. They rode the elevator to the room and soon stood in the living room that separated two bedrooms.

"Where would you like your bags?" the bellboy asked.

Sterling looked at Rae. "Your choice." Clearly he wasn't going to press the issue of intimacy…for the moment. Rae wasn't sure if she should be relieved or insulted. She shrugged and pointed to the bedroom on the left side of the suite in answer to his question. "I'd be happy to pay for my half," she offered sincerely as the bellhop went to drop her bag in the room.

Sterling slid his sunglasses onto the coffee table and turned to address her. "I invited you on this trip, and I intend to pay. Don't feel as if it obligates you in any way."

Rae scoffed. "Right. You and I both know how this works, Sterling." She sank onto the comfortable couch.

The bellhop dropped Sterling's single bag in his room and headed for the door. "Will there be anything else?" he asked.

Sterling slipped a couple of bills into the man's hand and sent him off with a polite, "Thank you."

Rae liked that he wasn't flashy with his cash. He was classy. But no man was too classy to pay for a woman to come to Vegas and expect nothing of her. "Tell the truth, Sterling. Was this room comped?"

"Complimentary?" he asked. His smile was a slow, lazy affair, as was his descent onto the couch beside her. "Yeah. I dropped so much cash my last two trips, they gave me the room for free this time. You're quick," he said. His tone held admiration.

"Just the same, I know that airplane wasn't courtesy of the house, so my offer to pay my portion still stands."

"And so does mine." His hand touched her cheek. "But I have to admit, this'll be something new for me."

"Not having sex on the first date?" Rae asked. "Yeah, me too."

Sterling laughed. "You are refreshingly honest."

"Yeah." Rae narrowed her eyes. "What about you? How is it you're rolling around in all this cheddar?"

Sinking back against the sofa, he gave her a steady look. "You're a smart lady. How do you think I made my money?"

Rae shrugged. "I don't see you pushing a record label, so my guess is drugs…crack to be specific."

Sterling didn't blink and didn't deny. Instead, he looked her straight in the eyes and admitted, "You're absolutely right. That's exactly how I got started."

"But that's not what you do now?" Rae was hopeful. This man intrigued her, but she couldn't date a dope dealer. Not even her strained morals would allow that.

"Not since I lost my baby brother to an overdose," he answered simply. "I'd be happy to tell you more, but dinner's at seven." He checked his watch. "Unless you don't need time to…"

"Oh…no…yes. I'd like to freshen up." She shot up from her seat. "I'll be with you in fifteen minutes."

True to her word, she was out of her room a quarter of an hour later.

Sterling walked out of his room, looking wonderful in a tan linen suit and collarless shirt. He stopped short when he saw her. "Wow."

"I know. I'm very low maintenance," Rae guessed at his surprise. "Makes me fast."

"Evil. That's what you are," he said. His eyes traveled the length of her, finally resting on the low scoop of her top. "You tell me we're not having sex, then you wear…that."

She hadn't thought her simple black halter and wide-legged slacks would get such a reaction out of him. "You want me to change?" she offered sincerely.

"Hell naw," he shot back, a crooked grin on his face. "Let's get out of here so I can show you off."

The restaurant was perfect, the food divine, the service impeccable, and Sterling was turning out to be a real winner. Except his personal life was still a mystery. Rae took one last indulgent mouthful of flourless chocolate cake and sat back in her chair. "That's really good."

"I'm impressed." Sterling also tossed his napkin on the table. "Most women pick at their food. You actually ate yours."

Rae laughed. "I'm not real shy around food. You'll learn that about me."

"What else will I learn about you?" He seemed genuinely interested.

"I can't sing, dance or rap, but I can play basketball like nobody's business. When I played in Europe I even had fans. They liked that I could shoot a three-pointer from anywhere on the floor. I've been coaching high school girls for the past few years, but starting this season, I'll be the head coach for the San Antonio Silver Spurs."

"WNBA?"

She nodded proudly.

"Impressive. I'll be sure to buy season tickets."

"And what about you, Sterling LeRoi?"

"What about me?" he asked coyly.

"Is that even your real name? I don't know any Black folks with that kind of last name."

"Actually, my given name is Leroy James Sterling. I changed it when I started investing. Seems to give me an advantage…an air of mystery. In fact," he leaned forward and pointed past her out the open French doors, "I was allowed to become a partner of interest in that property across the street because the others think I'm European—and white."

Turning, Rae looked out the balcony to see a dark and uninteresting older casino. "No offense, Sterling, but that doesn't look like the hottest property on the Strip."

"You don't think so? We're turning it into a luxury condominium high rise. That way, people with money can own their own piece of the Strip. We've got advance sales in excess of two million dollars."

"Two what?" Rae was astounded. "Sight unseen? I'd at least want to see a model before I laid out that kind of cash."

"Well, there you go." Sterling tossed his hands in the air, then let them drop. "You know a little somethin' about me, I know a little somethin' about you. How about we do somethin' fun now?"

"Like what?"

Sterling rose and offered her his hand. "How about I show you some fireworks?"

Rae grew warm under his smoldering gaze. "But what about our vow of temporary chastity?"

He lifted an eyebrow. "I wasn't talkin' about that kind of fireworks. I was being literal."

"Oh." Embarrassed that she'd let her mind slip so quickly into the gutter, Rae tried to cover by lying. "I knew that."

Sterling escorted her to the restaurant's balcony. She was dazzled by the sight and immensity of the Las Vegas Strip and its magnificent casinos below them, except the one Sterling had said he was buying. Police cars bordered the building, along with other emergency vehicles, and a crowd of people had gathered.

"What's going on?" Rae asked.

"Pay attention." Sterling gave a nod to the darkened building. You don't want to miss this."

Suddenly, light drenched the building from four sides. A man in a tuxedo rose above the crowd in a cherry picker and recited a bit of history about the casino. Turned out the place was one of the old haunts back in Bugsy Siegel's day. On the announcer's cue, the crowed started a countdown. Sterling and Rae joined in, along with others who now filled the restaurant's balconies.

"Three, two, one, zero" they said at once.

Explosions went off, forcing Rae to cover her ears. A second later, the brick and mortar casino simply melted straight into the ground. A cloud of dust mushroomed just as fireworks went blazing into the night sky.

It was spectacular—better than any Fourth of July display Rae had ever witnessed. And while the fireworks filled her eyes, Sterling stood on the balcony next to her, his arm wrapped around her waist.

The next day, they awakened late, had breakfast in their room, then went down to the casino to play craps, blackjack and poker.

In honor of her wishes, Sterling didn't try to make a single move on her the entire weekend. Not even a kiss.

Rae was officially insulted. Here Sterling was taking her home from the airport, and he seemed quite happy and content.

"Nice neighborhood," he said as he steered his sporty Catera through the winding turns.

Encino Park wasn't one of the most expensive neighborhoods in northeast San Antonio, but it was populated with upper middle-class families and a ton of oak trees. The local school district had offered her a coaching position in the high school nearby, but she'd refused. She had seen a greater need for strong Black women leaders in the San Antonio Independent School District that catered to the lower income neighborhoods.

The thought of leaving her high school girls to accept her new coaching position sent a pain through her heart. But they would be proud of her…she knew that. She'd promised to get them tickets to the WNBA games when she could. It was a promise she planned to keep.

"It's this one, right?" Sterling pulled up to her modest, one-story brown brick home.

"Yeah," she said, searching her purse for keys. "Thanks, Sterling."

"Let me get your bag for you." He jumped out of the car before she could refuse.

"It's only one small bag," she protested lightly as she exited the car and headed for the front door. "And it's on rollers."

Closing the trunk, Sterling was quickly by her side. "Forgive me, but my Southern upbringing insists on at least a bit of chivalry," he offered with one of his slow, lazy, sexy smiles.

"You're from the South?" she asked. "What part?"

"Alabama. Montgomery."

"You don't have much of a drawl," she observed.

"I've learned that it helps to be able to blend into one's surroundings," he offered by way of explanation.

Rae wondered more and more about his chameleon-like qualities. How much of him was real? How much was pure front? Before she could ask, the air filled with gleeful squeals.

"Hi, Rae!" A small Hispanic girl with dark hair flying around her face in wild ringlets ran across the street. Her younger brother took off running on tiny five-year-old legs to catch her.

"Hi, Leti!" Rae opened her arms wide to swoop the child up and into the air. "Did you miss me?"

"Yes," she said, giggling and nodding enthusiastically. "Did you wins lots of money?" she asked sticking a little pink tongue through the gap where her two front teeth used to reside.

"Just enough to treat you to a huge Popsicle." Rae could hear the ice-cream truck as it rounded the corner and headed their way.

"Me too, Rae?" The younger tyke tugged at her skirt and looked at her with wide brown eyes that matched his sister's.

Bending to his height, Rae reached into her purse for three

dollars. "You, too, Roland."

"Who's he?" Roland Rodriquez asked, squinting against the sun in his eyes at Sterling.

"That's Sterling. He's a friend of mine," Rae offered.

"Nice to meet you, Roland," Sterling bent down to offer a handshake. Roland's tiny hand disappeared in Sterling's as he pumped his arm with enthusiasm.

"You're really, really tall," Leti said, taking her turn shaking Sterling's hand.

"I ate lots of vegetables when I was a kid," Sterling said with a wide grin. Leti and Roland both screwed their faces into grimaces. "And ice cream," he added quickly. Smiles spread like liquid sunshine on the two smooth brown faces. He had effectively salvaged his new friendships.

On cue, Rae handed the money to the older child. She received two wet kisses for her generosity before the pair raced down the street, along with the half dozen other children who had appeared magically from their own homes.

Rae chuckled as she walked inside the air-conditioned comfort of her house. Sterling followed her inside.

"You can just leave the bag by the door," Rae said. "I'll take it from here." She looked at him with new appreciation. He was great with kids.

Sterling stepped closer to her. "I had a very good time this weekend, Rae," he said.

His slanted brown eyes reminded Rae of fine brandy. "I did, too," she said sincerely, feeling a tug of desire at his proximity. "I had no idea what a fine poker player you are," she said, recalling their big win at the table.

"As are you." He gave her a nod of respect. "That last bluff was a thing of beauty."

Rae smiled, wanting him now more than ever to make a move on her. "Everyone fell for it but you."

They stood smiling at one another for a moment. Because she found the moment awkward, Rae took a step toward him.

He studied her lips a moment, licked his own, then backed

away. "I guess I'd better go," he said. "I'm feeling mighty pleased with myself for being such a gentleman all weekend. I wouldn't want to ruin my reputation now."

"You couldn't," Rae assured him. "In fact, I should give you a reward for being such a good boy." She hoped he didn't miss her attempt at sexual innuendo. "We can still catch the ice cream truck."

"Thanks, babe, but I'll save my licks for something—tastier."

The glimmer of mischief in his eyes heated Rae to her core. "Why wait?" she asked, not knowing why she was trying so hard.

" 'Cause everything's so much sweeter when you have to wait for it," Sterling said. "I'll call you later."

"Sterling?" Rae stopped him just as he was about to open the door. He smelled like fresh laundry and light musk.

"Yeah?"

They were so close now, all Rae had to do was lean in to kiss him. "You're not gay, are you?"

His lips tilted upward. "No," he stated simply.

"Have plans on becoming incarcerated any time soon?" she asked.

Sterling's eyebrows lifted with his surprise. "No."

"Married?" Rae continued her fishing expedition.

Crossing his arms now, Sterling looked a little perturbed. "No. Do you put all men through this kind of inquisition?" he asked.

Sighing, Rae stepped back and gave him free access to the door. "No. Usually, I just fall for their good looks, get a few good lays in and dump 'em for being trifling," she said honestly.

"So why do I suddenly get the fifth degree when I've been such a good boy?" he asked good-naturedly.

Rae shrugged. "Thought I might be a bit more careful going forward. I'm pushing forty. Gotta' grow up some time, you know?"

He studied her with renewed interest, stroking the small scar on his jaw. "I know exactly what you mean," he said. "I've gotta go." He gave her a light, lingering kiss on her cheek that nearly blinded her with delight. "Later." He closed the door softly behind him.

Rae moved to her front window and watched him back out of the driveway and steer his Catera CTS down the street. Moving from the window, she retrieved her bag and began to analyze her new find. "He's good-looking," she said to herself as she walked toward her bedroom. "Well-mannered, doesn't do drugs…I hope." She flung the suitcase on the bed and unzipped it. "Yeah," she decided. "He'll do just fine. Just fine."

And, just like that, she'd managed to solve a two-year-old problem. She'd finally found a suitable man to be her child's father. Now all she had to do was get him into bed.

And there was one other concern. How would the WNBA feel about having an unwed mother as a coach of their newest expansion team? "Only time will tell, Rae Paris," she said to herself. Her job was secure, for the moment. A trip to the playoffs would cement it for at least a second season. However, if worse came to worst, she could always go back to coaching high school basketball.

For now, she wanted a child too badly to wait any longer. If Sterling didn't call her, she'd be sure to call him. First things first.

Jewel surveyed the conference room. They rarely had use for it as real estate contracts were usually reviewed and signed in clients' homes or in her or Trevor's offices. Today, it would host the most important contract negotiations of her career…of her life. SADI was a viable initiative as of today. With the fifteen investors she'd invited to become partners, they had over thirteen million dollars with which to purchase the land and start renovations on the three-block site.

Sterling LeRoi and Rae were the first to arrive. After an exchange of pleasantries, they headed for the coffee urn and pastries on the back credenza. Sterling spoke in friendly, quiet tones while Rae smiled and laughed and found reasons to touch him on the arm or chest anytime she could. Frankly, Jewel was relieved to see how much interest Rae seemed to be taking in the tall stranger. Rae's comment the other night about loving Trevor was not meant in the way Jewel had feared.

Trevor moved up behind her at that moment. "You sure you want him involved in this project?" he whispered in her ear. "He doesn't look respectable."

Jewel was a bit peeved at his comment. "He's got an extremely

impressive portfolio. I looked into it thoroughly. He's quite legitimate...
sold a chain of restaurants to buy a lot of rundown houses around our
site. He renovated them to make them livable and rents them out to
low-income folks under Section 8. He's going to be a major investor
in luxury condos in Vegas, and now he's investing in SADI. Besides
that, he'll occupy Rae's time and keep her out of our refrigerator for a
while," she added, only half teasing.

"Fine." Trevor sighed. "I trust your judgment. It's Rae's I don't
care for. Did I tell you she's giving serious consideration to having that
man's child?"

"They're getting married?" Jewel asked in surprise. "They just
met."

"Shh." Trevor put a finger on her lips. "They're not getting
married, and he's not supposed to know about the baby. Rae sprang
this news on me last night when she called."

"Oh." Jewel looked at the couple across the room with renewed
interest. "It's going to get awfully interesting in this conference room
in a few months," she predicted.

"Damned sure will if I have anything to do with it," Trevor
agreed. "I'd better go over and pretend to be the happy host while I
pry Rae's fingers off the man's a—."

"Trevor." Jewel gave him a backhand to the chest. "Be nice,"
she insisted.

Trevor smiled and crossed the room. He gave a loud, open-
armed greeting to Rae and Sterling as he forced himself between them
and drilled the other man with a warning glare.

Not for the first time, Jewel felt a pang of jealousy at the
amount of interest he showed in Rae's affairs. The woman was grown.
He needed to let her handle her own business. Right after this meeting,
she'd be sure to let her husband hear her thoughts on the matter.

Time to be the happy hostess, she decided as more investors
arrived. "Mr. and Mrs. McWilliams," she beamed and ushered the older
couple into the room. "Help yourself to coffee and pastries. Pick any
seat."

"Pastries?" Marva McWilliams bit her lower lip as she craned
her neck to see what was laid out on the credenza. "You evil little thing.

I just started my diet."

"Not to worry, Marva, dear. You'll just start again tomorrow," Daniel McWilliams said with a dig as he escorted his pleasantly plump wife toward the treats.

The room filled with the lively chatter of the ladies from the investment club, Darlene Liberty, Shirley Justice and Monique Forall. They had a habit of talking over one another and finishing one another's sentences. To Jewel, it was like talking to one person with a lot of heads, arms and legs.

"Oh, Jewel, honey, this is so exciting," began Darlene.

"Yes, we hope to make a sizable profit on this venture," chimed in Shirley.

"Sizable. We've done quite well in the markets. Moved from stocks to bonds just as the market was crashing, you know?" bragged Monique. "It was like a sixth sense—"

"We knew just when to get out," they all chimed in unison.

"Find a seat, girls," Darlene instructed with a wave of her dark, arthritic fingers. "I'll see if there's decaf."

The two ladies did as instructed, confirming the leader of the aging trio.

In the next moment, Jewel ushered in the Reverend Samuel Redwine who was followed by two local attorneys, and three other citizens of the community.

At exactly ten o'clock, the room was filled. Jewel went to close the doors just as Eloise walked in in a cloud of White Diamond perfume.

"I'm not late, am I, darling?" She offered her daughter a wide-eyed look.

"Oh no, you don't," Jewel whispered between tight lips. "You have no business being here."

"Don't be rude, dear. I have every right to be here. I'm here on behalf of the restoration guild." Eloise surveyed the room with narrowed eyes. They were green eyes. Her father's eyes, Granny had always said. Didn't matter. They'd always looked evil to Jewel.

"Why is the guild interested in what we're doing?"

Eloise gave her a shrinking look. "Don't be naïve, child. The property you're proposing to buy is in the historic King Williams district. We have to make sure you keep everything as close to the original architecture as possible if you want the city council to approve the project. That's all."

Eloise found an empty chair near Daniel McWilliams, introduced herself politely to the gentleman and his wife, and sat down with the elegance of a queen at court.

Jewel held tight to her disgust as she watched all the men give her mother an appreciative glance or nod. The woman was in her mid-fifties and could still have men drooling like the infants they were.

In that moment, it occurred to Jewel quite vividly, how totally opposite she and her mother were, in both appearance and manner. Jewel was dark-skinned, like semi-sweet chocolate Trevor always told her. Eloise was pale as milk toast. Her mother put on airs…played the quiet sophisticate while manipulating everyone around her, while Jewel preferred to be open, direct and honest. *And I would honestly like to bounce her arrogant butt right out of here.*

As if sensing her thoughts, Trevor sent Jewel a warning glance from the other side of the room and quickly walked over to stand beside her. He slid an arm around her waist and set the tone for the meeting. "Welcome, everyone. Welcome to the first official board meeting of the SADI Initiative. My beautiful wife and I are thrilled that each of you has chosen to join us in this venture. Make no mistake that this will be a worthwhile project for us collectively and individually as well as for the community the Initiative will serve. Isn't that right, Jewel?"

It was a smooth rescue. Trevor bought her just enough time to set her mind straight. Just enough comfort in the strong arm circling her waist to calm her down. "That's right, Trevor." She took his lead, making certain to overlook her mother as she looked around the conference table.

A grateful smile and nod to Trevor let him know she would be fine. He took a seat to her side. No doubt he thought it wise not to be too far from her. But Jewel was fine. She facilitated the meeting with practiced ease as she warmed to her topic. She outlined each step of the project, the first being to choose a design. The next, which businesses would occupy each space. The people in the room who wanted to bring their business into the venture, as well as their investment money, had their pick of prime corner office spaces. They then needed to pick a façade. As Eloise leaned in attentively, Jewel rolled out the design from a local Black architect to the oohs and aahhs of the participants around the table.

"You'll notice," Jewel said, pointing at the drawing, "the design is in keeping with the architecture of the historic era." She directed a glance straight into her mother's green gaze. "I'm sure the restoration guild will be happy for the foresight."

"Looks lovely," Eloise offered almost graciously. "I'd like a copy of the blueprint to take back with me," she stated pleasantly.

"Of course," Jewel agreed, feeling a little heady for being one step ahead of her. "Well, that's all for this meeting. I'll be representing our group at the next city council meeting to personally request their support of our proposal."

"Oh, darling?" Eloise pushed an envelope across the table at Jewel. "Here's my share of the investment money and my signed contract. I'm thrilled to be a joining such an important project." She beamed an electric smile around the table at those assembled.

Jewel felt as if she'd just been sucker-punched. Her mother was investing?

"Oh, and could you please give me a call with the date and time of the next board meeting?" Eloise rose from her seat, as did the men in the room. "I've got an eleven o'clock and just can't be late. See you, Trevor." She wiggled her fingers at her son-in-law and left the room, leaving silence in her wake.

That was, until Marva McWilliams threw an elbow into her husband's ribs.

"Oof!" Daniel clutched his side. "What the hell'd ya do that for?" he whined.

Darlene, Shirley and Monique giggled into their hands. It had escaped no one's attention that Daniel McWilliams had watched every move of Eloise's behind as she'd made her exit.

Marva just glared at her husband. "Are we nearly through here?" she asked Jewel, her tone full of irritation.

"Yes," Jewel said. "We'll schedule another meeting for two

weeks from now. We still have a few things to settle before we can begin building. I'll give you all a call."

"Is two weeks good for us?" Darlene turned to her friends.

"Should be." Shirley nodded her pressed salt and pepper hair. "Don't go cruising 'til—"

"'Til end of April, girls," Monique added, tugging her flowered dress from her hind parts. "This one's the Gulf cruise, right?"

The room emptied out as Jewel and Trevor shook hands and exchanged pleasant good-byes. Feeling her husband tense suddenly at her side, Jewel followed his glare to Rae and Sterling who stood near their seats talking quietly.

Trevor took a step in their direction. Jewel caught him by his arm and pulled him back. He turned a questioning glance at her.

"Grown people," she said directly. "It's none of our business. Let's go."

Trevor's eyes fell to the large manila envelope that still sat on the table. "What about that?"

Jewel stared at it for a moment. Sighing, she went over and snatched the envelope from the table. "If it does have a check and a contract, I'm ripping them up." She headed out of the room and across the hallway to her office.

"I suppose that's none of my business either," Trevor said as he followed her. He leaned against the doorjamb as she tossed the envelope on her desk.

"She just wants to cause trouble, Trevor. I know it," Jewel insisted.

"Maybe," Trevor shrugged. His attention was diverted for a moment as Rae and Sterling left the conference room and headed out the front door. The wrinkles on his forehead eased as he turned back to Jewel and continued his train of thought. "Maybe your mother just wants to do the right thing. Who are we to deny her an opportunity to give back to the community that has been so good to her?"

Jewel leaned forward and narrowed her eyes. "We're her estranged daughter and son-in-law. That means she's not allowed to come play in our sandbox."

"I love when you're evil." Trevor smiled and licked his lips slowly. "So, that sandbox you're referring to..." He walked over to where she sat and spun her chair around until she faced him. "I don't have any houses to show until four today. I can play all day 'til then."

Because he was making her hot, Jewel pushed him away. "I don't have time for distractions, Trevor St. John." She eyed him up and down. God, he looked good today. And his dark brown eyes all full of warm lust... "No matter how tempting," she added. "I've got work to do. Go stand in a corner or something." She waved him away and pretended to find something interesting on her desk.

Trevor lifted her chin with a finger and turned her to face him. He planted a warm, wet, sexy kiss on her mouth before backing slowly out of the room. "If you change your mind, I'll be right next door." His tone was deep and sexy.

Jewel just shook her head and sighed helplessly. "I'll be there in a few minutes." She couldn't defend herself with all that testosterone being thrown in her direction. "But it's not a good idea in the middle of the day."

"I'll have Linda go get us all lunch. Tell her we'll be in my office when she gets back. Working on stuff." He wiggled his eyebrows suggestively.

"Send her someplace far," Jewel insisted. She eyed him hungrily as he first gave money to Linda, gave her their lunch order then walked deliberately into the next office.

Jewel pushed her thighs together and closed her eyes. She thought about Trevor waiting for her and wondered why their office assistant was taking so long to get her keys and purse together.

Jewel waited until Linda had pulled out of the parking lot before she ran to lock the front door. "This is insane," she shouted and raced back to Trevor's office. "We're too old to be acting like horny teenagers, Trevor!" she laughed and pushed aside the door. For a moment, Jewel could do nothing except look on in admiration.

Trevor leaned back against his desk wearing nothing but a red power tie and a wicked grin. The tie looked good hanging between Trevor's cinnamon-brown muscles. Jewel let her eyes wander indulgently down the solid planes of his stomach, loving how a sprinkling of hair began just below his belly button. Her eyes fell even lower. "I see someone is anxious to come out and play," she teased, as her body warmed at the sight of her magnificent man. She advanced toward him slowly.

"I've shown you mine." Trevor spread his arms wide. "Now let me see yours." His eyes narrowed with mischief and lust.

Jewel suddenly felt as if she were floating and not fully in control. She stripped for Trevor, slowly, encouraged by his rapt attention and quiet murmurs. It was heady stuff, to feel so much love for another person...and to feel it reciprocated with such intensity.

Jewel eased out of her tiny bikini underwear and stood only inches away from Trevor's pulsing erection.

"That's it, baby. Just stand there for a minute and let me take you in." Trevor's eyes should have seared her flesh as he scanned her frame from breasts to toes. Jewel trembled. "Time's up, Sir Trevor." She tugged gently on his member. "Now, let me take you in."

Chapter Five

Sterling was a man of great lusts. He didn't believe in denying himself anything, women, drink, drugs, money… Whatever made him feel good at the time was what he was after. But unlike the brother he'd just buried a month ago, the flames of his more dangerous impulses had never burned him completely. He'd been singed on occasion, but was still standing because his impulses only lasted a short time. Sterling didn't believe in forever.

His current moneymaking venture had made him a multi-millionaire through the acquisition of worthless properties that he renovated and turned into rentals or re-sold at a profit. The St. Johns' Initiative had seemed interesting and new, so he'd decided to dive in. He hadn't counted on meeting Rae.

He was giving serious thought to making Rae his next girl-of-the-moment,…but for the first time in his life, warning bells were going off in his brain.

He squirmed from his seat atop the hard metal bench of the gymnasium risers. He'd watched the basketball game between Rae's championship team and the underdogs of Judson High with interest. A sucker for all competitive sports, Sterling bet on many, lost on most, but if he'd been given odds on this game, he'd be raking in the dough. Rae's girls were stomping Judson 100 to 82 in the second half.

Sterling admired Rae in her tan suit that showed off the long, lean lines of her body. Every time she strode from the bench to the foul line to challenge a referee's call or knelt down to draw the next play for her team, Sterling had to take a long, deep breath. This woman was clearly in command of the game, her team, and her life.

Maybe not all aspects of her life.

Beside him, Trevor St. John rose to his feet as Rae's team ended the game with an outrageous three-point shot from half court. Following the lead of the cheering crowd, Sterling jumped up and applauded. He noted that Rae, in her enthusiasm, first sought Trevor's eyes, then his, before being engulfed by a team of adolescent girls celebrating their championship win.

That telling sign gave him pause...put his desire in check. It was one thing to obsess about a woman, but quite another to obsess about one who loved someone else.

"Good game, huh?" Trevor slapped him on the back heartily.

"Great," Sterling acknowledged.

"We may as well sit back down, man. She'll be a while before getting out of that." Trevor pointed toward the girls who had swarmed their coach and were now leading her in a screaming, jumping, laughing stampede into the locker room. "They love her. For some of those girls, Rae's been their mama, sister, friend and mentor."

Sterling noted the light in the man's eyes, the way he shook his head in admiration, or was it love? "Yeah, she's something," he agreed.

"So, what's up with you and Rae?" Trevor asked. The seriousness of his tone wasn't hidden beneath his easy smile.

Sterling shrugged. "You know, man. Just getting to know one another."

"Uh-huh." Trevor leaned his forearms on his knees, clearly wanting to say more. "How well you getting to know one another?"

"That's none of your damn business," Sterling offered simply. He wasn't mad but didn't appreciate Trevor stepping to him like that. "Why don't you tell me what's on your mind."

Trevor looked at him quizzically. "What d'ya mean?"

Sterling settled back against the steel, placing his elbows on the riser above him. "It's just that you've been sweatin' me ever since Rae and I met. If I'm treadin' on your territory—"

"Hold up! You've got the wrong idea." Trevor waved both hands emphatically. "Rae and I've been best friends since junior high. We've been through a lot together. If I've been sweatin' you, it's because I've seen too many men walk into her life, walk all over her, then walk out. I know she looks tough, but on the inside, she's just as soft as any other woman." Trevor now stared at him in challenge. "She's got no one else to look out for her, that's all."

Sterling studied him closely. "That's all?" he asked, skeptically.

Trevor frowned deeply. "In case you haven't noticed, I've got a wife. A beautiful one. A pregnant one."

The iron in Trevor's eyes made Sterling believe. He had to admit that every time he looked, the man was hugged up on his fine wife. "I had noticed," Sterling said by way of standing down. "I thought you was just bein', you know, greedy and shit." Sterling laughed and was glad to see Trevor follow suit. "Listen man, I ain't out to hurt anyone, but I can't offer any guarantees either. Relationships are complicated, dog."

"True," Trevor acknowledged. "Until Jewel came along, I had a string of not-quite-rights. Just when I'd decided to be a devout bachelor, she showed up...all full of sauce and sass...and changed my mind." Trevor's face lit up as he spoke about his wife. It was a rare occasion to see a married man so full of love. "Listen," Trevor's words were friendly but stern. "I care about Rae."

Sterling nodded. "I can respect that. All I'm askin' is for you to cut me a little slack."

"All right." Trevor sat up. "But if it don't work out, will you treat her with respect?"

"No problem, man. I ain't nothing if I ain't respectful. My mama taught me right."

Rae walked up the steps of the risers to find Trevor and Sterling shaking hands and grinning like two old friends. "What'd I miss?" she asked, her eyes still alight from her win.

Both men rose as she came to stand just below them.

"Nothing," Trevor said. He leaned over and hugged her tight. "Nice job, Coach. You're gonna give 'em hell in the WNBA."

Despite their recent conversation, Sterling couldn't help feeling a pang of jealousy at the congratulatory gesture. He rose and took his turn hugging Rae. She felt warm and smelled like cocoa butter. "Congratulations," he whispered in her ear. "You were great."

"Thanks." Rae beamed. "Did you see Renee?" she asked, referring to her star center. "Was she amazing or what? Ten assists, five rebounds, twenty-three points…she's been given a full ride scholarship to Tennessee State."

"That's great." Sterling smiled because she was smiling and because she had taken his arm as they walked out of the gym.

In the parking lot, Trevor said something about having to make an early showing and said his good-byes.

Sterling held the door open as Rae slid into his CTS. It seemed as if she belonged there, in the seat beside him, and Sterling savored their time alone. He listened as she recounted each play of the game and expressed her pride in her girls all the way to the restaurant. He liked the sound of her voice, a tad husky and somehow soothing…like warm brandy on a cold night.

They reached the restaurant and were immediately escorted to the table Sterling had reserved. They had a good meal topped off with champagne. "Get used to this," Sterling told her as he filled her glass with the bubbling liquid for a second time. "I have a feeling you'll be having a lot more winning seasons coming up. You coached a brilliant game."

Rae dipped her head a little. "I had great players."

"That you coached very well," Sterling insisted. "You're bad, girl."

Rae sobered and sat back in her chair. "That's probably the best compliment I've ever had," she said quietly. "Most men are kind of funny about me being a coach." She cocked her head to the side and folded her arms as she watched him sip his champagne. "Do you like me, Sterling?"

Because it seemed an odd time for the question, Sterling laughed a little. "Yeah. If I didn't, I wouldn't be treating you to a victory dinner."

Rae gave a quick nod of her corkscrew curls. The hairdo accented her striking features, the high cheekbones and full lips. "I like you, too."

They were simple words that had an unexpected effect on him. Sterling's heart revved up a few beats a minute as Rae pushed aside her empty plate and glass and leaned across the table.

"I want you to come home with me tonight." Her dark eyes narrowed with lust as she bit her lower lip.

Sterling's throat went dry as he imagined the damage they could do to one another. "I thought you wanted to take this slowly."

"I do…I did…I mean…" Rae shook her head. "I've changed my mind."

"Why?"

"Does there have to be a reason?"

"Yeah. There has to be a reason," he insisted.

"I want you," she answered simply.

It was Sterling's turn to lean across the table until their faces were only inches apart. "And whose arms will you be imagining as I hold you? Whose face will you see when you come?" he whispered intensely. He grabbed her hands and held tight. "Who do you really love?" He knew, even if Trevor didn't, Trevor was the man Rae wanted. He could see longing in her eyes every time the man was around. He didn't see it now as she stared at him, though. No. He saw only confusion turning to anger.

Rae pulled her hands away and retreated in irritation. "Listen, Sterling, if you're not feelin' me, that's fine. Take me home."

"I'll take you home," Sterling pulled out a Visa and laid it on the table, "but I'm feelin' every inch of you, Rae. Way too much."

"What's that supposed to mean?" Rae looked confused. "Do I scare you or something?"

"Baby, you terrify the hell out of me," he answered honestly. One night would be all he needed for Rae to become his next addiction. But this time, he wasn't sure it would be a quick encounter.

Rae watched the waiter retrieve Sterling's Visa and walk off. She dropped her gaze to the napkin she was wringing in her hands and tried to decide what to do now that her date had complicated things. The truth was she did want him…quite badly in fact. But the man was acting like he wanted something more permanent than a night in the sack, and that wasn't part of her plan.

"Listen, Sterling," she began, "I don't want to lead you on or anything. I just thought we could have some fun, you know?" And then get pregnant, and have a baby...

"I ain't got nothing against havin' fun, Rae," Sterling said as he signed off on the bill and returned his credit card to his wallet. "But there's something you gotta know about me. I've got an addictive personality. Whatever I like, I like to excess. You understand?"

Rae shrugged. "Not really."

"It means I'll gamble until I have no money left, I'll party 'til the joint closes down, and I'll love a woman 'til I use her up. If you're ready for that, say the word. If you're not, we may as well part ways now."

Rae smiled because now it was all coming clear. "How many girlfriends have you had, Sterling?"

"What's that got to do with anything?" he asked.

"Just answer me."

"I dunno." Sterling looked toward the ceiling of the dim room as if to find the answer. "I'd say maybe fifteen or so."

Rae nodded. "That's probably a conservative number, but okay. And exactly how much money did you lose playing poker in Vegas when we went?"

Sterling smiled and relaxed in his seat. "Nothing. I made six hundred. I see where you're going with this." He gave her a nod. "You're trying to make me out a liar."

"Aren't you?" Rae found herself more amused than angry.

"No. I do have an addictive personality. I was hooked on crack for three years and alcohol for five. I used to steal my dad's Colt 45 malt liquor when he had bid whist parties."

"How'd you get the crack?"

"Told you. I used to deal a little," he smiled sheepishly, "'til I got busted. I did a turn in juvie and decided to clean up my act. Didn't want to go back to jail, didn't want to end up broke like my folks, and I sure the f...sure didn't want to end up dead."

"So the moral of your story is that you learned to control your addictions because you knew the path you were on would lead to your destruction. Lots of people never learn that lesson." Rae found herself admiring the man.

Sterling's slow smile spread wide. "You make me sound noble or somethin'. I just made up my mind to quit...and I quit."

"Hmm. Sounds simple," Rae acknowledged. "Still doesn't explain your reaction to my proposal. What's the matter, Sterling? You never had a woman come on to you so strong before?" She doubted it.

"Pssst." Sterling rolled his eyes. "More'n I can count. It's just that none of 'em were tryin' to break my heart. That's all." He placed a hand over his chest melodramatically to make his point.

"I'm not out to break your heart, Sterling. We barely know each other."

"I know." He rose and helped her out of her chair. "And I'm not so sure we shouldn't keep it that way."

Standing so close to him, she couldn't help seeing the insecurity in his eyes. Standing so close, she couldn't help running a hand along his smoothly shaven cheek and admiring the strong line of his jaw. Standing so close...

Some force of nature too strong to stop drew her lips to his. Not that Rae wanted to stop.

The kiss was soft, gentle, intoxicating. If anyone in the restaurant was looking, Rae hoped they were dying with envy. Nothing mattered anymore except this moment, this man, this kiss. As they slowly separated, she struggled to feel her limbs, to find her breath.

Despite his outwardly calm appearance, she could feel Sterling's heart racing beneath her palm as if he'd just run a full court press. He said nothing for a moment, just looked stunned. Rae smiled. When he placed a hand on the rise of her behind and led her from the restaurant, she was certain he'd changed his mind about staying over.

As he drove, Rae watched his hands. They looked strong as they gripped the wheel to turn out of the parking lot. She imagined how those hands would feel all over her body, and it gave her a rush of pleasure. She pressed her legs together tightly, as if the movement could suppress her growing desire.

Sterling leaned against the armrest on the door and moved a

hand casually over his mouth. He cleared his throat a few times on the way to her house but didn't say a word.

The kiss had made things strange and uncomfortable between them. But it had been such a great kiss. Rae closed her eyes and relived every delicious moment. The soft feel of his lips, the sweet and tart taste of his mouth, the thrill of his tongue as it had barely skimmed hers. Rae's thighs were clenched so tight by the time they pulled into her driveway, a slip of paper wouldn't fit between them.

Before she could place a hand on the door handle, Sterling was out of the car and on his way to open it for her. He walked her to her door. She dropped her house keys into his open palm. Biting her lip, she silently bid him to hurry.

He pushed the door open and handed her back her keys. "You have a good night, Rae. Again, congratulations on the championship."

"Thanks," she said, disappointed. She'd been certain he'd come in after that kiss. But she wouldn't ask again, wouldn't lower herself to the point of begging a man for sex. "I had a good time. See you around, huh?" She took a step back into her entryway.

Sterling stood tentatively in the doorway looking her up and down for a moment, as if memorizing the way she looked.

Rae held her breath hopefully.

"Yeah," he said abruptly. "Car's running," he offered weakly.

Rae couldn't believe she'd missed that detail. He'd left the car running. He'd had no intention of coming inside.

"Gotta go," he said, pointing at the car with both hands.

"Sure. If you gotta go." Rae smiled through her declining spirits. She offered a half-hearted wave as she closed the door. It was all she could do not to slam the thing.

Turning to face her empty house, she kicked her right shoe into the next room. The other followed suit quickly. "What the hell is wrong with that man? I practically dropped my drawers for him, and he backed off like I had a disease or something."

She stormed into her bedroom, stripped naked, threw her damp panties into the hamper and forced herself under a shower of cold water. His leaving was better, she decided. Sterling LeRoi was too complicated. He came across like the player of the decade, but he was just a scared little boy afraid of being hurt. She didn't need that. Didn't need him. There were other ways to get pregnant. That's all she'd wanted from him anyway, she told herself. He was a would-be sperm donor. Nothing more. Besides, there was a real sperm bank in town. She hadn't wanted to resort to that; it seemed so cold and impersonal. But she was running out of options. Tomorrow, she decided. She'd go shopping for her baby daddy at the sperm bank.

Trevor straightened his tie and held it against his chest as he leaned over to kiss his wife. "Better enjoy that bathtub while you can. In a few months, it'll take a forklift to get you out," he teased.

Jewel gave him an evil look and flicked water at him. She didn't believe in showers. "I hate showers. It's like being attacked. Baths are soothing and gentle."

Trevor had to admit he liked the way she looked sitting in the tub, all that dark, shiny skin surrounded by snow-white bubbles. "Gotta show the Canyon Lake property this morning." He switched the subject to hold down an erection.

"To the Roberts? Tough customers," she warned, as she ran the washcloth up a long, ebony leg.

"I know. I've shown them over a dozen homes that should've had them drooling, but they've never been quite right. The ceilings are too high, the deck is too red, the master bathroom is too blue," he mimicked Mrs. Roberts comments.

"They're gonna love this one. It's perfect for them," Jewel insisted.

"How do you know?" Trevor asked, taking the opportunity to plant another kiss on her tasty lips.

"I have a sense about these things, you know?"

"I know," he acknowledged. "You've got the gift…"

"Got to use it," she finished, taking a line from Miss Dupree on the Tom Joyner morning show. "Watch that Mr. Roberts, hon. He'll try to knock down the price so far we'll be paying for the place," she spoke as he left the room.

Trevor threw on his suit coat. "I won't give up the farm, babe. Negotiations are my strong suit."

"I know," Jewel smiled. "Mr. Soft Sell."

"By the time I'm done, they'll think they stole this house from me," he said, cocky with confidence.

"Give 'em hell, honey!" she shouted.

No sooner had the front door closed than the pain hit—vicious and strong. Jewel doubled over her bubbles and gripped the sides of the tub and let out a low howl. "Trevorrrr!" Maybe he could still hear her.

"Oh, God. Trevor!" she screamed as her mouth dried and her head began to swim. "Help me. I'm...I'm dying!" She thought about getting out of the tub, but couldn't. Couldn't move, couldn't do anything but squeeze her eyes shut and cry against the pain that gripped her abdomen with steel claws.

Just as suddenly as it had come, the pain was gone.

Jewel relaxed her grip on the tub and opened her eyes slowly. Horror filled her as she witnessed the tendrils of blood filling the water and staining the bubbles red.

Trevor wasn't all that religious but had always believed there was a greater power—a greater force—in the universe than man. He'd forgotten his briefcase that morning...and he never forgot his briefcase, or anything else. Chiding himself, he'd performed a quick U-turn right before he reached the gated exit. Irritation had followed him all the way back to his house, but panic met him at the door. Something wasn't quite right—he could feel it. He ran into the bathroom where he'd left his wife just minutes before.

Now, days later, he recalled the loss of all rational thought the moment he saw Jewel lying in the tub unconscious—surrounded by blood-stained bubbles...

Sucking in a deep breath, Trevor let the air ease out of his body in a slow stream. The few days had been long and agonizing as he'd waited to hear that Jewel had pulled out of surgery and would live. Opening the back hatch of his SUV, he reached inside a bag he'd left there for what had seemed ages ago. Pulling out the soft powder blue stuffed puppy he'd bought for his child, he gently squeezed it. He'd planned to show it to Jewel, but now…

Quickly, he shoved the toy deeper into the corner of the space, then pulled out the small rolling luggage bag containing Jewel's toiletries and nightgown. He pinched the tears from his eyes and took a few deep breaths before entering the house for the second time that evening.

His shoes tapped loudly on the large granite tiles of the mudroom floor. He slipped out of them before passing through the kitchen to the spacious living room.

Jewel sat in her favorite overstuffed chair, wearing her terry robe, her feet tucked under the thick, flowered material. She looked so small as she sat staring at the flickering flames of a three-wick candle on the sofa table.

Her grief carried across the room and hit Trevor like a hammer, rocking him back on his heels. Something fierce and protective rose up from his gut, ready to slay the dragon causing her unhappiness. Trevor approached Jewel and knelt in front of her chair. It was then that he saw her hand wrapped tightly around a wad of tissues; the box lay on the floor beside her chair. "Are you going to be all right?" he asked.

Her face contorted with grief for long moments before she was able to answer. "I wasn't sure if I wanted to be a mother, Trevor." She looked at him apologetically. "I can't help but think this is God's way of punishing me for not appreciating the miracle of that baby."

For a moment, Trevor's strength faltered. The doctor had said Jewel or the child. Trevor had to choose which life he deemed more precious. He gripped Jewel's hand and squeezed it desperately. "It's all right, Jewel." He struggled to make it feel true. "These things happen. It wasn't your fault."

"Why can't I do this one thing?" Jewel said hopelessly. "Something every other woman can do without trying?"

"Shhh." Trevor rose to his feet and pulled Jewel from her chair and into his arms. He couldn't bear the hopelessness in her voice. Couldn't take her hurt that partnered with his. "It just wasn't meant to be, babe. That's all."

"I wanted to give you this baby more than anything, Trevor. I'm sorry I let you down." She fell limply against him, her warm, wet cheek against his shoulder.

Trevor closed his eyes and wrapped his arms around his wife, pulling her close. He laid his cheek against the soft curls of Jewel's hair and began to sway gently. It hadn't escaped his attention that her grief was for his loss...not her own. Jewel had pretended to want a child, but Trevor knew the truth. She thought she wouldn't be a good mother, but she wanted to make him a father. He loved her for that.

Gently, he held her as she moved with him, bringing her arms around his neck. Words weren't necessary—would've seemed intrusive at the moment. The night approached silently as they held one another, swaying to the slow, soothing rhythm of silence and flickering candlelight.

Jewel lifted her head and softly whispered in Trevor's ear, "I'm sorry."

A great lump formed in Trevor's throat, and it took a deep breath to ease the discomfort. Nodding his understanding, Trevor didn't dare speak. He couldn't add to her guilt, but the pain of losing the one thing he'd wanted so badly...the only thing he'd ever really wanted besides Jewel...was tearing his heart to shreds. He gripped the cloth of her robe in his fists and closed his eyes tightly until the peak of his pain eased enough to tell his wife what she needed to hear. "You don't have to be sorry, Jewel. I love you, babe. I always will."

His wife's body relaxed against his and her sobbing eased.

Silence fell between them once again as they resumed their dance. They moved in unison, each needing the other desperately to heal their hurt, each wanting to ease the other's pain. Both knowing it would be a long time before the hurt would heal.

Chapter Six

Rae tossed the profile of the sperm donor onto the table and slid onto the cool leather of the restaurant booth opposite Trevor. "There he is." She gave a nod at the folder. "Mr. Perfect: six-foot-one, forty-three years old, Black, stockbroker…bald. Perfect," she repeated. "Except for that last part. But hey, no one said bald wasn't beautiful, right?"

Trevor took a sip of his coffee. He looked tired. Very tired. "I take it Sterling LeRoi didn't make the cut?"

"You are correct," Rae confirmed with an exaggerated nod. "I think I scared him. Before I actually slept with him. It's a first for me." The comment was meant to make her friend smile. In the weeks since he and Jewel had lost their unborn baby, Trevor hadn't smiled since. Jewel seemed to be getting along fine, but Trevor was wallowing in a deep-blue funk, which was breaking Rae's heart.

"Thing is, I'm not sure about this in vitro stuff. It involves taking drugs, timing my cycle, going in and having my eggs harvested, fertilizing them and then having them implanted." She shook her head. "The doctor tells me it's unpleasant. Hell, he says it flat out hurts."

Trevor simply shrugged. "Price you gotta pay, I guess."

"The price is another thing." Rae looked down to avoid meeting his eyes. It was insane what she was about to propose, but it might help. Might help her and Trevor both. "The procedure is going to cost around nine, ten thousand dollars. I wouldn't mind, but it kind of drains the funds I saved to decorate the spare room and buy baby things."

Trevor winced. His eyes looked pained, as if he'd just been stabbed or something. "I'm sorry, Rae." He sat back against the high back of the booth. "I know how important this is to you, but I…I—"

"Trev, listen. I'm not trying to make you feel bad. I want to help you."

Confusion twisted his handsome brown features. "How's this going to help me?"

She swallowed hard and forced the words out of her mouth. "I don't want Mr. Perfect's sperm. I don't want to go through in vitro fertilization for a stranger's baby. I want you to be my baby's father. I want you and me to have a baby, Trevor."

He sat looking at her in dumb silence.

Rae's heart was racing. He was going to say no, she could feel it. "Please think about it, Trevor. I want a baby…you want a baby. I know you. Know everything about you, where you're from, what you believe, what kind of man you are. I won't know all of that about this guy." She pointed at the folder on the table.

"Rae, I could never leave Jewel."

"I never said I wanted you to leave Jewel. I don't expect that. I just think this is the way for both of us to have what we want."

Trevor rolled his coffee cup between his palms. His forehead was wrinkled as he considered her statements. "Why are you doing this, Rae?" he asked. "What do you want?"

"I told you—"

"I know what you said. I want to know what you mean." He stared at her suspiciously.

When he looked at her that way, he was expecting an honest answer. Rae wanted to come clean about her true intentions, but how could she? What kind of woman offers to have a baby as a way to buy a man's love? What kind of friend breaks up another friend's marriage? Yet that was what she was proposing.

Trevor continued to stare at her with his gorgeous eyes. Eyes that were demanding an answer. "I'm offering this to you because…I love you, Trevor St. John…and you know it." Rae fought against the sting of welling tears. "You've always known it."

Trevor took a deep breath and sighed heavily. He nodded slowly, as if he'd predicted her answer. "And I've always loved you, Rae." He reached across the table and took both of her hands. "Just not in the same way that I love Jewel," he said softly. "And you've always known that."

Rae nodded, buying herself time to clear the thick lump from her throat. "I know, Trevor. I do know that," she admitted. "And I wouldn't do anything to come between the two of you because I see how happy she makes you."

"Then what's this all about?"

Rae pulled away because she had to. Trevor had clearly defined his feelings, and now that it was out in the open, she had to deal with it. "I see how much you're hurting about losing that baby. I just thought I could help. I want to help. It doesn't have to be any more complicated than that, Trev, really."

Trevor blew a long breath, but he seemed satisfied with her answer. "So let me get this straight, all right? You want me to donate sperm, you have in vitro to get you pregnant, we have a baby...we'd have joint custody?" he questioned.

"Sure. I'm over at your house most of the time anyway. How hard would that be?"

"Not hard at all." Trevor's mood lightened. He looked hopeful. "Where does that leave Jewel?"

"Seems to me she's taking the miscarriage a lot better than you," she offered tentatively. Because he didn't protest the truth of her observation, she continued, "I'm not sure, but I think she might be relieved to only be a stepmother." She played with her folder, not daring to look at him.

"I, uh, would have to talk to Jewel about this." Trevor cleared his throat. "I'm not sure how she'd feel about it."

Rae smiled. "Tell her we can go halfsies on the cost of the in vitro."

For the first time in weeks, Trevor smiled. "Doesn't hurt to ask, right? I'll let you know what she says."

"Cool." Rae breathed easier. She'd gone out on a long limb on this one, but her friendship with Trevor was still intact. And she might be having his baby. Happiness made her stomach rumble. She looked around the table for the menu. "Now I believe you owe me dinner, Dad."

He'd rehearsed his sales pitch for two days, but just when he thought he was ready to convince Jewel to let Rae have his baby, Trevor couldn't remember how to start the conversation. He hadn't been this nervous when he'd asked her to marry him.

"How's your steak?" he asked because he couldn't think of what else to say.

"It's good."

They sat on the deck to eat the steaks Trevor had just finished barbecuing. He cut his steak into small pieces then cut each piece again. Next he reached for the tossed salad and offered some to Jewel...who already had a helping.

"No, thanks." Jewel waved off the bowl. "What is it, Trevor?" she asked. "I've never seen you so agitated."

Trevor shook his head and opened his mouth, but not a sound came out. He inserted a large piece of lettuce into his gaping mouth. "Good salad," he said pathetically.

Jewel studied him closely. She knew he'd taken the loss of the baby hard, but the look on his face wasn't the same as it had been for the past few weeks. He didn't look tired and sad tonight. Something else hovered in his eyes...something she'd never seen before. A sort of desperation, a panic. "Trevor," she could feel her pulse quicken, "what is it?"

"I've tried a thousand times to figure out just how to say this, Jewel." Dropping his fork and knife, he brought clenched fists to meet at the middle of his chest. "All I know is that if I don't tell you what I'm holding in, I'm going to burst."

Swallowing, Jewel felt her mouth go dry. "So tell me." She took a large swig of wine to prepare for whatever was coming.

"Rae made a suggestion...a request really...and...and I want to give it to her...I mean...I'd like for us to consider it."

He moved his chair around the table until he was sitting right next to her. Whatever it was, Jewel knew she wasn't going to like it. "What does she want?" she asked warily.

"A baby."

"What's that got to do with us?" Jewel's hands went cold.

"She wants me to be the father." Trevor took her hands in his warm, damp palms. "I want to be the father."

Jewel couldn't think of a single response. Here was her husband of five years, looking her square in the eye and telling her he wanted to have a child with someone else. He couldn't have hurt her more if he'd driven a dagger straight through her heart.

"You want to have a baby with Rae?" she finally managed.

His eyes were bright with hope. "Yes."

"And what am I supposed to do when the two of you have this child? Babysit?" She pulled her hands free of him and pushed to standing. "I can't believe you're asking this, Trevor."

"Jewel," Trevor rose to stand beside her, "I need you to understand. When we lost that baby…when I heard you could never have children again…it was like my whole world turned inside out. Like a lifelong dream had just been shattered. It's important to Rae to have a child. Just as important as it is to me. Can't you see? It just makes sense."

"Yeah, I see." Jewel blinked through the tears that had started to roll down her face. "I wasn't woman enough to give you a child, so now you turn to the woman who's always there, the one who always has your back. That sure does make sense. I should've seen it coming."

"It's not like that," Trevor denied. "Rae and I don't have that kind of relationship, and you know that."

"I don't know anything," Jewel snapped. "I didn't know the two of you were capable of hurting me this badly." She pushed back her chair and headed inside.

"Jewel." Trevor followed her. "Jewel, stop. Listen. I love you!"

The bedroom door slammed shut just as he reached it.

"Shiiiit!" Trevor shouted to the walls. This wasn't how it was supposed to go. Not at all.

The house felt empty, soulless. Though spotless and smelling of orange cleaner indicating Priscilla had been there, there was no scent of Jewel's perfume mingling with the orange. No high heels left carelessly on the living room rug, no humming or singing coming from the bedroom.

Trevor pulled off his tie and sat heavily on the bed. She hadn't come to the office either. Instead, she'd done her showings and faxed all the paperwork to Linda from the copy store. Of course, he knew where to find her. She'd be at her granny's house…the one Glendora had refused to sell. The older woman had insisted, when she could walk easily again, she would leave the assisted living apartment and move back into the home she treasured.

The front door opened and closed. "Jewel?" He nearly leapt from the bed and ran out to the living room.

"No. It's me, Trevor." Rae walked in with sacks of groceries. She'd stopped buzzing at the gate to warn him she was coming over a week ago. Now she just entered the code and came on in. Trevor didn't care. He liked having her around. He didn't like being alone.

"Any word from her yet?" Rae asked as she dropped the bags on the kitchen counter.

Trevor, sad and tired, sank onto the living room couch. "No."

"Well, she'll be at the meeting tomorrow, right? She wouldn't risk the Initiative, would she?"

The thought brightened his spirits. "No. You're right, Rae. She'll show up at the meeting. I don't think she'll let her feelings about me get in the way of that."

"If it helps, I'll talk to her. Tell her I didn't intend to hurt her feelings," Rae offered.

"Somehow, I don't think she wants to see you any more than she wants to see me. No offense," he added. He pulled off his tie.

Rae should've looked away when he began to remove his shirt but she couldn't. He was beautiful. All sexy brown muscles with a manly sprinkle of hair on his belly. "I don't offend easily," she said, a little distracted.

Trevor reached for his belt, then rose to carry his discarded clothes to the bedroom.

Rae was disappointed when he closed the door behind him. Her disappointment deepened when she realized he hadn't considered that she was in the room when he'd begun to disrobe. She pushed fingers into her temples. "Get over it, Rae," she said angrily. "It's not you he wants."

"What did you say?" he shouted from the opposite side of the door.

She dropped her hands to her sides. It was best if he didn't know what she was thinking. "You want me fix a couple of steaks or something?" she shouted.

"I've got some leftover Chinese in the fridge," he offered.

"My man," she said cheerfully. Rae wasn't one for cooking. She'd given serious consideration to making planters out of the burners on her stove at home. "I'll go warm it up," she offered.

Just as she opened the refrigerator, the front door opened. Jewel glared at Rae then slammed the door shut.

If looks could kill, she'd be in a casket. "Hey, J," Rae said weakly. "I was just going to warm up some Chinese. Want some?" Of course she didn't.

"I need some things from my office." Jewel's tone dripped venom. "Don't mind me."

Rae raised her hands in a gesture of acquiescence as Jewel entered the office across the hallway. "You know Trevor's all tore up that you disappeared," she said, trying to break the tension.

Jewel continued rummaging through the papers in her office.

Rae pulled the containers from the refrigerator and dumped the contents onto plates. She put the first one in the microwave. "Neither one of us meant to hurt you, Jewel. You know that, don't you?"

The other woman was in the kitchen faster than Rae could blink.

"What is this, Rae?" Jewel challenged. "Is this your attempt to make everything all right so you can show Trevor you're the reasonable one? Is that it? I didn't think you were so low."

"I didn't think you were so stupid," Rae shot back. "That man loves you more than any man will ever love me."

"And that hurts like hell, doesn't it, Rae?"

It hurt, but Rae didn't want to admit it to her. "He loves you, Jewel. He thought you would understand."

"You and I both understand," Jewel said quietly. "He wants a baby more than anything else in the world, and that's why you came up with this scheme. So you could have him forever."

Rae leaned across the counter and spoke in very distinct tones. "He's not mine to have, Jewel. Even if I had his child, I would never have his heart."

"If you had his child, neither would I."

Rae could tell by the stunned look on Jewel's face that she hadn't meant to make that confession. "You don't actually believe that, do you?" she asked Jewel.

Turning in a huff, Jewel went back inside her office, stuffed some papers into her open shoulder bag and headed for the door.

Trevor picked that moment to walk out of the bedroom dressed in his old sweat pants and a worn T-shirt. "Jewel." His face brightened.

"I'm not staying, Trevor."

He drilled Rae with an accusatory glare. "What happened?"

"I was apologizing." Rae lifted her hands innocently.

Trevor jumped over the couch to catch his wife at the door. "Jewel, can't we talk?"

Jewel hesitated. "Maybe later. Not now."

"Tomorrow?" Trevor pressed.

"Yeah, uh, okay." Jewel gave Rae a hard look before leaving.

Trevor raced to the counter and challenged Rae. "What happened?"

Rae swapped the hot food in the microwave with the containers still needing to be reheated. "I tried to apologize. She wasn't hearing it." She didn't look at Trevor as she tried to digest what Jewel had just revealed to her. She was jealous of the baby, not another woman. Rae knew Jewel didn't want her to tell Trevor, could tell by the last look she'd shot at her before leaving. Jewel needed to let her husband know about her insecurities on her own.

"If she would just sit still and listen to me. I know we can work this out." Defeated, Trevor sank onto a stool across the counter from Rae.

"If it's any consolation to you, I'd take it as a good sign that she's so hurt."

"You're crazy," Trevor countered.

"Means she still loves you, dummy," Rae said, pushing an empty paper plate at him. "Eat something. You're gonna need your strength when you go begging at her feet tomorrow."

"Smart-a—"

"Ah, ah, ah!" Rae stopped him. "Keep a civil tongue, you dog. This is an upscale establishment." She opened and closed a few drawers but couldn't find what she was looking for. "You got any plastic forks?"

"Cabinet above the stove." Trevor pointed. "Upscale my behind," he teased. He twirled his plate on the granite countertop for a moment before speaking again. "I'm sorry the whole baby idea didn't work out, Rae." He lifted grateful eyes to her. "But thank you."

Rae dished out a huge portion of Kung Pao Chicken, suddenly ravenous. "It was just an idea. Not that big a deal," she lied, feeling her own hopes shrivel like raisins. But what had she expected? For her to have a normal, happy personal life wasn't in the cards. Sometimes she wondered why she kept trying.

The morning was a pleasant sixty-degrees. Jewel pushed Glendora's new wheelchair down the street in front of Greenview, unable to see too far ahead due to the fog. The blanket of mist was just thick enough to bring a feeling of intimacy as they talked. "I decided last night I can't go back to Trevor, Granny."

"Why on earth would you decide such a foolish thing, child?" Glendora adjusted the shawl around her shoulders. "It wasn't like he cheated on you."

"Isn't it?" Jewel asked hopelessly. "Just because he asked

permission to have Rae's child doesn't make it any less disrespectful."

"He was just asking a question, Jewel," Glendora insisted.

"He was telling me I wasn't woman enough to make him happy," Jewel insisted.

"Men think differently than we do," Glendora countered. "He probably thought it was an innocent enough thing to ask. The man has never made a secret about how much he wants children."

"I don't buy it," Jewel sighed, thinking her poor grandmother was just a victim of her upbringing. Back in her day, if men cheated on their wives, the woman turned a blind eye, happy to keep her man. That didn't work for Jewel. "And even if that's true, what's Rae's excuse?" she said aloud. "You can't tell me she didn't mean to drive a wedge through Trevor's and my relationship."

"Maybe," Granny stated, "that's the nature of some women, sure 'nuf. But here you are ready to give her what she wants wrapped up with a bow. Don't make no sense to me."

Because she didn't have a good reply, Jewel said nothing.

"Seems to me like if Trevor had wanted to start something with Rae, he had plenty chances before he ever met you." Granny stated.

It was a good point, Jewel admitted only to herself.

"Then again, it may not be Rae you're worried about." Glendora twisted slightly in her chair, making a point of looking at Rae as she spoke.

Jewel gave a soft curse at the woman's questioning gaze. Not for the first time, Jewel thought the woman's instinctive interrogation style would have made her a great operative for the CIA. That had been one of the many theories debated by their family about Glendora's time in Europe. "Who woulda gave two thoughts about a dumb colored gal from the South?" her great aunt had asked often. "Wouldn't surprise me none if she'd been a spy," someone else would chime in. "How else you explain her comin' home years later and with all that money?" Of course, the discussion only went on from there.

"What's that?" Glendora lifted her head as if to hear better."

"Nothing," she said.

"What's really bothering you, Jewel Marie? You and I both

know Trevor worships the ground you walk on. So what is it?"

Jewel was ashamed to say but couldn't help releasing the thoughts that had weighed her down for the past couple of weeks. "I'm afraid I'll never be a good enough wife for Trevor, Granny. That's what's bothering me."

"Why are you feeling like that?"

"I killed that baby," she confessed. Guilt stabbed at her gut like a thousand needles. "Killed it with my negativity and my fear. That child sensed what I would be like as a mother. It chose death over me."

"Oh, baby, you can't believe that." Glendora reached a hand up for Jewel.

Grabbing it as if it were a life raft, Jewel squeezed the strong hand and stood still for a moment, unable to continue walking. "It's true, Granny. I'm a horrible person. Trevor deserves way better than me."

"Don't be silly, child. You're a good person…the best." Glendora shook her head. "Lord, Lord, Lord. This is my fault."

Jewel's hand trembled in her grandmother's hand as she moved around the wheelchair and knelt before her. "What are you talking about, Granny? You did your best to raise me to be a good person, but I…I let you down." Because she couldn't hold back the heartache any longer, Jewel dropped her head to her grandmother's knees. The comforting strokes of her grandmother's hand on her head released her tightly wound emotions, and she sobbed.

"You and Eloise. It's my fault the two of you don't believe in love or lasting marriages. I wasn't much of a role model."

"This isn't your fault. If it's anyone's, it's my mother's."

"Ain't no need in blamin' her, child. She only knows what she's seen, same as you." Glendora sighed. "The blame's on me. I just don't know what to do about it."

"There's nothing you can do, Granny. Nothing at all." Resigned to her fate, Jewel wiped her eyes and reached up to kiss her grandmother's cheek. Walking around to the back of the wheelchair, she resumed their slow stroll through the fog.

"I got an invitation the other day," Glendora said softly after a long silence.

"An invitation to what?" Jewel asked, relieved to have something other than her own failures as a wife to talk about.

"An awards ceremony in London."

"Really?"

"They want to deliver a lifetime achievement award to one of my close friends. 'Course, I can't go by myself." She patted the arms of the chair.

"Are you asking me to go with you?" Jewel hoped so. It sounded exciting...a way to escape her problems for a while.

"Yes. Can you get away?" Glendora asked.

"Yeah. I'll let Linda know I'll be gone for—"

"About a month," Glendora interrupted. "I thought while I was there, I'd visit with a few people. Do you mind?"

"No, not at all," Jewel answered honestly. It sounded like a nice break. It would give her time to think about how to end her marriage before the man of her dreams discovered the monster she truly was.

Chapter Seven

Jewel smoothed her blood-red suit for the hundredth time, struggling to keep her emotions in check. She had to facilitate this meeting for the Initiative, and it would be the first time in two weeks she had been face-to-face with either Trevor or Rae.

She'd managed to keep her time in the office limited by doing work from Granny Glen's old house and calling and faxing things in to Linda. She'd made sure that when she was in the office she had clients meeting with her. That way, Trevor couldn't communicate with her.

All this planning and walking around on eggshells was exhausting, but Jewel knew she couldn't relent. Until she felt strong enough to deal with this mess, she couldn't talk to her husband or their supposed friend.

Carefully, she kept her eyes averted from Rae, who was seated at the conference table flipping impatiently through the agenda.

Jewel couldn't ask Rae or Trevor to leave the investment group now; contracts had been signed. At least that's what her lawyer had told her. Still, she didn't know how she would be able to endure the sight of them for the duration of the two-year project.

Trevor entered the conference room and, as his presence always did these days, sent Jewel's pulse skittering.

"I think we need to talk before the meeting starts," he whispered as other board members trickled in behind him. He smelled divine.

Like aftershave and fresh laundry.

"No time," she said quickly, allowing her eyes to dart around the room. If she talked to him now, she'd never regain her composure enough to hold the meeting.

"After, then," Trevor stated with quiet insistence. He then took his time moving away from her to greet the few people who had already arrived.

He looked cool and poised as he talked first with Rae and then walked over to give Sterling a warm greeting and handshake. It was the thing she'd always admired about Trevor, depended upon really, that he would be solid and calm in the midst of chaos.

But today, it was really ticking her off.

As the room filled, Jewel made adjustments to her skirt. Red was the color of confidence and power. She massaged the light wool of the suit as if by osmosis those things would be infused into her veins.

"Looks like we're all here," she said aloud. Placing her most confident smile in place, Jewel tried to appear normal...whatever that was. "Let's all find a seat and get started. We have a full agenda today. Lots of decisions to make." She took a sip of lukewarm coffee to ease the tightness in her throat as the board members carried pastries and cups of coffee from the back credenza to their seats.

It didn't escape her attention that Sterling and Rae sat as far away from one another as possible. They'd barely spoken a word to one another since they'd arrived.

Jewel's concern deepened. Rae's actions were speaking louder than her lying tongue. Not in all the years she'd known her had the woman ever let a single man she was interested in get away. If she wasn't interested in Sterling, then she was definitely after Trevor. Well, she could have him. Jewel wasn't about to become the hysterical jealous wife featured on Jerry Springer shows. She wouldn't dream of giving Trevor the satisfaction of having two women fight over him.

Suddenly noticing that all eyes were directed her way, Jewel knew she'd have to pull the knives out of her back later. Now was the time for business.

At that moment, Eloise sailed into the room in a cloud of

Coco Chanel and her signature winter white. Mr. McWilliams nearly jumped from his chair to assist the overly elegant Eloise into another right beside him.

Mrs. McWilliams deepened the worry lines around her mouth.

Jewel knew just how she felt.

"Sorry for being a little late, everyone." Eloise beamed a gorgeous smile at Jewel before acknowledging everyone else at the table. "Have I missed much?"

"Oh, no," Mr. McWilliams offered. His chest puffed just slightly more than usual. "We were just starting," he offered.

"Right," Jewel added, feeling the need to take control of this meeting as quickly as possible. "As I was saying, we have a full agenda. Let's start with old business and move on." She sat down and led the group through some lively discussions regarding space planning, building design and cost for storefront and office space.

For a full two hours, Jewel managed to forget everything but the Initiative. More than before, she admired the diverse opinions, expertise and backgrounds each individual brought to the group. Even Trevor and Rae had managed to make suggestions she'd grudgingly had to agree with.

Most impressive was Eloise. Jewel had no idea of what a great business mind her mother possessed. Her contribution had been very insightful as she'd led the discussion on ways to gain funding from the San Antonio Historic Restoration Guild as well as the City of San Antonio if they kept their renovation within specific guidelines.

Jewel had decided that her mother's motives for being an investor were legitimate when she'd opened the manila envelope she'd given her at the last meeting and found a sizable check inside. Trevor, always the sane one, had talked her out of shredding the contract and check. As he'd pointed out, the woman wouldn't sabotage anything that she'd invested such a healthy amount of money in and that had the potential of lining her pockets.

Jewel had to admit, Eloise was a lot of things, but stupid wasn't one of them. She collected her notes and surveyed the table, ready to end the meeting. "Great job, everyone. I think we've made real progress today."

Her comments were met with nods and general agreement.

"Next meeting is a month from today. Ten A.M. sharp. Linda will send out minutes of today's meeting no later than the end of the week for your review and approval." She gave a nod to her assistant who was putting away her mini-recorder and tapes.

With the meeting adjourned, everyone pushed away from the table, mingled a bit, and found their way out of the room. Eloise walked past Jewel, stopped and came back. The two women looked at one another. There was no animosity or hostility in her mother's green-eyed gaze. "Good job," Eloise offered before making a quick exit.

For a moment, Jewel stood in stunned silence. It was a first—a compliment from her mother. Before she could figure out what had motivated her mother to make this unnecessary move, Rae was in front of her. "Nice to see you, Jewel." She looked hopeful.

Jewel held no charity in her heart for the woman she used to think of as a friend. She gave an unenthusiastic tilt of her chin to acknowledge Rae's comment then dropped her eyes to her papers to discourage further conversation.

Rae left, blowing a long breath on her way out the door.

The room was blessedly silent. Jewel shoved her paperwork into her shoulder bag, disturbed by the powerful presence she felt in the room. As always, she felt Trevor with every fiber of her being, even when he wasn't touching her. They were alone. She was afraid to raise her head to look at him. Afraid he'd see who she really was.

Trevor crossed the room to close the door. Deliberately, he moved to stand beside her. "Jewel...baby..." His voice was quiet, soothing.

Jewel wanted to fall into his arms and bury her face in his shoulder, but she didn't move.

He reached for her hands.

Jewel quickly took a step back. "Whatever you've got to say, do it without touching me," she said more harshly than she'd intended. Her nerves were on end, and she was holding on to her control with tremendous effort.

Dropping his hands, Trevor sighed. "I just wanted to tell you how sorry I am. I had no idea how strongly you'd feel about…" He faltered.

"How could you not know?" Jewel folded her arms, still hurt at his and Rae's insensitivity. "I really wanted to be the one to give you a child," she admitted honestly.

"I know—"

"Let me finish," she insisted. "I also know that now that there's no possibility of us having a child together…" She took an intensely punishing breath before continuing. "…It means that you won't ever be happy with me, Trevor."

"I am happy with you, Jewel. Completely." He closed the distance between them and attempted to pull her into his arms.

Jewel retreated again. "Don't do that, Trevor." His embrace was too tempting. "Don't lie to yourself like that."

"I'm not lying, Jewel. You're not listening. Why are you being so difficult?" he asked. His patience was clearly thinning.

Jewel finally looked deep into his dark brown eyes and melted a little to see the love still there. "I'm just being real, Trevor. Real enough for both of us."

"Look," Trevor tried again, "maybe my timing was off in asking you to consider the possibility of Rae and me having a child. I know that you were devastated when you lost that baby, Jewel. Weren't you?"

She dropped her head and nodded. He was right on the money but not for the reason he thought.

"Honey, how could I do anything but love and admire you for wanting to bear my child? For suffering through what you did because you wanted me to have what I've longed for all my life?"

This time, she didn't back away when he moved closer and pulled her hands out of their defensive posture and into his warm, assuring palms. "I'll always love you for that, Jewel. Always."

Lifting tear-filled eyes to his, Jewel let go of pretense and opened her heart to him as she always had. "I feel so inadequate, Trevor. I can't bear the thought of some other woman giving you a child."

"Oh, baby," he said softly, pulling her into his arms. "You'll never be inadequate. Not to me."

It was heaven being wrapped inside his hug. It soothed the hurt, eased the guilt she'd been carrying for weeks. Jewel brought her arms around his waist and laid her head on his shoulder.

"Rae feels bad that she caused problems between us, Jewel. She didn't mean to."

"I know." Jewel pulled away to look at her husband, a little perturbed that he chose that moment to defend his friend. "It was a helluva thing to offer, though, wasn't it?" she asked pointedly.

"Yeah, it was," Trevor admitted. "But you have to understand where she's coming from," he explained. "She wants a child so badly that she visited the sperm bank to pick out a donor."

"Really?" This was news to Jewel, but she wasn't impressed. "Why didn't she go through with it?"

Trevor shrugged. "She showed me the file on the donor she'd picked out. Then said it felt so cold and impersonal that she was having second thoughts. That plus the high cost."

"How much?" Jewel asked with interest.

"Around nine or ten thousand."

"Wow," Jewel said, feeling less and less sympathy for Rae Paris. The woman had just purchased a Hummer. What was nine or ten grand?

"She figured if I was the donor, the two of us would have what we always wanted and could split the cost of the in vitro fertilization procedure," Trevor continued. "It sounded like the answer to our prayers at the time."

His arms began to feel like a vice around Jewel's waist.

"I hadn't thought through how it might feel to you. I'm sorry."

Jewel's anger deepened. Maybe it wasn't she who was at fault in this. The man was so selfish. "And that's what bothers me most, Trevor." She stepped out of his embrace. "That one day it'll come to this again. What you want will overshadow how I feel, and I won't be able to take that. Do you understand?"

"Jewel—"

"I don't want to talk about this right now, Trevor." She headed back to her paperwork. "Granny Glen has asked me to accompany her to Europe for a reunion with her friends and to attend an awards ceremony. I'll be gone for a month starting next Saturday."

"When were you going to tell me about this?" Trevor placed his hands on his hips.

"I'm telling you now," she shot back.

"How the hell are we supposed to solve this if you keep running out on me?" The normally calm, cool Trevor was now shouting.

Jewel found it a little unnerving to know she'd made him so angry. "We'll talk when I get back."

"In a f-- In a month?" The cinnamon brown of his face was tinted with red. "If you leave me now, don't bother coming back, Jewel."

Her heart stuttered in her chest. "What did you say?"

"I said, if you leave, don't come back." His eyes were hard as granite as he enunciated each word.

Jewel was too hurt to respond in any way but to pick up her bag and leave. Forever.

Eloise hummed happily as she pulled her Mercedes into the long drive toward the gate of The Dominion. She felt good about the Initiative and how Jewel was handling it. She'd looked so confident as she'd facilitated the meeting and had no problems challenging anyone who took a wrong turn in their discussions. Her mother had been correct—the apple hadn't fallen far from the tree. Still, it would be hard getting back into Jewel's good graces after so many years and so many hurts. Yet she knew it was time.

Lately, Eloise had been lonesome—even in large groups of people when she acted as if she were the belle of the ball. It didn't really matter anymore whom she impressed, whom she charmed or whom she forged a business relationship with.

Lately, all she felt was lonely, and no amount of charity functions or business meetings could fill the void. Today, working alongside her daughter, was the first time in a long time that she'd felt connected with anyone. Perhaps she'd call her mother and schedule time to visit with her as well.

Approaching the gate, Eloise flitted her fingers at George, the guard. The man came out of the tiny building and held up a hand to stop her.

Irritation was instant. She'd told the man a long time ago that she wasn't interested in any ideas he had about the two of them becoming an item. "Now listen, George, I'm in quite a hurry—" she began before she noticed the worried look on his round brown face.

"Yes, ma'am. I know," he said, "but there's a guy over there." He pointed across the street to a tall Black man dressed in white leather and leaning against the gleaming white and chrome panels of a magnificent Ducati motorcycle. "Says he's your husband. I told him you didn't have no husband, but he said he'd just been away for awhile." George said the last sarcastically. "'Course I didn't believe that, Ms. Hunt, but still he said he'd wait."

As George spoke, the Black man pulled off his sunglasses and looked right at her. Eloise felt his eyes pull her closer, though neither of them moved.

"You want I should call the police, ma'am?" George asked.

It was tough to hear with her heart pounding so loudly in her ears, but eventually George's question sank in. "Uh...no, George. It's all right." Eloise pulled her eyes away from Charles Hunt long enough to give a tepid smile to the guard. The last thing she needed was to have her dirty laundry aired in front of someone with a wagging tongue. "He's not dangerous," she lied.

Charles Hunt was the one person in the world who had the power to make her lose the one thing she cherished more than anything...her self-control.

Charles donned his sunglasses once more and swung a long leg over the white leather seat of his motorcycle and had it purring to life within seconds.

Presumptuous cad, she thought. Without so much as a signal from her, he'd assumed she'd let him in. Eloise sat the eternity it took for the gate to open, trying desperately to think of how to get rid of him once and for all.

It would only take a few moments for her to escort her unwanted visitor to her house. Eloise glanced discreetly in her rearview mirror at the man at least a half-dozen times. He still looked good, damn him. He looked sexy in his helmet and dark goggles and was still the most magnificent man she'd ever laid eyes on.

Eloise pulled into the garage, while Charles parked behind her in the driveway. She walked to her back door and stood there, waiting for him to join her.

When he was within arm's reach, Charles stopped and took an appraising look, from Eloise's $700 heels to her recently pampered, auburn-rinsed hair. His eyes had always been narrow in that sexy Clint Eastwood kind of way, but now they had tiny crow's feet at the edges, making them even more attractive. And the fact that he was looking at her as if he wanted to have her for lunch was making Eloise a little woozy.

"You're still the best-looking woman on the planet, Elle," he said in his deep-as-the-ocean voice.

Eloise's legs weakened. "It's cold out here. Let's go inside." She needed time to pull herself together. She entered the house and took a couple of deep breaths to keep the panic from taking over.

Walking quickly through the mudroom, the kitchen, and into the living room, she headed for the wet bar to pour herself a glass of wine. As she rounded the bar, she realized that he wasn't there.

"Nice place you got here," he called from another room.

Eloise couldn't tell which one. "Would you like a drink?" She finished pouring her wine and took a long swallow.

"Sure," he said, finally sauntering into the living room. "Got any beer?" he asked as he surveyed her high ceilings and nine-foot picture windows.

"No."

"Johnny Walker?" He walked around her spacious living room, running a hand along the fine upholstery of her couch and chairs.

"Yes. I have that," she said, a little punchy from the intimate way he was touching her things. "On the rocks, right?"

He looked at her and smiled. "You remembered."

Dropping her head to protect herself from the effects of his charming smile, Eloise fumbled around behind the bar to locate the whiskey. The bottle had never been opened because none of her friends drank the stuff. She'd only kept it because…

Her hands trembled a little as she ran a fingernail along the paper around the top. They shook a bit more as she opened the bottle and poured the amber liquid into a glass. Eloise hated herself for being so weak…for wanting him so badly.

" 'Preciate it," he said, taking the glass from the bar with his large, strong hands.

Because she couldn't handle another moment of awkward suspense, Eloise blurted out in a rush, "Why are you here? What do you want, Charles?"

He made a satisfied moan as the liquor made its way down his throat. Charles sat the glass down, folded his arms on the bar and leaned toward his estranged wife. "I'm here because you never came to see me. I've waited years for you to forgive me for what I did to you. Every year, I invited you to Vegas, to make up with you, to hold you. To make love to you." His smile widened, his sexy eyes narrowed, and Eloise felt herself fill with want.

"Then your mama called and asked me what the hell kind of man I was."

"My mother?" Eloise asked, taking the moment to find a bar stool to lean against. "My mother called you?" How dare she interfere?

"Yep. Said a real man wouldn't be sitting around waiting for what he wanted. He'd go after it."

"So, my mother challenged you and you had to step up," Eloise concluded. "That's so typical of you, Charles. Never could resist a dare, could you?" Eloise took a sip of her own drink.

Charles rose to his full height and sent a searing look into her eyes. "Truth is, I was already on my way when she caught up with me."

Eloise gripped her glass a little tighter. He was telling the truth. She knew because he wasn't pleading with her to believe him. Still, she didn't hold any hope that anything good would become of his re-entry into her life. She'd learned during their marriage that all she could count on with Charles Hunt was that the bottom would fall out. Eloise clutched the seat of her stool and drained her wineglass.

"I can't wait anymore, Elle." His voice sounded weary. "I need you."

And she needed him. And her growing need made Eloise feel like a deer staring into the headlights of an oncoming semi-truck. "You've never needed me before, Charles. Why now?"

"That's not true, Elle." He made his way around the bar. "I've always needed you." He placed his hands on her hips.

"Even when you were making love to all those other women?" she tried not to sound as wounded as she felt.

"Especially then." His tone sank to the depths of dark and sexy. "I thought I could make up for feeling worthless by showing you how much other women adored me."

"Since when did you ever feel worthless, Charles?" Eloise wasn't buying a word of this.

"From the moment I laid eyes on you, Elle."

Again, he wasn't urging her to believe him. Eloise smelled the scent of liquor on his breath and the road on his clothes and allowed herself to enjoy the feeling of being held again.

"Here you were, this beautiful, rich girl who had everything," he continued and pulled her closer. "And I was a poor boy from the wrong side of the tracks—"

"Who was the star running back of the University of Texas Longhorns," Eloise placed her hands on his chest and felt the still hard muscles beneath his sweater. "All the girls, White and Black, hated my guts the instant you decided to date me. Did you know that?" she asked softly.

"No." He drew his knuckles gently down her cheek and ran his thumb across her chin. "I'm sorry."

Shaking her head, Eloise swallowed hard to find the right words. "I didn't tell you because I liked it." Eloise looked him directly in his deep brown eyes. "I loved the fact that I was the only one you wanted, Charles." A lump formed in her throat as she remembered how much in love she'd been with this man. "It's all I ever needed from you," she admitted.

"I'm so sorry I hurt you," Charles whispered as he planted a kiss on her cheek.

"Don't, Charles," she pleaded with closed eyes. His hands were hot over the material of her skirt, awakening yearnings she'd kept dormant for years.

"I can't wait any longer," he insisted, nudging his cheek against hers. Kissing her softly on the temple, on the lips, on the neck.

He smelled like leather and sweat and lust. His hands moved her skirt up around her waist, and he ran his hands along the satin of her underwear.

Eloise couldn't fight the overwhelming need rushing through her. She didn't want to anymore. "Not here, Charles," she said, maneuvering around him and heading out of the bar. "The bedroom's this way." She held a hand out for him.

Charles followed her willingly. "Bedroom, huh? That's one we've never tried before."

That much was true.

When they were first married, they hadn't been able to keep their hands off each other long enough to reach the bedroom most of the time. Eloise remembered making love to him on the hood of her first car with only the moon and stars for light, and there had been several close encounters in the elevator of their apartment building, and the hammock at her mother's house…

Eloise went to close the shades on the French doors and windows of her bedroom to ensure there were no prying eyes. Before she could perform the task, Charles was behind her at the door.

"That's your backyard?" he asked.

It was her own private Garden of Eden. Eloise appreciated the appropriate level of awe in his voice as they both looked from the pool with a waterfall to the gardens leading up to the oak trees, crepe myrtles and eight-foot privacy fence surrounding the yard. "This is my sanctuary," she said quietly.

"I always pictured you in a place like this, princess," he said, calling her by the nickname he'd given her back when they'd been dating. "Always knew it wouldn't be me who'd give it to you."

Because he seemed sad in his admission, Eloise turned to face him. "Why do you say that?"

The tiny lines around his eyes softened, as did the soft brown of his irises. "We've always been two different people, Eloise. The only thing we've ever had in common was our love for one another."

"That's true." Eloise moved her hands inside his jacket to feel his warmth. "But there was a time I would've done anything for you, Charles Hunt. Anything," she whispered as she nipped at his full lips.

"And what about now?" he asked. His eyes met hers with a sincerity she'd rarely seen.

"Now?" Eloise realized that he didn't quite have the same effect on her as he had in the past. She could see him for what he was now. A man. Good looking with the gray at his temple but still sheltering the boy within him. Fingering the stud that sparkled in his left ear, she knew that the intrigue this rogue had held for her when she was young wasn't as strong now that more than a decade had passed. She was stronger now, wiser for having been on her own for so long. Yet she couldn't lie to him and tell him that he no longer mattered to her. There was still something about him that sent everything all akimbo inside her.

"I'm not sure," she answered honestly. "The jury's still out."

"Well, while the jury's contemplating, how's about you and me giving them something to talk about?" His smile was devilish. His hand was now firmly planted between her legs, touching her just the way she liked.

"Ohhhh, all right." Eloise leaned back against the glass of the door and let waves of joy run from his fingers right through her body. Arms up, legs wide, she let Charles have his way with her.

Charles had one hand working her panties off her hips, while the other unbuttoned her blouse. Soon her bra hung loose as Charles paid full homage to her breasts with his kisses and breathless praises.

Eloise stepped out of the panties that were dangling at her ankles and suffered in heavenly anguish as his fingers worked miracles beneath the skirt that was now hopelessly bunched at her waist. If there were neighbors watching, she hoped they enjoyed the show because there was no way she was going to stop him now.

At some point, Charles had managed to remove his pants. They were now a pool of white lying atop his black leather boots. He lifted her legs effortlessly and positioned himself to slide inside her slick walls.

Eloise cried out as he filled her. She'd forgotten how good he felt, how perfectly they fit together. He moved inside her again and again with an urgency that wasn't normal for Charles. His lovemaking had always been slow, calculated for optimal pleasure, but not today. His movements were more desperate, more needy, and she liked it.

Holding to his shoulders, Eloise held on for the ride, unable to hold back her cries of insane pleasure. It didn't take long for her to reach the edge of insanity. She heralded its arrival with screams, for the first time unashamed of the power of her passion. No sooner had she finished than she felt Charles tense beneath her and spasm uncontrollably inside her depths.

Panting, he slowly released her to stand on her own. Eloise led Charles to the unused bed, and they both lay in each other's arms in silence. Eloise knew that what they'd just done had changed nothing. This was typical Charles, positioning himself to enter her life once more, only to leave her heart shattered in a thousand pieces.

This time, she would have the strength to let him go. Permanently.

The telephone rang and interrupted Eloise's thoughts.

"Hello?"

"Eloise, it's your mother. I need a favor."

Chapter Eight

The morning sun stretched through the bay windows of Eloise's kitchen, its sole purpose seemingly to showcase Charles's magnificent chocolate physique. At more than sixty, his shoulders were wide, his waist narrow, and his stomach, while no longer chiseled, was nearly flat. But the fact that his middle had softened over the years was small comfort.

Eloise blew out an exasperated breath. At nearly the same age, she knew better than to give his looks and charm too much credence. "You can't stay here while I'm gone," she repeated for the third time. It had been two weeks since she'd agreed to go to London with her mother. Surprisingly, her mother had volunteered to take care of buying the airline tickets, saying she found surfing the Internet fascinating. The last thing she needed was to have her ex-husband have run of the house while she was gone.

Charles was undaunted. "I promise not to have any wild parties or mess up the rug, princess." He donned a white sweater and adjusted it over black jeans. "I stopped that some ten years ago. I've changed in a lot of ways," he said sincerely.

For a moment, Eloise was tempted to believe him. He wasn't a morning person, never had been, so she found it slightly endearing that he'd made her breakfast that morning…after he'd made her body sing with those talented fingers yet again.

Stop it, she commanded the delightful but decadent memories that filled her head. "I told you not to get comfortable," she said aloud, not knowing if she spoke to her estranged husband or to herself. Feigning a search for some item in her purse, she struggled to find the words that would help Charles understand she was serious about him leaving.

"Oh come on, Elle." Charles moved closer. "Let me watch the house while you're gone. At least until I find a place of my own. I'll clean the pool," he offered.

"I have a service for that." She brushed aside the hand that reached out to her.

"What's the harm? I promise to leave when you get back."

"Listen, Charles." She leaned her weight to one side and looked him straight in the eyes. "We've both had our fun, now it's time to part ways before...well...before something happens."

"You mean you've been holdin' back?" A hand went to his chest dramatically. "I'm an old man, Elle. You gotta take it easy."

Eloise wasn't amused. She checked her watch. It was getting late. If she didn't hurry, she wouldn't be able to pick up her mother and get to the airport in time to get through the security lines, and they'd miss their plane. "I don't have time to argue with you, Charles. If you want to find your next sugar mama, do what you have to do, but not in my house. Not this time." It was vicious and low and not at all what she'd expected to come out of her mouth. But she couldn't take it back now. Instead, she grabbed the handle of her rolling luggage and pretended she'd meant the snipe.

"Let me get that for you," Charles offered with such unaffected cordiality, Eloise wondered if he'd heard what she'd said.

"I've got it." Eloise swatted away his hand to hide her shame. Opening the garage door, she took a step toward the car.

Charles quickly put a hand around her waist. "Let me drive. I haven't seen your mother, my daughter, or anyone but you since I've been here." His eyes darkened as the humor left his face. "And for the record, I'm not looking for a sugar mama. I came for you."

It was a reaction, but not what she'd expected. A dark, stormy feeling took hold of Eloise as Charles' hand wandered down her waist to rest gently on her behind.

"It's too late, Charles," she whispered as the weight of sadness filled her heart. "You came too late for me."

"No, Elle," he insisted softly, "I'm just in time." His gentle grope on her behind ignited a dangerous fire in the pit of her belly. His sexy lips parted just enough for the scent of mint to reach her.

The floor tilted slightly beneath her feet, and Eloise moved with it. Her tongue plunged inside his waiting mouth before she had time to catch her balance. Releasing the nuisance of her luggage handle, she fell inside his open arms.

Charles pulled his wife closer, reveled in the warm softness of her body and wondered how he'd lived so long without her. It had been decades since the woman in his arms had mattered to him for more than the fifteen minutes it took to sate his desire. He'd had an unhealthy dose of young, pretty women in the past decade. More than a man with any sense would have had, he chided himself. They'd been pretty enough. Sexy enough. Accommodating enough. But each time he'd tried to find out who they were, he'd been disappointed to find the outer décor served only as a shell to vacuous souls.

But this was real. Eloise was real. A real woman with real strength and beauty. He'd known it since the day he'd met and fallen madly in love with her. Somehow he'd managed to let pride and insecurity chip away, then destroy, all that was good about their relationship. All he knew was that Eloise made him whole, complete, content. Problem was, she had every right to turn him away, to say hateful things after his years of indiscretion. Hell, being let inside her bed, inside her body, so quickly had been an unexpected gift.

Charles felt, rather than heard, her sigh as she sank softly against him. It was sexy as hell, and he gave thought to having a round right there in the garage. He checked the space in her back seat. It wouldn't be the first time.

Eloise allowed herself one last, indulgent taste. She'd be in Europe for a month with her mother. But when she got back, she'd deal once and for all with Charles Hunt.

For now, she enjoyed his warm embrace and the way his arms around her felt like a warm bed on a chilly morning. No matter what Charles said, this time she wouldn't allow him to reopen old wounds that had taken twenty years to heal. This time she would be in control.

Eloise deepened the kiss and pressed tightly against him, hoping like the devil that the cocky sucker burned for her while she was gone.

"I have to go," she said with significantly less bite than before. Eloise pulled away and licked his taste from her lips. "You're going to be the death of me, Charles Hunt," she said, picking up her discarded bag.

"Death by chocolate, baby. No better way to go." He couldn't lie. The way she wanted him was giving him a hard on...and a boost of confidence. Maybe winning his way back into her heart wouldn't be as difficult as he'd first thought. "I'll take good care of things while you're gone," he said, assuming her comment to mean acquiescence. He opened the trunk and stowed her suitcase, then held his hand open for her keys. "Let me drive." His tone was soft yet insistent.

"All right. But we've got to hurry. I hear the security on these international flights is ten times worse than domestic."

They made the drive to her mother's house in twenty minutes flat. Charles pulled into a parking space beside a Jaguar. Eloise recognized the car as Jewel's and Trevor's and was instantly irritated. "Looks like you get your wish, Charles," she said.

He gave her a quizzical look.

"Jewel is here," she explained as a bad taste bathed her mouth.

"Really?" His face beamed with pleasure. "Fantastic!" He nearly leapt from the car and ran to open her door. He was shifting from foot-to-foot in anticipation by the time they reached Glendora's door.

Jewel opened it. "Daddy!" she squealed as she threw her arms around her father's neck.

Charles lifted her into his arms and spun her with delight.

Eloise stepped back to avoid being hit by the spinning duo who'd blurred into one person. She felt old resentment creeping inside, cooling her blood. Charles had the same idiotic look on his face the day Jewel was born. Anxious, ecstatic and madly in love with the small person they'd created.

It seemed only moments ago that Charles had proclaimed his arms were made for Eloise alone. But then Jewel had come along, and everything changed. He'd rarely put the child down—he had always been singing to her, playing with her, taking her places. And not long afterward, it seemed any woman could find her way inside his arms.

And Jewel. Jewel had always looked at her father with love in her eyes. Eyes that had never allowed themselves to see the worst part of the man...only the best.

Eloise was irritated that adulthood hadn't changed the rose-tinted hue in her daughter's gaze. The only color Eloise could see at the moment was a distasteful green.

She averted her eyes that were quickly filling. Shame and guilt became her heart's companions for resenting something as wonderful as a father's love for his only child. None of what had happened between her and Charles had been Jewel's fault. She knew that—now.

"Come in. Come in." Jewel led her father by the hand into Glendora's small apartment. Not once did she bother to look in Eloise's direction.

Eloise was hurt.

"Granny, look who's here," she said with the uncensored delight of a ten year old.

Eloise closed the door quietly behind her and stood by to watch the reunion. Feeling like an outsider looking in as Charles leaned closer to Glendora to hear words meant only for him, Eloise fell back on the role she was most comfortable playing...the timekeeper. She cleared her throat. "We've got to be going, Mother, or we'll miss the plane." She scanned the four suitcases sitting near the door. "You're not taking all of those, are you? We'll be charged extra for—"

"Two of those are Jewel's." Glendora turned back to her son-in-law as if she hadn't just delivered a bomb.

"Jewel's coming?" Eloise's reaction was automatic and much too quick to reel back in.

Jewel frowned. "Don't worry, Eloise. You weren't the only one who was surprised."

"Hush now," Glendora sputtered irritably. "Why don't you put those in the car for us, Charles, honey?" she instructed by way of dismissal.

With a knowing nod, he eased her back to her seat on the couch and moved to do her bidding. The task should've taken two trips, but Charles managed to take all four bags at once. "I'll be waiting in the car," he said to Eloise with a wink.

Eloise felt duped and irritated. She hated surprises and her mother knew it. "Well, aren't we just one big, happy family?" she murmured.

"We are and it's about time we acted like it." Glendora's chin rose obstinately. "You two are my family, and I love you, though I haven't done right by raising you." She held up a weathered hand as they protested in unison. "No. I taught you to be independent, and you both learned that lesson well. Just look at you, Eloise." Pride shone in her watery brown eyes. "A successful investment banker living in a big, pretty house."

Eloise swallowed hard against the lump of guilt in her throat. She couldn't tell Glendora now how she'd mistimed the stock market. Couldn't tell her that she'd recently called in some favors, hoping to get a job in order to continue making payments on her immodest estate. Unfortunately, she feared her age made any real offers slow in coming. Her current savings wouldn't last through the year unless there was a generous bull market in the immediate future. It would take that, plus a healthy return on Jewel's Initiative, to recover the tens of thousands of dollars she'd lost of her mother's retirement nest egg.

"And, Jewel," Glendora continued, "you run one of the most prestigious and profitable real estate offices in the city. I'm so proud of you."

Jewel ducked her head at the praise.

"And both of you found the one man who was perfect for you." She looked at one woman, then the other. Jewel tried to avoid eye contact.

"And you're both ready to piss that love away," Glendora concluded angrily.

Eloise rolled her eyes. "Oh, I'm not listening to this," she said, reaching for the doorknob. "Charles is a no-good womanizer who wasn't worth the years I spent with him."

"Well, maybe if you hadn't been so hard on him, he wouldn't have left!" Jewel fumed.

Eloise turned on her daughter. "That's right. Charles left. Left you and me. But I stayed and did my best to raise you."

An incredulous look crossed Jewel's face. "You sent me to stay with Granny Glen when I was ten."

"Because you were an absolute terror!" Eloise could feel her blood running hot.

"I was a terror because I missed my father."

"All I was trying to do was keep a roof over our heads, Jewel. Meanwhile, you skipped school, smoked dope and started having sex with any boy that looked your way."

"That's not true." Jewel took a step toward her mother. "I skipped school one time on Senior Ditch Day, and I would hardly call smoking marijuana that one time a big problem. And let's not forget, Eloise, that the one person I wanted to sleep with when I was in high school, you slept with instead."

Silence reigned as Eloise reeled from the impact of her daughter's words. "You wanted to have sex with your father?" The words barely made their way out of her mouth.

"Don't be sick." Jewel looked as if she'd swallowed something foul. "My boyfriend, Eloise. You slept with him at our family reunion." She gestured emphatically. "I was completely humiliated."

Memories came flooding back to Eloise in vivid detail. The boy had been barely legal at age twenty-two and much too old for her sixteen-year-old daughter.

The tryst with the boy hadn't been planned. And she'd realized soon after that it had been nothing but a vain attempt to heal her wounded pride following one of Charles's affairs. She'd needed desperately to prove, if only to herself, that she was still attractive to other men. She'd never intended to hurt Jewel, but she hadn't counted on the indiscretion of that twenty-two year old who couldn't wait to brag about his perceived sexual conquest of Jewel's "hot" mother.

Glendora finally broke the awkward silence. "I think you owe Jewel an explanation for that, Eloise. But now is not the time. Jewel, fetch my overcoat. Eloise, help me to my wheelchair," she instructed. "We'll all have plenty of time to talk on the way to London."

Conversation on the plane was impossible. With Eloise's frosty demeanor and Glendora sitting between them, Jewel found the flight to Heathrow long and uncomfortable. It was a relief to finally exit the plane and stretch her legs.

The air in London was wet and thick upon their arrival. Still, the sky, though dreary, carried an exciting scent, and Jewel could almost feel the electric pulse of the city as they exited the terminal behind their limo driver.

It seemed Glendora felt it as well. The moment she left the terminal and laid eyes on the city, years washed from her face as a rosy glow tinted her yellow-brown cheeks and a smile brightened her eyes. She rose to stand on the sidewalk and seemed to breathe in the fog and cold with delight.

The limo driver, a portly, red-cheeked fellow, offered Glendora a hand as Eloise collapsed the chair to fit into the trunk.

"Wait just a minute." Glendora waved off the driver's assistance and lifted her face to the sky. She continued to breathe deeply. "Smells just the same," she said with pleasure.

All Jewel could smell was exhaust from the cars and shuttles that were jockeying for position along the curb. "It's cold, Granny Glen. Let's get in the limo before you catch something."

"Don't worry 'bout me, baby." Glendora scanned the city once more with loving eyes. "I'm feelin' just fine."

"Well, the rest of us can't feel our toes, Mother," Eloise piped up irritably. "I'm sure the view is just as lovely from the hotel, so can we go now?"

"Yes, yes," Glendora said, irritated to be rushed. The driver helped her inside the car with a "There we are, now," and then offered a hand to Eloise.

Jewel's ears and nose were frozen by the time it was her turn.

Warmth was welcome as she slid in beside her grandmother.

"Hilton Paddington Hotel," Eloise instructed as the driver removed his hat and put the car in drive.

"Awright, then," he chimed cheerfully. "And if you don't mind me saying so, Miss Jubilee, it's my honor to be drivin' you today." His smile was directed into the rearview mirror at Glendora.

The old woman beamed. "That's kind of you…what did you say your name is?"

"William, ma'am. You're here for the Laurence Olivier Awards, isn't that so?"

"Yes, it is. I must say, I'm surprised you know of me. I was no star and you seem a bit young."

"Oh yes, but my folks were big fans. They have old playbills and pictures from all of the old shows," he offered by way of explanation. "You took a picture with me ma and dad a while back. Signed their playbill. They say you created quite the scandal."

Jewel watched and listened intently to the conversation. She thought she detected a heavy dose of "star-struck" in William's lovely accent and looked at Eloise for an explanation.

Eloise frowned and shrugged to indicate a shared ignorance.

In tandem, Jewel and her mother turned questioning looks on Glendora even as she continued her conversation with William. She offered them a pleasant cat-who-ate-the-canary look but nothing more. To the limo driver, she shot question after question about people and places and events that she'd known before.

William would have served well as a tour guide, Jewel decided, for the seeming wealth of information, past and present, at his disposal. Glendora turned sideways and leaned over the seat to facilitate their conversation. It seemed she was totally enamored with William by the time they finally arrived at their hotel.

"You simply must be my driver for the rest of my stay here in London," Glendora said as William helped her out of the car and into her wheelchair.

"I think that can be arranged, ma'am." William seemed to be fairly flying as he insisted on wheeling Glendora inside the hotel. Eloise followed along quickly to take care of their check-in. Jewel hung back to look at the spectacular architecture of the building.

It was a beautiful building, standing about five stories high. The details above the doors and windows were spectacular and quite different from the buildings in San Antonio. On either end of the building were two towers that seemed to add elegance to the entire structure. It was the kind of building Trevor would've loved… something with history.

Sighing at the thought of her husband, Jewel let the chill air blow past her for a moment. This was what it was going to be like without Trevor. Cold and lonely. But it couldn't be helped. It was better to end it now than suffer through a heartless, loveless marriage for years before finally bringing things to an even sadder end. She walked inside. Rich taupe and ivory tiles in diamond shapes led her from the lobby to the semi-circular desk of polished mahogany. Jewel overheard her mother question if the suite had three beds, still complaining that her daughter had come along unexpectedly.

Jewel smiled. Granny Glen was a pip all right. She'd duped both of them. Jewel knew what the old woman expected, that if she and Eloise spent time together, they would reconcile their differences and become closer. Jewel hated to disappoint her grandmother, but she knew that wasn't in the cards. Her mother's selfishness and cold heart had erased any relationship they'd had a long time ago.

Apologetically, the woman behind the desk informed Eloise that she was unable to locate an available room with three beds. They would have to make do with the king-size bed in one room and the queen in the other. Glendora announced that Jewel would sleep with her while Eloise would have the other room to herself.

The suite was luxurious with polished chestnut furniture and large windows overlooking nearby Hyde Park. Jewel unpacked, placing her clothing in the top two dresser drawers, wishing she'd never come on this trip. Things felt unsettled at home. She'd contacted their attorney, who'd refused to draw up divorce papers without speaking to her first. At least she'd left the business during the slow season. People relocated and moved in spring and summer more often than winter. And the Initiative would have to move ahead in her absence. Trevor had promised to attend the city council meeting to lobby for approval to purchase the land and start building.

Thoughts of Trevor pierced her heart like a razor. Sinking to the bed, she covered her face with the folded clothing in her hand. He'd looked so angry and confused when she'd left the office two days ago. His threat that, if she left, she shouldn't come back had hung heavy in the air, though he hadn't repeated it. Though they'd tried to be professional while working, it was apparent from Linda's gentle questions and concerned eyes over her reading glasses that she knew all was not well.

Jewel fell back onto the bed, tossing the clothes onto the pillows. She'd thought she'd feel better, having put some distance between them, but instead found irritability and sadness had sunk into her bones as deeply as the wet, chilly weather outside the window. Leaving San Antonio in sixty-degree weather to arrive at Heathrow Airport in freezing weather had come as a shock to her system. At least she'd packed a heavy overcoat, gloves, hat and scarf, as Granny had instructed. She could wrap herself snugly to combat the effects of the weather, but little seemed to warm the icy grip on her heart.

Granny wheeled herself in from the sitting room of their suite. A delightful smile filled her face, wiping years from her countenance. "What're you doing, child? Not unpacked yet? We've got things to do, places to go. We'll be having dinner with some of my old friends downstairs. They'll be meeting me at seven sharp. Let's get dressed. Hurry, hurry." She clapped her hands and wheeled toward the small closet. "Take down my blue Chanel suit would you, Jewel? I want to make a good impression."

Glad to forget her problems for the moment, Jewel lifted herself from the bed and did as her grandmother asked. She found a dress of her own as well. "I don't know where you're finding all this energy, Granny Glen." She covered a yawn with her hand. "This time change is kicking my butt."

"Oh, young people," Glendora clucked, wheeling toward the bathroom. "You have no stamina. That's what happens when you have machines to do everything for you." She hummed happily as she eased out of the chair and walked, slowly but steadily, inside the bathroom.

Jewel shrugged. She was just about to offer some help, but it seemed Glendora was having one of her "good days" and decided the old gal was capable of getting herself cleaned up and ready for dinner on her own.

Fingering the phone, Jewel fought indecision. Should she call Trevor to let him know they'd arrived safely? Deciding he deserved no less than that, she followed the instructions on how to make an international call on her card.

He answered just before the machine was to pick up. "Hello?" he asked groggily.

"Oh, I'm sorry," Jewel said sincerely. "I forgot about the time change, Trevor. Did I wake you?"

"Yeah," he said, seemingly more alert. "So, you're in London?" his tone was flat and accusatory.

"Yeah. We're here."

"Listen, Jewel," Trevor paused. "I was a little harsh the last time we spoke. I didn't mean what I said."

"Don't…apologize, Trevor." Jewel couldn't take it if he was nice. It was easier to believe she was doing the right thing when he was angry. "Hey, you know who's in town?" she asked.

"London or here?"

"There. In San Antonio."

"Who?"

"My dad," she said delightedly. "He said he's staying at Eloise's house until he can find a place of his own. Isn't that great?"

"Yeah. That's good, Jewel."

Another uncomfortable silence fell between them.

"Well, I just called to let you know we're here," she explained unnecessarily. "And to make sure you know we're due in the city council meeting next Wednesday to get the green light on the Initiative."

"I'm fully prepared to present at the meeting," he assured her.

"You'll do great, I know," Jewel said honestly.

"When you get back, Jewel—" he began.

"When I get back, we'll get a divorce," she interrupted. Biting her bottom lip, she waited for his reaction. She hadn't wanted to blurt it out over the phone, but she could tell he was about to talk about reconciliation again. There was no future between them—couldn't be now that she knew his true feelings about children.

"You've lost your mind, woman," the normally unruffled Trevor was nearly yelling into the phone. "We're going to work this out. There'll be no divorce."

"I wish we could work it out, Trevor, but…" She couldn't continue because heartbreak had brought tears to her eyes and choked her voice into silence.

"Give yourself time to think this through while you're there." Trevor's voice was trembling with emotion. "I miss you. You're my whole life, Jewel. I can't live without you. And I don't think you can live without me, baby. Think about it."

Jewel couldn't reply, could only curl into a tight ball and turn her face into the pillow to cry. Clutching the phone, she pulled it to her chest as it went dead. *Oh dear, God. What have I done?*

Eloise felt her heart shatter. She'd tried not to listen to her daughter in the next room as she spoke to her husband. Such things were private. But she sensed something had gone wrong and walked to the doorway. Her daughter was lying in a fetal position, shaking the king-sized bed with her sobbing.

Eloise walked over, pulled the phone out of her hand gently and laid it back in its cradle. She then slid onto the bed next to Jewel and cradled her head on her chest. Knowing there were no words that would ease the pain, Eloise said only, "I know. I know, sweetie. I know just how you feel."

Whatever energy Glendora had felt when she'd first entered the bathroom left immediately when she exited. There was her poor Jewel, crying her heart out and clinging to her mother. It was the first time the two had touched one another in ten years, and it was clear that something tragic had led them to finally connect. "What happened?" she asked, fearing the worst.

Eloise turned tear-filled eyes in her mother's direction. "Jewel just asked Trevor for a divorce."

Glendora walked to the bed on weakening legs. "Now why

you want to go and do something foolish like that?" she asked Jewel sadly. She didn't expect an answer and didn't get one, though Jewel seemed to be quieting down. Easing onto the bed, Glendora patted her granddaughter's back. "It'll be all right, child. Granny's going to make it right." *If it's the last thing I do.*

Chapter Nine

The music was good, "old school," the crowd noisy and lively, and Rae had never felt lonelier in her entire life. It seemed Trevor was working 24/7 since Jewel had left. Even his weekends were filled with showing homes and doing paperwork. Days were fine, yet she could only put her team through so many hours of practice. Rae was thrilled with the talent on her team and couldn't wait to take the WNBA by storm when the season started.

But nights…nights were pure torture. She walked into Sunset Station at nine o'clock on Friday night just to drown the misery with loud music and heavy doses of alcohol. A couple of men asked her to dance, but she politely dismissed them. One was a little round and the other had nearly blinded her as strobe lights glinted off the gold teeth filling his mouth. Anybody with that many cavities couldn't be kissed, she decided.

Her fifth Long Island iced-tea went straight from her mouth to her bladder. Dang. Rae crossed her legs tightly and tried to force her fuzzy brain to think what to do. She had to go but didn't dare leave her stool. There were at least a hundred people milling around behind her, including one high-yellow floozy in a bad outfit that looked like she couldn't wait to pounce on her stool the second she left.

Opening her legs wide, Rae placed her feet on the foot rail to peer down the stool's length. It was a little dark, but she patiently let her eyes adjust and focus. The darned thing was bolted to the floor.

A man walked up beside her and ordered two drinks.

"'Scuse me." She patted his arm and struggled to bring herself upright.

The man turned in her direction and smiled. "Rae? How're you doing?"

It took a moment for her eyes to re-focus. When they did, she recognized him immediately. "Sterrrrliiing," she sang. "It's so good to sheee you," she slurred and wrapped an arm around his shoulder. "Hey, I've, I've gotta go to the restroom," she pushed herself onto her feet, a little unsteadily, "and I don't wanna lose my seat," she explained, though it was tough with her tongue being so thick all of a sudden. "Can you like...unscrew it from the floor," she pointed at the bolts so he wouldn't miss them, "so I can take it wid me?"

Sterling shifted a little. "Wait," he said. "You want to take the barstool with you to the restroom?"

"Yes." She nodded and her head felt heavy. "Can you do dat for me?" She patted him reassuringly as she headed for the ladies' room. "I gotta go so I'll meet you outside the door...gotta go." She thought she saw him nod, so she made a beeline for the restroom as the urge to release the imprisoned liquor became unbearable. "When I get back, I'll buy you a drink, 'kay?"

The door was heavy, and it seemed to take an unnatural effort to push it open. Rae raced across the tile floor. In relief she saw that for once there wasn't a line in the restroom. She was able to find an open stall immediately. Dancing a bit, she managed to pull down her underwear just before reaching the toilet seat. Rae laid her head back in ecstasy as her bladder emptied in a long stream. "Whewww! Oh, that feels much better," she said aloud.

Someone snickered outside the stall. "What? You never had to go bad before?" she asked irritably. She wiped herself, pulled up her underwear and pushed out of the stall. To her surprise, there were several men there, one using a urinal in a row along the opposite wall. The men, showing differing levels of amusement, and the urinal had appeared from nowhere.

"Ohhh," Rae said, realizing her mistake. "I'm sorry, I'm sorry. I thought...I thought this was the ladies' room." She giggled. "My mishtake," she said and left the room as the men burst out laughing. Rae chuckled.

Sterling found it difficult not to smile as Rae walked drunkenly through the crowd back to the bar.

"You won't believe what I just did." She laughed and sat heavily on the bar stool he'd guarded during her absence.

"What's that?" he asked, loving the sexy way she looked in her short skirt and sheer top.

"I went in the men's room by accshident. Oops!" She laughed until her stomach hurt.

Sterling suddenly wished he hadn't come with a date. It was clear Rae wasn't fit to drive herself home, and she was an adorably happy drunk. "I'm sure that'll be real embarrassing in the mornin'," he said, smiling. "You want me to call someone to pick you up?" he asked.

Rae looked at him as if he'd grown a third eye. "For what?"

"To drive you home. I wouldn't want you wrecking that badass Humvee of yours." Or those killer curves, he thought.

Rae wagged her head sadly. "No. See, that's the problem, Sterling, I'm alone." She turned dark, hurting eyes on him. "Nobody's wid me...nobody stays...nobody wants me." She stared at him as if it would help him understand.

"I'm here," I want you. Sterling didn't add the last. "I think you're fine."

"So fine you ran away from me," she reminded him.

He was busted on that one, but how could he explain that he was afraid of getting close to her because he would always be her second choice? Sterling didn't settle for second. Maybe all the men in her life before had held the same feelings. "I wasn't running, Rae...I was—"

She shushed him with her hand. "Ish awright. If you ain't feelin' me, I'm cool wid that. I don't beg no man for love, 'kay?"

"It's not like that Rae." Sterling ran a hand up and down her arm.

"Ish not your fault." She patted his hand. "I play like I don't need nothin' and nobody, you know?"

Sterling simply nodded, painfully aware that his own date was probably wondering what had happened to him. But he couldn't leave Rae like this. "Everybody needs somebody," Sterling offered.

"Dat's right. You're right," she agreed, nodding her head with exaggeration. "And I thought I knew who I needed. I did think that," she assured him.

"I know," he said, picturing Trevor St. John.

"But he dudn't want me. Never has and...and that hurts. It hurts bad." Her voice was a mere whimper. "I've loved him all my life, but he loves Jewel," she cried, dropping her head onto her hands.

Shit. Sterling hated to see a woman cry. He rubbed her back soothingly and tried to think what to do. The only person he knew to call was Trevor, and he was the object of her pain. There was nothing to do but to take her home himself. "You wait right here, Rae," he told her. "Hear me?" he asked.

She made a motion with her head. Figuring that was as close to a "yes" as he was likely to get, Sterling went in search of his date. He found her flirting with another man at their table. It didn't surprise him—Chianti was all about having men fall at her feet. Sterling wanted to be upset, but found it hard, given what he was about to ask.

Turned out, he'd had no reason to sweat. Chianti's reaction was relatively painless. She called him an insensitive, two-timing son-of-a-dog and threw the drink he'd given her in his face before storming off into some dark corner to meet the man who'd been mackin' on her when Sterling had arrived.

Picking up a napkin from the table, Sterling wiped his face and the front of his suit as he headed back to the bar. A small panic hit him when he found a woman in a tacky liquid gold mini-dress on the stool where he'd left Rae. A quick look up and down the bar proved she was no longer there.

"Where the hell did she go?" he asked himself. Quickly, he checked out the couples on the dance floor before heading toward the door. He pushed out of the club and scanned the parking lot. The black and gold Hummer was nowhere in sight. "Jesus," he cursed. He hoped she didn't kill herself. Pulling his own keys from his pocket, he unlocked his car and headed toward her home in Encino Park.

Trevor flipped mindlessly through the many channels of his satellite service and wondered why he paid so much to get a hundred channels of infomercials instead of the ten he'd had with cable. The phone rang. Hoping it was Jewel, he leapt across his bed to answer. "Hello?"

"Oh my God, Trevor," came Rae's sob across the line. "I had an accident. Can you come and get me?"

Fear shot through his veins. "Yeah, Rae. Are you all right? Where are you, hon?"

A few more choked sobs hit the line, raising Trevor's anxiety. "Tell me where you are, Rae and I'll be right there."

"I'm at Redland Road and Highway 281 in the ditch…yeah… in the ditch," she said as if she were checking to make certain. "Are you coming to get me?"

"I'll be right there. Don't worry. I'll call you back on my cell, okay?"

"'Kay," she said.

Trevor threw on a sweater and jeans and raced out the door. Rae had only been drunk twice in her life that he knew of. For a woman who was so tough in many ways, Rae Paris couldn't hold her liquor. Thing was, the only times she'd tried had been when she was in extreme emotional pain. One was when her mother died, and the second was on his wedding day. Trevor wondered guiltily if he was once again the cause of her unhappiness. He hadn't seen much of her since Jewel left. He'd intentionally stayed away from his oldest friend in hopes that Jewel could see that she was the most important thing in his life. It hadn't worked and it hadn't been fair to Rae.

It took ten minutes for him to find the Hummer and its owner sitting exactly where she'd said she'd be. He'd expected to see an accident, emergency vehicles, but there were none.

He parked on the shoulder and ran to see about her. "Are you all right?" he asked.

She nodded but remained seated inside her car with the door

open. "I feel stupid," she said, shaking her head. "I must've fallen asleep at the wheel. I woke up just as I hit the ditch. It scared me." Her face twisted as she tried not to cry. "I'm sorry for waking you."

Trevor reached inside to hug her. "It's all right. I haven't been sleeping well lately anyway. May I ask what had you out drinking tonight?"

"Sure," she said, shades of her old self rising to the occasion, "as long as you don't expect an answer."

It made Trevor smile. "How 'bout we get you home?"

"I'm all right, really," she said. "I'm pretty much sober now."

"Oh no." He pulled her out and escorted her to the passenger side of her vehicle. "You get me out this hour of the morning, and the least you can do is make me feel like I'm rescuing you."

At that moment, another vehicle pulled onto the side of the road in front of Trevor's SUV. Sterling LeRoi exited the car and walked up to the Hummer. "She all right?" he asked Trevor.

"Yeah," Trevor answered, noting the slight panic in the man's eyes. It didn't escape his attention that Rae seemed to be avoiding the newcomer.

"Good." Sterling raised his voice to speak to Rae, "Why'd you leave? I was going to give you a ride home."

Rae turned to look at him then. "I'm sorry, Sterling. I didn't want to be a bother...I...I don't know what I was thinking," she finished, letting her hands drop into her lap.

"Well, I'm glad you didn't get hurt."

"Thanks," she said weakly.

Sterling looked at her a moment longer before backing away. "Looks like you're in good hands now. You need any help, man?"

"No, I think I've got it," Trevor said as his respect for Sterling rose a couple of notches. "Thanks for trying to look after her." He shook hands with Sterling, "But she's got a hard head, man."

"Word," Sterling acknowledged. "Well, ya'll take care," he said as he walked back to his car. The Cadillac pulled back onto the highway, and Trevor followed suit. Rae's house was only a few miles away, so it only took five minutes to reach her house and get her safely inside.

Dropping her keys onto the entry table, he watched his friend drag herself into the darkness of her living room. "You going to be all right?" he asked, still concerned.

"I don't know, Trevor," she answered wearily. "I really don't know."

He'd never heard Rae sound so down, never seen her so listless. Trevor couldn't stand to see her this way and certainly couldn't leave her in such a melancholy mood.

Removing his shoes, he walked barefoot into the dark room and sat down next to her on the couch. He pulled her into his arms and kissed the top of her head. "Tell me what's going on," he insisted. "I know you're hurting. What can I do to help?"

"Make love to me," she whispered softly. "Just one time."

For the second time that night, Rae had Trevor in a panic. "Make love to you?" he asked, still not believing he'd heard her right. "Why would you ask such a thing, Rae? Just because Jewel is away doesn't mean I take my vows less seriously."

"I know that," Rae said as she eased out of his embrace and looked at him in the dim light of the room. "And I know it's not even fair for me to ask you, but it's what I need tonight, Trevor."

Baffled, Trevor stood up and paced the room. "I don't get it, Rae. What will our making love do for you, huh? How can it do anything but make things more complicated? I'm trying to figure out a way to get Jewel back, not push her further away."

"Who said Jewel has to know anything about it?" Rae asked quietly. "This isn't something you're doing to Jewel, Trevor. This is something you're doing for me. It's that simple."

"Nothing's that simple!" Trevor hated that he was shouting, but the women in his life were driving him crazy. "Why is it that no one thinks about me and my feelings, huh? Why do I have to be the one who bows to everyone else's crazy whims?"

"Trev—"

"No, no. You listen to me," he insisted. "All I wanted was a child. Is that so crazy? No, it's not," he answered himself, "and my best friend decides that she'll help me out. For some odd reason, this

Council

Blue Anchor Library

Title: You Can't Plan Love
ID: 20473303

Title: Never say never
ID: 20473370

Total items: 2
19/08/2014 17:31

Thank you for visiting Southwark Libraries

sounds rational when I hear it, but it drives my wife into an absolute frenzy. She's so upset about it that now she thinks there's no hope for us and she wants a divorce."

"She asked you for a divorce?" Rae asked incredulously.

"Yes!" Trevor shouted. "She thinks she'll never be enough for me now, thinks I'll hold it against her because she can't have children."

"Well, would you?" Rae asked.

"No!" Trevor brushed a hand over his fade. "But because I can't prove that, I now have to suffer without my wife whom I live for, whom I'd die for!"

"See, that's what I don't get, Trevor." Rae left the couch and stood in front of him. "How can any woman have you and then throw you away? You think I hate your wife, don't you?"

"Naw, I don't." Trevor dismissed the idea, though he knew Rae had only tolerated Jewel from the beginning of their relationship.

"Well, I don't," Rae said softly. "The only thing I ever had against Jewel is—she got you."

Trevor had no idea how to respond so didn't try.

"She doesn't get that you're perfect in every way a man can be," Rae continued. "That you were, and are, willing to fight for her love, for your marriage, no matter how unreasonable she is. It's not fair, Trevor." Her hands cupped his face. "She's loved you for a minute… and I…" She swallowed hard and her eyes filled with tears before she continued, "I've loved you for a lifetime. It hurts to know that you've never loved me back."

Trevor slowly grasped her wrists and pulled them gently from his face as his heart broke in a dozen pieces. He kissed each palm in turn. "I love you, Rae. I always have." Because she got a hopeful look, he continued quickly, "But it's the kind of love that's enduring because…because…you're my best friend. I can be myself with you, tell you my darkest secrets, even the things I don't dare tell my wife because I'm afraid she'll think me less of a man. Make no mistake, Rae Angelique, the love I have for you is just as precious as what I have for Jewel. It's just different. Don't make me choose between you," he pleaded.

"You don't have to, Trevor." A tear slid down her cinnamon brown cheek slowly. "Because I can't live like this anymore. I can't live comparing every man I meet to you...the dream of you...the fantasy of you. All I've ever wanted, Trevor—was you," she said, shaking her head. "And if I'm ever going to be free of this want, I need the opportunity to get you out of my system. And then Jewel can have you all to herself. I promise."

"Rae, I can't—" Trevor backed away.

"Don't make me beg, Trevor." Rae closed the distance between them, the look in her eyes desperate. "You know I don't beg anyone for anything. But I need you...just for tonight." Her lips trembled as she pressed them against his.

It was nothing like Trevor expected; their kiss didn't seem poisonous and wrong. Instead, it was gentle and sweet...and somehow familiar...as if they'd kissed before. He tasted the alcohol on her tongue and found it pleasingly tart as he followed the pace of her rolling tongue.

Rae moaned and stepped back to look at him for a moment. "Have you always been able to kiss like that?" she asked.

"Naw," he admitted. "I had a couple of real good teachers along the way." He thought back to his first two girlfriends for a moment.

Trevor placed a hand against Rae's cheek and assessed her for the first time. She was quite attractive. She had large, dark eyes, high cheekbones and an angular jaw that should've made her look manly, but didn't. Her skin was a warm brown color that was soft under his palm. "You're very pretty," he said honestly.

Rae ducked her head so he couldn't see her reaction. "You told me that one other time," she said as she slowly began unzipping her skirt.

Panic sent Trevor's pulse skittering.

Now she looked at him, her dark brown eyes filled with emotion. "It was prom night," she continued. "I'd worked my behind off sacking groceries to buy my dress only to have my mamma steal the money from my room and blow it on booze. I had to wear my cousin's hand-me-down dress, which made me miserable."

"I remember." Trevor nodded, "The top hugged your breasts

and the skirt was a noisy blue puff of a thing that showed off your legs. It was nice."

"It was hideous." Rae laughed a little as tears pooled in her eyes. "I walked into the ballroom with crooked-tooth Adrian holding onto me like a hot TV." Her skirt fell to the floor, and she began to unbutton her sheer black blouse. "And when you saw me, you left your date for a minute just to walk over and tell me…I was pretty." She smiled at the memory. "And later, when you asked me to dance, I felt like Cinderella," she confessed.

Shaking his head, Trevor wished he could move. His feet seemed to be stuck to the floor. Rae dropped her blouse on the floor, and her bra followed quickly. It was shocking to see her standing there nude. "I'm not a prince, Rae." He swallowed hard as he fought the urge to look away. Rae's sleek, athletic build was quite the opposite of Jewel's outrageous curves, yet he found her uncomfortably attractive.

As Trevor allowed himself a long look, he expected lightning, thunder, or at the very least the voice of God to enter the room and warn him to go no further. Yet there were no forces of heaven or earth present to intervene and keep him from breaking all the sacred covenants of his marriage. There was only his will, which was taking a horrific beating at that moment.

Rae stepped up to him and whispered, "Come with me." Desire filled his senses. Fighting to force aside his doubt, guilt, and conscience, he let his friend lead him to her bedroom. When she turned on the light, the walls vibrated with a sensuous chili color. Her bedding held the same color, with splashy accents of amber and sage in the pillows she tossed to the floor in haste.

Rae pulled back the covers and slid inside the sheets. "You coming?" she asked, a bit unsure.

Trevor stripped off his shirt slowly. "You know this will change everything?"

She nodded her head. "It'll give us a new beginning."

He slid off his jeans and boxers and took his place on the other side of the bed. He leaned over to kiss her gently. She moved to fill his arms and Trevor felt her trembling. "I don't want you to feel bad about this afterward, Trevor."

He pulled her tight against his chest and kissed her soft, fuzzy head. "I've always wondered what it would be like to make love to you."

"You don't have to say that," she said bravely, but her trembling bottom lip and her glistening eyes told him she'd needed to hear that. "But this doesn't have to take long, I want you too bad."

Trevor covered her mouth with his fingers. "If we're going to do this...and it sure looks like we are...," he said, taking a look at his rigid member, "I want to do it right, if it's all the same to you. That way, there'll be no regrets for either of us."

A tear fell from each eye down the sides of her face as she nodded.

This time when Trevor kissed her, he put his whole heart and soul into it. And the soft, easy rolling of their tongues set the pace for their lovemaking.

Rae was sitting outside on her deck, wrapped in a blanket when the sun rose. Her body still hummed with happiness from Trevor's skillful touch. There was a peace inside her like she'd never felt before. The restlessness that had always lived deep within her gut was gone. Trevor had started it. Now he'd ended it.

She heard movement inside her house, a banging of the kitchen cabinet as it closed. A few moments later, Trevor was outside.

"Thanks for the coffee," he said, raising his steaming mug in salute.

Rae never drank the stuff. She only kept it around for company. "You're welcome," she said. "Have a seat," she offered, patting the space next to her on the porch swing.

"Pretty sunrise," he said, easing onto the cushion.

"Yeah," Rae nodded.

Trevor fidgeted with his jeans and shirt and shifted uncomfortably on the swing. "Last night was...nice, Rae. Really nice."

Because he was so sincere, Rae felt her breath catch a little.

"Yeah. You were right, too. Hate to admit it."

He looked at her curiously.

"It did change everything." She smiled.

Trevor took a deep breath and stood up. "Listen, Rae—"

"Don't get scairt," she teased. "Sit down."

Reluctantly, he sank back onto the swing.

Rae looked over at her friend and nudged him with her shoulder. "Don't start acting all stupid on me, okay? It'll make last night...weird."

"It wasn't right for me to make love to you last night, Rae, but I don't regret it. It'll be one of the moments of my life I'll always cherish."

"Thanks," she said. "It meant a lot to me too, Trevor. Now I know how it feels to make love to a man who matters to me. And... and I don't think I'll be able to settle for less," she confessed.

There was a sudden hardened look in his eyes. "Listen, Rae, it'll take an act of God to get Jewel back after this, but I love my wife. I love her and I need her," he said with such conviction Rae wanted to kiss him.

"I know that, Trev. And I want you to work it out with Jewel. I mean it," she added when she saw skepticism change his features. "I just meant that I'm done with picking up men just because they're men. I think I'll be choosier in the future. I deserve to have someone love me the way you love Jewel."

"Yes, Rae, you do." Trevor cupped her chin in his hand and kissed her cheek, then her forehead. "And if it took last night for you to finally realize that, then it was worth it."

Rae was even more certain that she'd never find a man as fine in face or character as Trevor St. John, but she was more convinced than ever that she wanted one all her own.

"I've gotta go." He threw back the last of his coffee. "I have to pitch our Initiative to the city council today. If I get approval for the project, I'm sure it'll help soften Jewel's feelings toward me." He left the swing and headed for the back door. "Give me a ride to my car, Rae, before someone decides they like the look of my rims."

"Those raggedy things?" Rae followed behind him. "Your rims

ain't worth spit compared to mine. Lucky for me you picked the right vehicle to bring back here."

"Yeah, well, if my Escalade is gone, my new chauffer drives a Hummer," he shot back as they fell into a companionable banter.

Rae grabbed her keys and pushed on her slides. She was surprised to be so happy and content when she would've bet her last dollar yesterday that she would be more obsessed with Trevor this morning than ever. It was funny how things worked out. But no funnier than to have Trevor open her front door and find Sterling LeRoi standing there, hand poised ready to knock.

"Sterling," she said, noting that Trevor said absolutely nothing.

The man looked from Trevor to Rae before speaking. "I just stopped by to see how you're doing this morning," he explained. "I see you're still in good hands."

There was a chilled tone to his voice. "Oh, yeah. It was so late, I asked Trevor to stay last night," Rae lied. "I was just taking him to his car."

Sterling flipped his keys around his forefinger once. "I can save you the trouble if you like. I was just making a quick stop. I'm on my way downtown to meet a real estate broker. I could take you to your car, Trevor," he offered, a polite smile stuck to his face.

"Oh. Well…sure." Trevor shrugged, hoping to appear nonchalant instead of like a child who'd been caught sneaking out of an adult bar. "I'll see you later, Rae," he said and followed Sterling to his car. "Thanks for this, man."

"No problem."

It was a short, uncomfortable ride to the place where he'd left his SUV on the side of the road. Trevor could tell by the sullen look on Sterling's face and the way he tapped his steering wheel with his fingers that the man had things he wanted to say. "Say it, man."

"What?" Sterling asked irritably.

"Whatever's on your mind?"

"You don't wanna know."

"Say it," Trevor pressed.

"All right." Sterling pulled onto the gravel on the side of the road, stopping abruptly. "What the hell kind of man takes advantage of a woman when she's three sheets to the wind, man?"

"I didn't take advantage of her," Trevor stated calmly. "If anything, I'm the one feeling used today," he said honestly.

"That's a bunch a bull!" Sterling twisted violently to face Trevor head-on. "Rae was feelin' down and lonely last night, and your wife bein' out of town, you decided to make her feel better, is that it?"

Despite asking for Sterling's opinion, Trevor was growing defensive. "You know what? You don't know anything about it. It's none of your damn business." Trevor opened the door.

"I know about men like you. My father was a man like you. Treated my mama like a damned slave. He made her wait on him hand and foot, cursed her every day and made her take care of other women's children. And she never fought back and swore she loved him till her dying day. You don't take advantage of a woman's love, Trevor."

"I'm not like that." Trevor argued.

"The hell you're not. You play around with Rae's emotions by making sure she's nobody's business but yours, isn't that so, Trevor?

Trevor turned and stuck a finger in Sterling's face. "If you want to know Rae's business, if you want to know what happened last night, ask her!" He slammed the car door shut and got inside his own vehicle. His tires spewed gravel as he put distance between himself and Sterling. "No regrets?" he said aloud, repeating his vow from the previous night. "Who the hell did I think I was fooling?"

Chapter Ten

Jewel stared past the windows of the limo into the ever-present fog of London. It had been a week since they'd arrived, and each trip into the city found them cocooned by the misty clouds of air. Jewel hated the place...hated the cold...hated the dreariness.

She looked over at her Granny Glen who was talking animatedly with William, the driver. Glendora seemed to know every member of nobility of a certain age—at least those still living. William was a great fan of the tabloids and enthusiastically recited recent deaths, weddings and scandals. Eloise sat on the edge of her seat, obviously fascinated by the conversation.

Glendora seemed to have regained her youth in seven days. As it were, they'd had tea, dinner or brunch at a different home, estate, villa or bungalow every day of the week. She'd met more royalty, ladies, countesses and duchesses than she could count.

Jewel sighed and turned back to the otherworldly view outside the window. Reluctantly, she admitted that her mood had more to do with Trevor than the weather. Every time she had a thought about him, which was every two minutes, an aching pain filled her chest and tears stung the backs of her eyes. Maybe it had been a mistake to tell him she wanted a divorce while she was here. Now it was this "thing" hanging out there that she couldn't do anything about. Jewel liked getting things done quickly. Waiting to finish the deal when she got home was torture.

Tucking her misery away, Jewel took in the sight as they arrived at the Royal Lyceum Theatre and William navigated behind a line of limousines. There was a mob of press and fans lining the walk in front of the ornate, Victorian building. The throng went crazy each time someone exited a car and hit the red carpet.

The rapid-fire camera flashes and excited crowd piqued Jewel's interest.

"Here we are then." William pulled closer to the curb. "When we reach the carpet area, I'll be round to help you out, Miss Jubilee," he said.

Glendora sat taller in her seat and took deep breaths. Eloise checked her makeup, though she looked perfect, as usual.

Jewel pulled out her compact mirror, fixed a smudge of lipstick before dropping the item back inside her tiny purse. William stopped the car, opened the door and assisted Glendora onto the red carpet, where it seemed the London fog didn't even dare to linger.

The crowd went crazy, pushing pens, paper, old playbills and T-shirts in Glendora's direction. Jewel saw a different Glendora standing tall and regal. Waving, smiling, and blowing kisses, she posed for the hundreds of cameras flashing in her direction.

"I knew it," Eloise said in awe as she exited the limo to join her mother.

"You knew what?" Jewel asked, still stunned at all the attention her grandmother's presence created. It was thrilling to bask in the excitement alongside her Granny Glen as she and her mother each took an arm to support her as she made her way slowly down the carpet. Glendora moved first toward the screaming fans of all ages, and then toward the reporters dancing impatiently on the sidelines. She stopped to offer each reporter a laugh and a sound bite or two.

Jewel was amazed at the woman's transformation from tottering grandmother to cherished celebrity. She'd always had a regal grace to her carriage, but now Jewel knew why; this wasn't the first time Glendora had been surrounded by fans.

Jewel listened intently as Glendora was questioned in turn by the reporters. They asked how she was feeling and how she'd felt leaving London so many years ago. She'd danced on stage with famous stage actors and even was the opening act for the great Josephine Baker for a few years.

"Harold Knightly of the BBC, Miss Jubilee," one reporter with a crooked-toothed grin introduced himself. "How are those fabulous legs of yours? Still dancing, eh?"

"Not lately, Mr. Knightly." Glendora was stately in her sky blue gown that accentuated her still slender frame. She pulled aside the slit of her skirt to reveal a shapely leg wrapped in sheer support hose. "Most days it's all I can do to walk on these traitors, I'm afraid," she answered with a beaming smile.

Knightly laughed. "Well, they're just lovely, and you look to be getting along just fine to me, Miss Jubilee," he said genuinely.

A tall white man with slightly rounded shoulders walked up behind Glendora at that moment. His appearance sent a ripple of excitement through the crowd, and more cameras flashed. The man had a head full of wavy steel gray hair, and his lids sagged slightly over intense green eyes. His slender frame looked good in his black tuxedo. In his younger years, Jewel guessed he had been quite handsome.

"May I have the honor of escorting you inside," he asked Glendora just loudly enough to be heard over the din.

Turning, Glendora seemed frozen as she stared at him. Her jaw dropped slightly. "Arthur."

The awe in her grandmother's voice had Jewel taking another look at the man. His eyes were intense with emotion. He offered Glendora his arm gallantly.

Glendora shook her head slightly, as if waking from a dream. "Of course." She placed her gloved hand gently in the crook of his arm, and the two of them walked toward the theatre entrance.

The paparazzi burst into renewed frenzy, calling out "Lord Arthur! Miss Jubilee! May we have a word?"

Jewel nudged her mother, who relinquished her guiding hand from Glendora's other arm so that the couple could enter the theatre ahead of them.

"Who is that?" Jewel asked.

Eloise was staring just as intently at the man. "If I remember correctly, he's Lord Arthur of Windsor. Mother has pictures of him."

"She does?"

"Yes," Eloise said. "She's got a whole photo album full of pictures from when she lived here."

"Where?" Jewel asked. "I've never seen them."

Eloise hushed her as Jewel tried to ask more questions.

They entered the theatre through one of the arched doorways. It was a gorgeous place, with high ceilings and ornate tiled floors. An anxious young woman wearing an earpiece stepped up immediately to greet Glendora.

"Miss Jubilee, I'm Bridget Harkins. Please follow Deirdre here." She ushered a young Black woman with a heavy bosom forward. "She'll escort you backstage. Ms. Abbe is getting ready but can't wait to see you."

Glendora seemed exceptionally reluctant to leave Lord Arthur but obediently followed the assistant away from the lobby.

"Now then." Bridget pushed a wayward strand of brunette hair from her harried face. "We have a table reserved for you in the Wyndham Bar, Lord Arthur. For you as well, ladies, if you wish."

Arthur turned toward Eloise and Jewel. "Shall we, ladies?" he asked with a stiff yet gracious bow.

"I...uh...absolutely." Eloise seemed slightly awestruck.

Jewel couldn't imagine why. She was beginning to get frustrated. It seemed as if everyone was in on some secret except her.

The bar was lavish with deep red walls and brilliant white borders. A white stone fireplace with a mirror stood opposite it. Outside the windows, Jewel could see tall gray buildings that appeared to be apartments. It seemed odd to look out at common buildings while she was inside one so elegant. She imagined it kept a person grounded, though, knowing that there was a real world out there.

"I would be pleased if you joined my table. I'm alone this evening," Lord Arthur offered.

"You realize who we are?" Eloise asked suspiciously.

The old man nodded. "Of course." He pulled out a chair for Eloise, stealing the opportunity from the waiter who stood nearby.

Jewel watched her mother with interest. It seemed to take her a minute to make up her mind, but the moment she did, she slid easily onto the chair.

Lord Arthur pulled out another chair. "It's Jewel, isn't it?" he asked.

Jewel nodded. "Yes." She took the seat. "Thank you," she said politely, realizing her mother hadn't been so gracious. It was disarming to see her mother's abrupt loss of manners.

"May I bring you a bottle of wine for your table, Lord Arthur?" the waiter asked.

"Uh, champagne," he said, easing into his own chair. "This is my daughter and granddaughter's first time in London. I think it's only right to celebrate, don't you?" he said, offering a chuckle.

The waiter faltered. "I uh…of course, sir. Of course." He was off like a rabbit.

It was Jewel's turn to stare at Arthur. No wonder Eloise was acting so stiff. This was Eloise's father. Her father! Jewel wished she already had the drink. She sensed things were about to get very interesting.

"Eloise, dear. You don't look entirely thrilled to see me." Arthur laid a pale, liver-spotted hand on hers. "I must say, I don't blame you," he added soberly.

Eloise seemed transfixed by his touch on her hand. Her lips trembled and her voice shook with emotion. "Mother told me you were dead," she said quietly.

Arthur bit off a laugh. "Yes, well. She would then, wouldn't she?" He patted her hand. "She was quite angry with me when I last visited you in America. I'm certain she'd no thought of ever seeing me again. It's only because she's moving a little slower these days that I dared to approach her." His eyes twinkled a little.

Jewel liked his easy humor and quick smile. And she liked the softness she saw in his eyes when he looked at Eloise. It was the same look her father always had for her. Suddenly, she felt sorry for her mother. Sorry that she'd never felt her father's love before this moment. Sorry because Eloise didn't seem to know what to do now that she had. "The way Granny Glen was looking at you, Lord Arthur, I think she's forgiven you," she offered, to break the uncomfortable silence that Eloise didn't seem inclined to fill.

"Do you really think so?" He turned so that she could see the hope in his bright green eyes, eyes that matched Eloise's.

"Absolutely," she said, just as the waiter arrived with their champagne. When the man left again, she raised her full flute and lifted it in Arthur's direction. "Here's to family."

"Aren't you delightful?" he said with a brilliant smile. He lifted his cut crystal glass as well. "What do you say, Eloise? To family?"

Lifting her glass with one hand, Eloise dabbed at a small tear in the corner of her eye with the other. "I can't believe I'm sitting here with you," she managed as she clinked crystal to crystal.

Intrigued, Jewel leaned forward. "Lord Arthur, how is it that you know all about us, when we've never heard a word about you?" she asked.

A sad look dulled the man's eyes.

"I'm sorry, I shouldn't have been so forward," Jewel said.

Eloise offered her own apologies. "My daughter isn't known for her tact."

He waved off their comments. "It's all right. It hurts that Glendora hasn't told you anything about me, Jewel. She's all I've thought about for many, many years," he said sadly. "I suppose it's my own fault, really."

"You used to visit us when I was a child, didn't you?" Eloise asked.

"You remember?" The man was out of the dumps immediately. "Yes, I would travel to America periodically to see you and your mother, to make sure you didn't go without anything you needed. Of course, Glendora refused my help. She always insisted on doing everything on her own."

"Why didn't the two of you end up together?" Jewel asked, wondering if it had to do with her grandmother being Black and him being white.

"It's a maudlin tale…I was afraid mainly. Yes, that would have to be the crux of it." Arthur sighed and sipped his champagne. "Afraid of the scandal buzzing about us, of being ousted from the peerage, of losing my position in the House of Lords. I was engaged to another woman all the while I was having an affair with Glendora. When the paparazzi got wind of our relationship, I denied it totally. Glendora never forgave me and the relationship ended." He shrugged. "She didn't want to be second best. And she didn't deserve it."

"So, you married your fiancé?" Eloise stared into her champagne glass. "Even though mother was pregnant with me?"

Again, Arthur laid his hand on top of Eloise's. "After I broke my engagement to Catherine, I went begging to Glendora for forgiveness. I offered her marriage. She refused. It was some time later that I discovered she'd had you—my child." He squeezed her hand. "I eventually gave up trying to win her back. I finally realized Glendora's will was much stronger than my fortitude."

Arthur took a few long breaths and a half-hearted sip of his champagne before continuing. "As it was, Catherine was much more forgiving. I suppose we got married out of convenience, though. Not love. She'd already selected a wedding dress, you see? And in truth, though she was never the love of my life, nor I hers, we got on quite well while she lived."

It was clear to Jewel now why Glendora was so adamant about Eloise and her making their marriages work. Her grandmother regretted leaving Lord Arthur…it had been written all over her face the moment she'd laid eyes on him that evening.

"I always wondered," Arthur sounded tired, "if things would've been different had I been more persistent." He turned to Eloise. "I would've loved to see you grow up in person, not just in the pictures your mother sent every year."

"It's a wonder that you're sitting with us now, Lord Arthur. Won't this end up in the tabloids?" Eloise asked a bit contemptuously.

He lifted his hands. "Ah, there it is," he offered. "I've nothing to lose, you see? My dear Catherine is long deceased and cannot be hurt by the news. Besides, I've resigned my seat in the House of Lords… seems I'm quite scandal-proof. A coward to the end, I'm afraid."

Because he said it with such melancholy and regret, Jewel felt her heart break a little as they all tucked their chins and fell to their own thoughts.

"Ladies and gentlemen," Bridget entered the room in a rush, "the ceremony will be starting presently. Let's head to the theatre for seating, shall we?"

The theatre was large with plush, burgundy seats. The ceiling was domed and ornately designed, and the whole atmosphere was like something out of a fairy tale. Glendora was already seated in the first row, to which Eloise and Jewel were escorted. "You never said which of your friends was being honored tonight." Jewel cocked an eyebrow and studied her grandmother as she took her seat.

"Natache Abbe." Glendora adjusted her short, lacy evening gloves. "She was quite the celebrity back in the day."

"Was she good friends with Lord Arthur as well?" Jewel asked, fishing for more details.

"What does it matter?" Glendora asked.

"I'm just curious. But I'll let you keep your secret," she said, settling into her seat. "That way I won't feel bad about not telling you what my grandfather had to say about you."

Looking straight ahead, Jewel could feel the incredulous glare of her mother on one side and the shocked stare of her grandmother on the other.

"He told you what happened?" Glendora asked softly.

Seeing the tears that suddenly welled in Granny Glen's eyes made Jewel grasp her hand tightly. "Yeah. He did."

Glendora reached over Jewel to take Eloise's hand. "I'm sorry I told you he was dead," she said to her daughter.

Eloise just nodded and swallowed hard against emotion. She pulled a facial tissue from her purse and pressed it against her eyes just as the program began.

It was an amazing night. Jewel had never heard of most of the night's honorees, but she clapped heartily just the same. She felt as if she'd been caught up in some fairytale in a far-off land as she and Eloise escorted Glendora to the stage to present the lifetime achievement award to her friend. First, she read from Teleprompters, then she gave a spontaneous, sincere and very eloquent speech. If she'd practiced it at all, she'd kept it very secret…as she had most of her early years of adulthood.

Backstage, Glendora was offered a chair as her weakened legs finally gave out under the excess activity. The press kept her for interviews and photographs. Later, on the way to the hotel, they were all animated as they related the evening's events to William, their driver.

Back in the hotel room, Jewel ordered champagne as they all changed into their pajamas and bathrobes. She sank onto the sofa in the living area and pulled her feet beneath her. "Hurry up, Granny Glen, I have a million questions to ask you," she shouted to her grandmother. "Do you need some help?"

"No. I'm fine," Glendora said coming out of their bedroom, making slow but steady progress with her walker. "I'm exhausted," she declared, sinking onto the sofa next to her granddaughter.

"Well, just stay awake a little while longer. I think we need to celebrate." She poured the champagne into the three flutes that had been provided. "Come on, Eloise."

Her mother stood at the window of the room looking out at the cold London night, making no effort to turn her attention inside the room.

"Eloise?" Glendora spoke to her daughter. "Are you all right?" She worried how Eloise would react to finding out her father was an English lord. It wasn't a secret she'd ever wanted to reveal to her mother or sisters. It was easier to leave them guessing about what she'd done in Europe than to subject herself or Arthur to their hate.

Eloise turned. Her soft blue satin robe swished dramatically. "How could you do it, Mother?" she asked.

"Do what, baby?" Glendora felt her heart skip unhealthily.

Eloise sat opposite Glendora and Jewel. "How could you leave London? They love you here. Lord Arthur loved you. Why didn't you stay and make London our home?"

"Because it wouldn't have been right," Glendora said simply, allowing herself a moment to find relief. Her daughter didn't hate Arthur. That meant a lot. "I was living a fairytale here. I was well-off, I was somewhat famous and I had a man who loved me. My own Prince Charming." Her eyes went soft with remembrance. "Arthur was the love of my life...but he betrayed me."

"He begged for your forgiveness, didn't he?" Eloise asked. "Why didn't you make up with him?"

Realizing that Arthur had told them the complete story of

their fiery past, Glendora addressed the question. "You may find this hard to believe," she lifted the corner of her lip in a wry smile, "but I've always been hardheaded."

Encouraged by their smiles, she continued. "I was young then, thought no man could treat me like a two-dollah ho and get away with it. It was pride…and fear of being hurt once more that kept me from making up with him. I didn't think I could trust him again."

"Why didn't you ever tell me about him? Why didn't you ever let him stay when he visited?" Eloise asked.

"I didn't think he deserved you. A man that didn't acknowledge my love to start with didn't deserve the child that resulted from that love. I was pretty unforgiving back then. All I took from him was the money he put in my bank account every month."

"And now?" Eloise asked.

"I would give anything I have to get those years back." Glendora stared into her daughter's eyes. "I never let on, but I've been lonesome somethin' awful all these years. I never stopped thinking about what my life woulda been like with Arthur. Now, I'll never know."

"I could tell you what it would've been like." Eloise pulled back and poured herself a glass of champagne. "Arthur cheated on his fiancé with you, so he would've done the same to you. And every time he took another woman to his bed, it would've chipped away at your heart and made you feel more and more inadequate. It would've been hell, Mother." A tear made its way slowly down her pale cheek. It was clear she was struggling against past hurt inflicted by her husband. "You made the right choice," she said softly before draining her glass.

"I'm not so sure 'bout that, Eloise. Seems that time and old age cure a lot of ills. If my friends are to be believed, Arthur was completely faithful to his wife. They didn't know he came to the United States to visit with his mistress and illegitimate child for years before I made him stop. I think all the time about how alive I felt when I was with him. We talked about everything, had arguments too, but we always had the best time when we were together. I just miss talking to him."

"He must've missed you too. That's why he's been sending you flowers every year," Jewel interjected, pleased to have the mystery finally solved.

"No, child. None of those were mine, were they, Eloise?" She lifted an arched eyebrow at her daughter.

"They're from Daddy?" Jewel guessed when Eloise only offered a guilty look. "He's been sending them forever."

"Nearly thirty years," Eloise said dispassionately.

"That's right." Glendora told the rest. "Every year on their anniversary, he sends a bouquet of flowers and the number of his room in the hotel where they'd honeymooned. Every year he hoped she'd show up."

"That's so sweet." Jewel studied her mother. "Why didn't you ever go?" she asked, feeling bad for her father.

"Why do you think?" Eloise scoffed. "You don't see anything but the good in your father, Jewel...and I never wanted to take that away from you. But Charles...he..." She shook her head, unable to finish.

"He cheated on you." Jewel completed the sentence for her. "It must've torn you up inside."

Lifting her eyes in surprise, Eloise nodded. "Yeah, it hurt something awful. But worse was how you reacted to his leaving."

"I know. I was a beast. But how was I supposed to act?" Jewel defended. "All you did was yell at him and tell him you were grown and could do whatever the hell you wanted. You never gave him any time or attention, never cooked for him, or did anything he wanted to do. How do you think that made him feel?"

Eloise dropped her chin. "I know how it made him feel, Jewel. But I knew I was capable of so much more than having children, cleaning house, and hosting dinner parties. I am no man's servant. Not Charles's and not any other man's," Eloise insisted. "All I wanted was his support. Someone to share stories with me at the end of the day. Someone to see and appreciate my contributions."

She looked miserable as tears softened the hard look in her eyes. "Charles couldn't handle my success." Eloise tossed back a half-glass of champagne as if it were a shot. "I figured, if he felt emasculated by my accomplishments, that was something he needed to get over. Little did I know that he thought sleeping with other women was the solution."

Jewel decided that her father was a victim of his generation. She couldn't imagine Trevor ever feeling less of a man because of her success. If anything, he supported her efforts one hundred percent, as he was doing now with the Initiative. "Will you ever forgive him, do you think?" Jewel asked, a bit hopeful. Getting back with Eloise was always one of the topics of discussion whenever she and Charles were together. He loved her. Always had and always would.

Eloise shrugged and poured more liquor into her glass. "My heart says 'yes' every day. But my head says, 'Warning, Eloise, don't be a fool again.' When I came on this trip, I'd decided to have my fill of Charles Hunt, then divorce him and finally end that chapter of my life."

"Divorce." Jewel found the word left a bad taste in her mouth. "Sounds so final."

"What about you, child?" Glendora asked. "Still thinking that's the only solution for you and Trevor? The man hasn't done anything wrong, you know."

"At least he's never slept with another woman." Eloise supported her mother's statement.

"Maybe not," Jewel acknowledged. "But if I look at the two of you and your husbands as object lessons, I have to believe that if my husband is capable of asking to have a child by another woman, infidelity isn't far behind. He may decide that having a woman who can bear his children is more important than I am." There, she'd said it. Her deepest fear was out in the open. "I'm just beating him to the punch."

"So now you're a fortune teller, huh?" Glendora said with disgust. "Child, you don't know what a man will do 'til he does it. Fact is, neither does he."

"It doesn't matter, Granny." Jewel frowned and stabbed at the bubbles in her glass with a finger. "I'm too selfish to have a child. That's why God took away the one I was carrying."

"What'd I tell you about that talk?" Glendora began wagging her head back and forth.

"It's true, Granny. I'm sure of it. Every time I felt the least bit of movement from that tiny baby, I panicked." She put a hand over her stomach as if remembering the feeling. "I thought, what if Trevor loves this child more than me? I couldn't handle it. I know I would've grown to hate my own child." Jewel gave a pointed look at her mother. "You should understand that, Eloise."

"I do," her mother said sadly. "But it's a bad way to live, Jewel." She shook her head and stared off into space. "You remember that last family reunion we went to?"

"Vividly." Jewel stopped poking at the champagne, choosing to drink it instead.

Eloise had a far-off look in her eyes as she continued, "It was hot that day. One of those humid days when your clothes stick to your back and the only comfort is sitting in the shade under the big oak trees, waiting for a small breeze to bless you. You kids were swimming in Mother's little splash pool that day, and the adults were either playin' whist or shootin' the breeze.

"Anyway, I got thirsty and the lemonade pitcher had only a few drops left in it. So, I took it to the house to get more. Before filling it up, I decided to use the bathroom, but when I got there, I heard a man and woman grunting and moaning behind the bathroom door. I didn't have to guess what they were doing." She gave a knowing look. "I thought it was tacky and sleazy, whoever it was, but was going to leave them to their fun since I didn't have to go that bad. Then, I heard the woman say 'Oh, Charles,' and my heart stopped.

"I don't know what happened then. It was like I lost my mind or something." She looked around the room as if she could find it. "All I could think was that that low-down dirty skirt-chaser wasn't going to get the best of me that day. I was an attractive woman. Some other man would want me. So, I set out to prove it." Eloise slapped the blue satin on her knee. "The first man I found was that twenty-two-year-old boy. What was his name, Jewel?"

Jewel offered the name, "Sonny. My boyfriend," she added.

"I know," Eloise stated. "Anyway, I whispered something in his ear, and he followed me back into the house like a little puppy. And there came Charles adjusting his pants and smelling like my cousin Renee's perfume. I know because she was tramping her whorin' behind out the door with him. I turned around and kissed Sonny flat on the mouth right there in front of God and everybody.

"Charles just stood there. Didn't say a damn thing.

"That made me madder. That's when I practically dragged that boy into mother's room and forced him to have sex with me.

"The whole time, all I wanted was for Charles to run in and stop me, beat the crap outta the little boy bouncing on top of me like a trampoline, act like I meant something to him."

"I saw Daddy leave," Jewel offered. "I remember Reneé being mad at him, but I didn't know why. I figured you and he had another fight, and I was tired of it. That's why I went into the house looking for you. I nearly fell on the floor when I saw Sonny's bare behind on top of you." Jewel's face twisted as flashbacks of the disturbing image flooded her memory. "I must've called you ten thousand kinds of whore on my way to hide out in the cornfield."

"I felt like one," Eloise confessed. "The only thing that makes me smile about that day was how proud that boy Sonny looked when he lifted off of me, with his little weenie drippin," she gave a slight laugh before sobering. "I can only imagine how embarrassing it was for you, Jewel." She turned slightly glazed eyes on her daughter. "I'm sorry, baby. I never meant to hurt you."

It was honest, direct and human. Eloise's humility shattered the hard shell of resentment around Jewel's heart like a hammer on glass. For the first time, Jewel realized her mother was just another person, with frailties, feelings and faults like anyone else. Jewel couldn't stop the tears that filled her eyes any more than she could stop the newfound compassion from filling her soul. And when her mother reached out to give her a hug for the first time in years, she fell into her arms, finally able to accept her love.

"That's nice," Glendora cooed and patted her daughter and granddaughter on their arms. "Real nice," she repeated softly, feeling good that they had worked through this issue at long last. "Now let that be the last thing that ever comes between you," she said. "The last thing."

Chapter Eleven

"Well, children, I'm off to bed." Glendora struggled to her feet.

When her legs gave out, Jewel reached to support her. "Let me help you, Granny Glen." She sniffed and swiped at her still wet cheeks with her free hand.

"Thank you, baby." Glendora couldn't remember ever being so tired. She was grateful when Eloise took her other arm. It had been a thrilling but exhausting night. She couldn't wait to rest.

Glendora had nearly accomplished what she'd wanted for this trip; Eloise and Jewel were finally talking to one another instead of fighting, and she'd finally let her family know everything about the past she'd kept secret all these years.

In all honesty, Glendora had been a little anxious to see how Eloise and Jewel would react when they realized she'd danced bare-breasted right along with Josephine Baker in her early days. But her daughter and granddaughter didn't seem bothered in the least by seeing the film clips of her as a young dancer—probably because her face was hard to discern as she was grouped with the rest of the chorus line.

Funny, she'd feared telling of her time in London. Somehow, she'd thought that the telling of it would destroy the joy and comfort the memories held for her alone. In fact, telling the secret had released the feeling of triumph she'd held to herself for so long. It had been the happiest time of her life. Sharing it now made her feel closer to her girls than ever.

The trio made slow progress into the adjoining room. Glendora found she'd lost all feeling in her legs and wondered if she was walking or simply being carried by her girls. "Don't ever get old, children," she said, feeling her eyelids drop like lead curtains. With considerable effort she struggled into the bed.

Eloise arranged the sheets and blankets around her. "It's better than the alternative," she offered.

Glendora wasn't so sure. "Well, go ahead and get old then," she said, sinking back onto the pillow. "Just don't die alone."

"Hush that talk, Mama."

Glendora could feel her daughter's hand smooth the unruly strands of gray from her face. Glendora suddenly felt the need to further unburden herself of the thoughts weighing heavy on her heart. She forced her eyes open and took each of their hands in her own. "Listen to me, Eloise, Jewel." She looked from one to the other. "Lord, the two of you are so beautiful," she said, feeling as if she were seeing them for the first time in years. The two women couldn't have been more opposite. Eloise was the color of wheat under sunny skies with eyes that always reminded her of emeralds, while Jewel had deep brown, satiny skin and eyes nearly the color of coal.

Glendora's eyes dropped closed once again, but she forced her words to push through the fatigue. "I always taught you girls to look past the color of your skin, even when other folks couldn't. Eloise, everyone always fussed over you 'cause you were light. And Jewel, folks thought they were better than you 'cause you were dark. You both listened to me when I told you that color has nothing to do with character. You've never let anyone stop you from following your dreams, and I'm proud of you for that. But now you have to listen me again. Children, don't be a fool like I was."

"Mama—"

"Granny—"

Glendora shushed them. "Listen to me," she insisted. "I was full of pride when I was young. Thought I was smarter and prettier than everyone else around me. It made me reckless and I took risks no one else woulda dreamed of."

145

"But look at what you've achieved, Mama," Eloise insisted.

Glendora gave a nod. Her head felt so heavy. "My pride was my greatest strength and my greatest fault," she acknowledged. "I was too prideful. Too full of myself to find forgiveness when I thought I'd been slighted. I put myself above everyone else, and my reward is this…being alone instead of with the one man who made me happy."

"Let's not start that, Mama." Eloise sounded tired as well. "If you're trying to convince me to give Charles another chance, it's not happening. Keep in mind how long his infidelity lasted. He's hardly worthy of my forgiveness."

Glendora squeezed her hand. "I know that, baby. I'm not sayin' he did right by you. But look deeper, child. Behind every act of injury or insult, there's some powerful emotion drivin' it. Think of your own actions, the ones you just confessed to Jewel."

"I never did anything to Charles," she protested.

"Neither did I to Arthur. But he needed so desperately to be considered a fine, upstanding man with integrity that he was willing to denounce anything he thought would get in the way of that."

"And at that time, what was in the way was you," Jewel added.

"Yes. Until he decided our love was worth more to him than anything else. 'Course by the time he came to that realization, it was too late. My pride had hardened my heart. I refused to forgive him." The old woman sighed. "And my pride is a curse I passed along to the two of you."

"You taught us to stand up for ourselves, Mama. That's no curse," Eloise insisted. "I'm embarrassed that I put up with Charles's philandering for so long before I got rid of him. I felt like such a fool."

"I'm not sayin' I got all the answers, chile. All I'm sayin' is there's a fine line between being a fool for a man and not forgivin' him for being one. 'Cause that's all they are, children…they're just men.

"Talk to Charles, Eloise. Find out what's in his heart, that's all I'm sayin. And Jewel—"

"I know, Granny. You want me to talk to Trevor."

"That's right. He ain't done a thing wrong, except ask a favor of you. You chose to take it as an insult. Don't keep pushing him away 'cause of what you're scared he's gonna do. I tell you this for sure; a man who is punished ahead of time is likely to commit the crime he's been convicted of after a while."

Fatigue drifted through Glendora's body and mind like the London fog settling along the ground. "Don't be a fool for any man, but if they're redeemable…forgive 'em," she whispered as sleep carried her to blessed unconsciousness.

Trevor shuffled through the listings on his desk for the fifteenth time. He couldn't focus and couldn't sit still for longer than two minutes at a time. Pushing back from his desk, he blew a long breath and paced around the room.

The good news was, the city council had approved the Initiative and had even kicked in some tax benefits for the occupants once it was completed.

But there was also bad news. Despite his promise to Rae of no regrets for their night together, he was being torn up by guilt and anxiety. How would he tell Jewel about this without losing all hope of getting her back? Hell, the woman had been talking about divorce before he'd so much as kissed Rae.

Linda walked inside his office just as he was making his fourth trip around the desk. "Mr. St. John, there's a Charles Hunt here to see you."

"Charles? Really?" He stopped in mid-pace. "Send him in."

"Already here." Charles slid past Linda.

The woman gave him an appreciative look over her half-rims before turning back to the lobby.

"Hey, how're you doin', Charles?" Trevor ran over to shake the other man's hand and give him an enthusiastic hug. He'd always liked Charles, despite the fact that he was prone to drifting in and out of his daughter's life at whim. "I heard you were here. What's goin' on?"

"I need to find someplace to stay, son. I promised Eloise I'd be out by the time she got back from London." Charles took a seat while Trevor headed around the desk to his chair.

"Sure, I can help. A house, huh?" Trevor rifled through the

papers on his desk. "You here to stay, then?"

"Yeah. I'm getting too old for all this traveling. I want to settle down and spend my old age with my grandkids." Charles laughed. "Sounds silly coming from me, doesn't it?"

Trevor looked at his father-in-law, realizing he had no idea of their recent loss. "Listen, man." He put away the paper. "I've got some things to tell you."

Charles frowned. "Sounds serious."

Trevor blew out a breath. "It's very serious. How about I take you to lunch so we can catch up?"

Because Charles wanted fried catfish, Trevor took him to eat at the Acadiana off Loop 410. After they'd made small talk over their lunch, Trevor folded his hands and prepared to tell his father-in-law about losing the baby. Not knowing how to sugarcoat the story, Trevor jumped right in and told Charles about the pregnancy that nearly killed Jewel, how it had left her barren and how they'd fought over Rae's proposition.

"Jewel was in the hospital and I didn't know anything about it?" Charles sank back in his chair with an unreadable expression on his face. Finally, he shook his head. "I must've been moving. Glendora would've called me otherwise." He said the last to himself.

"Sorry, Charles," Trevor offered.

"Naw," he waved off Trevor's gentle apology. "I messed up so much over the years, Trevor, I don't deserve anyone's sympathy. In fact, I came home to see if I could set some stuff straight." He played mindlessly with his napkin, folding and unfolding it. "Maybe I came too late."

"Well, if it makes you feel better," Trevor said, "anytime you show up, Jewel is happy."

A smile crossed the older man's face for a moment before fading. "Yeah, but I wasn't here when she needed me." Charles fell silent for a few moments. "Well, I'm glad she has you, son."

Trevor hung his head. "I haven't told you all of the story yet," he admitted, wondering why he suddenly felt so keen on confession. "Two nights ago…I slept with Rae." He peered up at the man sheepishly, watching for his reaction. "It wasn't like cheating…" he continued. "I did it as a favor to Rae…to help her. Turns out she's got this obsession thing about me."

Charles said nothing, just sat looking at him with that same unreadable expression.

"And I think it worked," Trevor added hopefully, clearing his throat. "She said she's got me out of her system and will be looking for a man of her own…um…which I think is great. She says she deserves someone who loves her as much as I love Jewel." He stopped talking and took a long swallow of iced tea to clear the hot desert overtaking his mouth. His story sounded lame, even to his own ears, yet Charles said nothing. "I do love Jewel," he added, feeling like an ass. Trevor could think of nothing else to do but pull out his wallet and grab hold of the bill. "Well, that's it," he said weakly, "that's all I had to say. Wanna get out of here?"

Charles nodded and eased from his chair.

Trevor paid the bill at the cashier, and they left the building. Just as they stepped into the parking lot, Charles turned to face Trevor and swung a hard fist square into his jaw.

Trevor stumbled back a few steps and fought the reeling in his head and blinked against the stars floating before his eyes. "What the hell, Charles?" He held tight to the wood railing as his equilibrium came back.

"I know I'm no role model, son," Charles rubbed his knuckles, "but for the record, I don't like you cheatin' on my daughter. And no matter how you try to justify it, that's what you did."

Trevor looked into the older man's eyes but didn't see hate there, only sincerity. Charles offered him a hand. "This is the only time I want to have this discussion. Understood?"

Trevor nodded. "Understood." He took the other man's hand and shook on it.

"You all right?" Charles asked.

"Yeah." Trevor shook his head a little to clear the still-swirling stars in his eyes. "But you sure as hell hit hard for an old man."

With a smile, Charles jerked his head in the direction of the car. "Let's go."

Nursing his stinging jaw, Trevor pulled his keys out of his

pocket and followed Charles's long stride to the car. He beeped the remote to unlock the Escalade just as his father-in-law reached for the handle.

Trevor took his place behind the wheel and started the engine. "Still wanna look at some listings?" he asked, testing the waters.

"Yeah," Charles offered. "Man's gotta have a roof over his head." With that, he pulled a pack of gum from his jacket pocket and sank back against the seat with a satisfied sigh. "So," he started, "That story you told me about why you slept with Rae…"

"Yeah?"

"'Sthat what you're planning on telling Jewel?" he asked.

Trevor winced. "It's pretty weak, huh?"

Charles nodded. "Definitely needs some work, son."

"Got any suggestions?" Trevor asked, feeling grateful to have Charles as an ally.

"You don't wanna lie to Jewel…that would be worse," the older man offered. "I made that mistake one too many times," he admitted.

"Well, what I told you was the truth," Trevor insisted.

"I believe you, son," Charles acknowledged, "but I'm a man. Women don't think the same as we do. Let me give it some thought. It's all in how you deliver the message, really."

"Yeah?" Trevor was starting to feel like there was some hope.

"Let me think on it. We'll come up with something."

Trevor nodded and smiled. The motion made his face hurt. "While you're thinking, could you come up with a story for me to tell my clients when they see my swollen jaw?" he teased.

Charles laughed heartily. "Now that's where a lie will take you the farthest, son. The sky's the limit."

The two men fell into an easy banter after that. Trevor wondered if this was what it was like to be a father, to punish a child when he did wrong then help him back up when he was down. Yeah, he decided, that's the way it should be. He had so been looking forward to fatherhood. But it would never be, he reminded himself.

The thought of his lost child left an ache in his heart. He hoped time would ease the pain.

Charles sat leisurely sipping coffee the next morning, a routine he'd had all his life, looking at the listings for the two homes Trevor had suggested. He'd walked through both of them and decided that either would suit his needs, but he was finding it difficult to decide which one to place a bid on.

"It ain't the houses," he said scornfully, tossing the papers onto Eloise's round breakfast table. He looked around and sighed. He liked it here, among Eloise's things. She had such a way of making a home comfortable, even one as large as this.

The telephone rang and the answering machine started the recording of his wife's voice telling the caller to please leave a message. At the tone, a man identifying himself as a collector for her mortgage company was insisting that her house would be going into foreclosure if she continued to ignore his calls.

Charles frowned. That couldn't be right. How could Eloise have put her house at risk? It wasn't like her. Though he didn't want to get in her business, Charles decided that he needed to check further into this. First, he listened to all of the recordings on her machine. The mortgage company had called four times since she'd left town, and some man had called to say there were no job openings at her old office.

Moving to the kitchen desk, Charles shuffled through the pile of junk mail and bills he'd placed there daily. He found urgent notice after urgent notice. He remembered seeing the red stamps but had assumed it was a marketing gimmick.

By the look of things, her house payment wasn't the only thing she'd missed paying. She hadn't paid any of her bills the month prior to leaving for London, and now she was at least two months in arrears on everything. But her house...she was over four months late on her mortgage.

Eloise was in financial trouble. Charles shoved his hands in his jeans pockets and sighed. He'd bet she hadn't told a soul about this. The woman was too stubborn to ask for help—always insisting on standing on her own.

Well, not this time. Charles rushed to the bedroom, found his leather jacket and headed for his bike. He knew exactly what to do. It would piss Eloise off, but he was hoping in the end she would appreciate his help.

Lord Arthur's estate was just like a movie set, Jewel decided. The fog had been less insistent today, allowing her to see the sweep of lawn and shrubs around the massive home of her newly found grandfather.

"You should return in the spring," the old man said as he joined her on the stone-cobbled terrace that wrapped around the house. "There's always a blaze of glorious color when the bulbs open and the roses flower," he stated proudly.

"I'd love to see it," Jewel said truthfully. Looking up at the man, she shared a quiet smile with him. "When I was a kid, if I'd told anyone my grandfather was white, the kids would've laughed at me and called me a liar."

Arthur threw his head back when he laughed. "And what do you suppose your friends would say now?"

"They'd be envious." She turned her attention back to the acres of land. "You don't seem at all put off that I'm so dark-skinned. It's nice to be accepted so unconditionally."

"My dear child, if anyone fails to see how scrumptiously beautiful you are, they're stupid as well as blind." He gave her a gentle kiss on the forehead.

"Trust me, Grandpa Arthur, I've run into a lot of stupid people in my time." Jewel remembered briefly how many times she'd felt the disapproving glances of her great-aunts, Granny Glen's sisters, who were all so proud that their daughters and granddaughters were light-skinned and had "good hair."

To Jewel's delight, all of her cousins had worthless husbands—most had been incarcerated at one time or another—and bad kids. Lots of bad kids.

Only she had married well. Oh, it had been sweet when she'd

introduced Trevor to her great aunties at the wedding dinner. They couldn't say enough about how handsome he was... "And so well off," they'd said when they thought she couldn't hear. She'd felt like a princess on her wedding day. Her grandfather was making her feel the same way today. He had servants at her and Eloise's beck and call.

"Won't you and Eloise change your minds and stay awhile longer?" her grandfather asked seriously. "We're just getting to know one another."

"We thought we'd give you and Granny Glen time to make eyes at one another in private," she teased. "No need having us kids in the way." She tiptoed up to give the tall man a peck on the cheek. Besides, she was actually looking forward to the shopping trip she and Eloise had planned. A bond had started the previous week when Eloise had opened up to her, and she wanted—no, needed—to close the gap between them once and for all. That, plus the fact that it was their last week in London, and she couldn't live without doing a little shopping while she was here. "Are you ready to go, Eloise?" she called into the house.

Her mother walked onto the terrace wearing a frown. "I think I'll stay with Mama," she said apologetically. "She's not feeling well."

Alarmed, Jewel looked past her mother. "What's wrong?" she and Arthur asked at once.

Eloise shrugged. "She says she's just tired—overexerted herself."

"Oh, dear." Arthur lifted a hand to his cheek. "I have been keeping the old girl up nights I'm afraid. We've had the best time reminiscing. Not to worry." He clapped his hands together and smiled. "I've a friend who's a physician. I'll have him over for a look, eh? That way the two of you can have your shopping day."

Eloise looked relieved. "It would make me feel better to have a doctor take a look at her. Thank you, Lord Arthur."

The man frowned. "Come now. Such formality, my pet? If you can't manage Father, how about Arthur?"

Smiling, Eloise gave him a soft peck on the cheek. "Call us right away if there's anything really wrong—Father?"

His hazel eyes twinkled with delight. "As you wish, my dear.

As you wish."

Glendora tried to hide her fatigue behind a smile when Eloise, Jewel and Arthur reentered the room. By the concerned looks on their faces, she surmised that she'd failed. "The three of you need to do me a favor," she said with good humor.

"What's that, my love?" Arthur sat beside her on the sofa and took her hand gently.

"Stop looking at me like you're tryin' to plan the words for my headstone. I can't take it."

"Ain't nothing wrong with her." Jewel pretended not to be worried, seeing the dark circles beneath her eyes. She kissed her grandmother's cheek. "You're feisty as ever."

The worry line eased but didn't disappear from Eloise's forehead as they lingered a while longer.

"We'll only be gone a little while, Mother," Eloise assured Glendora and kissed her as well. "Unless you'd rather we stay."

Glendora gave her The Look.

Eloise flung her hands up in surrender. There was no arguing with the old woman now. "All right. Consider us gone."

Glendora gave a quick nod. "Good. See if you can find me some perfume. Something sweet and powdery, nothing that smells like bug spray."

Jewel waved good-bye to her grandmother who sat in the huge room with finely upholstered furniture, ornate wool rugs and floor-to-ceiling French doors that opened onto a stone patio. There were fresh flowers from Arthur's greenhouse arranged in an elegant spray on the table before her. And at her side was a man who gazed upon her with adoration and love. Despite her fatigue, Glendora looked happy and more content than Jewel had ever seen her.

It was an image that would burn in Jewel's memory forever.

"Good-bye, Mother." Eloise's voice held a hint of emotion.

"Bye, bye, babies. And before I forget, thank you for this trip. It meant a lot to me."

Glendora Jubilee died the evening before she was to return to America.

Chapter Twelve

Trevor checked his watch. Charles would arrive any minute. Their flight to London would be leaving in two-and-a-half hours. Trevor wasn't thrilled about flying—especially across an ocean—but Eloise had said that Jewel was absolutely distraught at her grandmother's passing.

Even if Jewel didn't want to see him, he had to be with her to offer whatever comfort he could. Plus, he had to pay his respects to Glendora. He'd loved the old woman as if she were his own grandmother.

The phone rang. Trevor didn't have time for chatting. "Hello."

"Trevor?" It was Rae.

"Yeah."

"Somethin' wrong? You sound rushed."

"Yeah, I am, Rae. Charles and I are headed out to the airport in a few minutes."

"Oh, yeah. The funeral. I would go…"

"I know, Rae. Don't worry about it." He carried the cordless into the bathroom to retrieve his shaving kit. "Anyway, what's up?"

She cleared her throat and blew out a breath on the other end of the line.

Something was wrong. Trevor packed the shaving kit and sat down on his bed. "What is it, Rae? What's going on?" The last time she stalled like this, she'd been in the hospital with her boyfriend's fists imprinted on her face and body.

"You know me too well, Trev. Anyway, I'm all right. I'll start off with that."

Losing patience, Trevor pressed, "Then what is it? Just tell me."

"I think we're pregnant."

Panic seized him. Trevor couldn't breathe. "Don't play like that, Rae." He prayed that this was one of her jokes. "That shit ain't funny."

"I'm not trying to be funny, Trev. I'm serious."

"Do you think or do you know?" he pressed.

"I had a blood test after I missed my period. I know I'm pregnant."

This couldn't be happening. "No chance it's somebody else's?" he asked desperately.

"You trying to piss me off?" she countered.

"No. No. Dammit, Rae. What are we going to do?"

"The nurse tells me I'm going to be sick and tired for the next nine months." She was short. "I don't know what the hell you're going to do."

The connection went dead.

Trevor gave a long, fiery curse and buried his face in his hands. He might as well kiss his marriage good-bye when he got to London. How the hell was he going to tell her this?

The servants in Lord Arthur's estate were bustling about, airing out rooms, changing linens and opening windows to accommodate Jewel and Eloise's move from the hotel and the guests that had yet to arrive from America.

Arthur was devastated at losing Glendora yet again, and he could tell the loss was taking its toll on his newfound family as well.

Jewel couldn't stop crying.

Eloise couldn't stop moving. "Jewel," she said, punching numbers on the phone for the hundredth time that day. "You've got to pull yourself together long enough to help me. We've got a ton of things to do—a thousand people to call."

Arthur stepped up beside his daughter and pulled the phone from her hand. He tucked it inside his coat pocket and shushed her protest with a long hug. "Why don't you lie down and rest, my dear. I've had my assistant cancel your airline tickets and start on the funeral arrangements. You've called your relatives, so why not have a rest, eh?"

"I've tried lying down. I can't rest." She pushed away from his arms and paced the large room of his home. Suddenly, she turned and looked at him. "Did you say your assistant was making funeral arrangements? How is that possible? He doesn't know the funeral homes in San Antonio, does he?"

Arthur shook his head. "No, Glendora wished to be buried here in London. We've both a nice plot in the country."

"You do?"

The revelation stifled Jewel's tears.

"Yes. We purchased the land long ago on a whim. We pledged our undying love for one another under a large tree one spring. As we looked up into the sky, we decided it was in that spot and that spot alone that we'd be buried side-by-side." He sighed, remembering the day that didn't seem all that long ago but was in fact a whole lifetime past. "Turns out I didn't please her much the whole of my life." The thought broke his heart anew. "It's the least I can do for her now." He couldn't keep the quiver from his lips or the tears from his eyes.

"That's so sweet, Grandpa." Jewel rose from her place on the sofa to throw her arms around his neck.

"It's out of the question," Eloise stated. "I can't leave my mother here all alone."

"Eloise," Jewel argued, "Granny Glen loved it here. You said so yourself. Besides, she won't be alone." She looked up at Arthur with kind, soft eyes. "I think that's what she was trying to tell us the other night."

"It's what she wanted," Arthur added. It had been what they'd discussed when they'd been alone the night she passed. Arthur could still feel her warm weight in his arms. The smell of her perfumed hair still lingered in his nostrils. The touch of her lips, still so soft, was permanently etched in his memory.

Such was his fate. To have his treasured love for brief moments before she drifted away. There had never been enough time for them when they lived. Maybe eternity would be enough time for him to finally capture and keep his one true love.

"Let me show you the land," Arthur insisted to his daughter. "Then you can make up your mind, hmm?"

It took longer for Jewel and Arthur to get Eloise out of the house than it did to reach the land. When Arthur's driver pulled to a stop and opened the door, Eloise took a long breath before exiting the car.

It's so serene, she thought. It was like some picture from a fable—the vast landscape of snowy hills dotted with massive trees. Though it was winter now and the trees were without leaves, she could imagine how pretty it must be in the spring and summer. Lord Arthur's estate could be seen in the distance, standing like a small castle under the crisp, blue sky.

Maybe it was the lack of sleep, or the sudden realization that her mother was gone, but something made her legs give out. Eloise felt the weight of grief flood her soul as she fell to her knees on the cold, hard ground.

Snow soaked her slacks, and the chill of the morning air wrapped around her as she lifted long, sorrowful wails into the skies. The wind captured her cries and carried her sorrow far beyond her immediate vicinity. Jewel fell alongside her to comfort and cry with her.

It seemed to Eloise that she cried for hours. When her weeping finally subsided, she was tired and ached all over. Her eyes were swollen nearly shut as she wobbled unsteadily to her feet.

"Poor, dear child." Her father moved over to her and hugged her shaking body tightly. "Let's get you warmed up, and then you can have a rest. A cup of tea would be lovely about now, wouldn't it?"

Eloise couldn't find the strength to answer and didn't really care, though she did feel some comfort when Jewel slipped her hand in hers as they walked back to the waiting car. It was just the two of them now, mother and daughter. She gripped Jewel's hand just a little tighter and bid a silent "Thank you" to her mother for bringing them together at last.

She thought of her mother's words about pride and relationships as they closed themselves into the warm interior of her father's car for the short trip back. As much as she wanted to honor her mother's dying wish, she had reservations. Was Charles redeemable, she wondered? Could she ever forgive him for what he'd done to her?

Memories of love and longing for her husband filled Eloise's thoughts for the duration of the ride…to the point where she believed she'd conjured him when she saw him standing in the circular drive of the estate. Vaguely, she registered the presence of another man, but there was no mistaking the square-shouldered stance of her husband. "Charles," she whispered at the window as the car slowed to a stop. The thickening mist swirled about the man who wore a black overcoat and his signature black jeans. Instead of the charming grin that usually graced his handsome face, he looked serious and sorrowful. He walked over to the car and opened the door to help her out.

When she was standing before him, all Eloise could do for long moments was look at him. She was so happy to see him. "Oh, Charles," was all she could manage.

His arms were around her the next moment. "I know, honey. I'm sorry." His deep voice was soft.

Eloise buried her face in the wool of his coat and inhaled the scent of his cologne. "I'm glad you're here," she admitted.

Trevor pushed past Charles and Eloise to get to Jewel. "Baby?" he called inside the car.

"Trevor!" She rushed from the car into his arms. "Oh, Trevor," she cried. "Granny's gone."

"Oh, baby, I know. I'm here." He kissed her forehead, her cheeks, her lips, filling his senses with her like a man with an addiction. "I'm here."

"Shall we go inside the house then, children?" Arthur said quietly.

Before doing so, Eloise and Jewel introduced Arthur to their respective husbands. Inside the estate, Arthur instructed the staff to start tea and to bring snacks until dinner was ready to be served.

Glendora's sisters arrived in London in time for dinner, and for the first time in many years, Arthur's home was filled with family. He and his wife had never had children; she'd been barren, and neither of them had large families, so it warmed his heart to have Glendora's family here. They asked him a thousand questions about his affair with Glendora and about her life in London. Re-telling the stories he'd cherished for so long was refreshing and somehow cathartic. He was surprised, actually, to discover how little they knew of their sister's time in London and wondered if Glendora had felt their time together had been too precious to share with others as he had.

As the hour grew late, Arthur had his housekeeper escort his guests off to the bedrooms that had been made to accommodate them. Only after all had been tucked into their rooms did he make way to his own. It would be when he was alone in his bed tonight that he would miss Glendora the most…he wasn't looking forward to the long, lonely hours ahead of him.

Charles was pleased that the housekeeper had his bags placed in Eloise's room. He wasn't so sure how his wife felt about it, however. "Looks like they assumed I'd be sleeping with you," he said, noting how tired she looked as she pulled off her clothes. "Is that all right?"

"It's fine, Charles." Her voice was hoarse with exhaustion. "It doesn't matter."

He didn't like the sound of that but decided now was not the time to go into a deep discussion about their relationship. For now, it would be enough to be with her.

"Who knew you were like the daughter of an English lord?" Charles asked, trying to keep conversation light. "Does it bother you that he's white?"

Eloise shrugged and pulled off her bra and placed it dutifully in the clothes hamper in the room. "No. I heard enough speculation about it from my aunties over the years. They all went on about how good my hair was and how pale my skin was. They said I could easily pass for white."

Charles turned his back and tried to hide the effect created by seeing his wife naked. A nice cool shower was what he needed, he decided. "Why didn't you try to pass?" he asked.

"It's not how I was raised. Mama would've had a fit to know I'd denied my heritage. She always said we had to live our lives as if color didn't matter."

"She grew up in the forties and fifties." Charles frowned. "Of course color matters. How could she say it didn't?"

Eloise had her nightgown on and was now under the covers. "Makes you think negatively, she always said. Roadblocks exist only as long as you believe they do. I think she was probably right about that."

Charles stared at the toile wallpaper and thought about how true that statement was. "Your mother was right about a lot of things," he agreed. It was Glendora who'd told him that, if he wanted to win his wife back, he had to act like it. She'd told him sending flowers every year was weak and proved nothing, except that he knew how to dial 1-800-FLOWERS.

Charles smiled as he headed for the bathroom. Maybe coming to London was one way to show Eloise he was serious about winning her back this time. And he really hoped she appreciated what he'd done back in San Antonio. Of course, only time would tell.

It had been an extremely long day, and he wanted to wash it away. The old-fashioned bathtub with claw feet he found in the black-and-white tiled bathroom amused him. It had a long pipe that curved like a swan's neck just at eye level. The only modern-looking fixture was the showerhead that had a dial to select the type of spray he wanted. He selected the pulse, finding its massaging effect very pleasant.

By the time he toweled off and slid into the bed beside Eloise, she was lost in sleep. Charles ran a hand down her arm and kissed her gently on the shoulder. He didn't want to wake her, just hold her for a while. Snuggling close, he draped his arm around her waist and closed his eyes, knowing that he could sleep with only this woman for the rest of his life. He wished he'd reached that conclusion a long time ago.

Trevor hadn't let more than a few moments pass without

touching his wife since he'd arrived. It seemed as if it had been years instead of weeks that she'd been gone. Now that they were alone in one of Lord Arthur's elegant bedrooms, he pulled her into his arms. "I've missed you so much, Jewel." He pressed his lips against hers and was relieved when she reciprocated the kiss.

Just the feel of her soft curves against him ignited hot lust within Trevor. "I need you, baby. I really need you," he whispered as he trailed hard kisses down her neck and onto the soft skin above her breasts.

Her hands dug into his shoulders as she laid her head back to allow him easier access to the flesh he sought. "I need you too, Trevor," she said in a strained voice.

His trembling hands nearly ripped the clothes from her body. There would be time enough later for the confession he needed to make about sleeping with Rae. He and Charles had been unable to come up with any words that would make the news more palatable, so Trevor had settled on telling his wife the plain truth. But not now—not yet.

His need was throbbing and insistent and beyond control at that moment. Only one thing could ease the pressure building inside him like steam awaiting release.

Jewel lay naked on the bed now, her dark ebony legs opened in welcome. "I'm waiting, Sir Trevor," she whispered seductively.

Trevor didn't let another second stand between him and ecstasy. He pushed inside her tight, wet folds and let out an unrestrained moan. "I'm sorry, baby, but this won't last long," he warned. "You feel too good."

"Don't talk, Trevor," Jewel ordered. "I just need to feel you. That's all."

It was a request he had no problem filling, over and over again. With each thrust, he felt closer to Jewel, ending the feeling of longing that time and distance had created. He was home. Home at last.

Oh, Trevor. My sweet Trevor. Jewel moaned each time he filled her, wrapping her arms and legs around him to intensify each thrust. She'd missed this…the sweet turmoil he created inside her, the crazy joy he made her feel.

162

Their bodies sliding and slamming against one another created heat, passion and desire. Jewel felt connected to her husband in the most intimate way possible when they made love. This was more than the joining of bodies. It was the joining of their souls, of their lives, of their love. She hadn't realized until that moment how much she'd missed him. How much she still loved him and how right Granny Glen had been. He hadn't done anything so bad that she couldn't forgive him. Nothing at all.

The thought freed her emotions and released her desire. "That's it, Trevor. Right there!" she screamed.

His cries joined hers, and Jewel rocketed to the cosmos on a streaming comet of light.

The next day was bright and sunny. Not even a hint of fog arrived to mar the occasion of Glendora Jubilee's death. The event was well attended by fans and members of the peerage alike.

At dusk, only Arthur remained to watch as the casket was buried beneath the fine dark dirt of London, followed by the many flowers the crowd had brought. His words of good-bye were too personal to express to anyone save the woman who'd held his heart for the whole of his life. And so, he whispered them into the wind in hopes that they would reach her ears and touch her soul.

Rae entered the restaurant, feeling a little anxious. She didn't quite know what to think of Jewel's lunch invitation so soon after she and Trevor had returned from London, but thought it was a good thing that this meeting was in a public place.

Checking her watch, Rae noted that she was nearly fifteen minutes early. Taking a seat at the bar, she ordered an iced tea and thought back to her meeting with Trevor earlier that morning.

As usual, they had met at the gym to work out. First, he'd decided to play a couple of games of basketball with the other over-forty guys who were clinging desperately to their youth. She had to give ole Trev props, though. He'd been bounding up and down the court like a kid on summer break.

Afterward, he'd had plenty of energy to see him through their upper body workout on the free weight circuit. All the while, Rae had to plaster a grin on her face as Trevor told her a bit more than she cared to know about his reconciliation with his wife.

"I'm sorry if I pissed you off the day I left," Trevor said between reps on the bench press.

"That's all right," she said, placing her hands just under the bar to spot him on his next set. "I wasn't really mad, just wanted you to be as happy about it as I was," she explained.

"Tell you the truth," Trevor grunted as he strained against the weight on the bar before placing it on the stand, "I want to be happy about it." He stared at her pelvis for a moment. "I want a baby so bad, but I feel guilty every time I think about it," he admitted. "I don't know how I'm going to tell Jewel about this."

Rae felt sorry for him. She knew exactly how it felt to want something you couldn't have. Yet she'd felt much better since they'd slept together. She'd stopped yearning for a man, Trevor in particular, to make her happy. It had become enough for her to know there was a new life growing inside her.

"I'll do anything I can to help you out, Trev," she told him, shooing him off the bench to take her turn. "I still think the best thing is not to tell Jewel a thing."

"I dunno." Trevor sighed and readied himself to spot her. "I don't like keeping secrets from my wife."

"So tell her," Rae said. "But it'll end bloody this time." She pushed the weight up and down five times before replacing the bar. It was always sweet to feel the burn of her muscles getting stronger. She planned on staying fit throughout her pregnancy.

"You think so?" Trevor sounded dismayed.

"Look at how homegirl went off on you just because you asked the question," Rae offered. "I can tell everyone the kid belongs to Tyree or someone I just met. I'm telling you, Trevor, no one has to know but us."

"Charles knows," he said flatly.

Rae rolled her eyes. "Are you tryin' to mess up your life?"

Trevor hung his head and cursed. "He knew about me sleeping

with you from before, but I told him about the baby on the way to London. I don't think he'll say anything. But he's expecting me to tell her. Says I've made a mess of things. I have to clean it up."

"Men," Rae muttered. "You're fixin' to step in a mess, that's what you're doing." She proceeded to do another rep of presses before sitting up and wiping the sweat from her face with her oversized T-shirt.

"How do I tell her, Rae?" Trevor asked, plopping onto the bench beside her. "You're a woman. What would it take for you to forgive me?"

Rae looked at her oldest and best friend and sighed. "It wouldn't take much for me, Trev," she admitted. "I look tough, but I'm a pushover where love is concerned. Your wife…well, she's a bit more excitable about things. It'll only hurt her, Trev," she'd told him. "And unless you want to lose her again, I wouldn't say a word."

"But that baby you're carrying is mine," he insisted. "I want to be a part of its life."

"Then be the best damned uncle you can be." It was the last thing she told him before kissing his bearded cheek and heading for the showers. She had to get to the gym to start her ladies on drills.

But now as she waited on his wife to arrive at the restaurant, Rae wondered if he'd taken her advice. The last thing she wanted was to get into another fight with Jewel St. John.

The few men sitting at the bar turned their heads toward the door in unison, signaling Jewel's arrival. The dark-skinned woman with skin as smooth as porcelain always turned men's heads.

In the past, Rae had felt gangly and boyish around her, but today she'd never felt more feminine. Rae left her seat and greeted Jewel with a wave.

Jewel noticed Rae had ordered a soda when they reached one another and apologized. "Am I late?" she asked.

"No. I'm early, as usual." Rae didn't know how to be anything but on time. Maybe it was a result of her athletic training; her coaches had always been merciless about punctuality. Not on time? You had to do laps. Miles of them. "Could we get a table?" Rae asked the hostess.

"Sure," the young woman answered. "Would you like smoking or non?"

"Non," Rae and Jewel said in unison.

"Jinx. You owe me a pop," Jewel teased as they followed the woman to a table.

Rae relaxed and smiled. So, it was meant to be a friendly meeting after all.

"So, how've you been?" Jewel asked after a thin young Hispanic waiter had taken their order.

"Fine. Started training with the ladies. It's a good squad," Rae answered honestly. She thought they had the right mix of seasoned professionals and fresh-faced college grads to make a good run in their freshman season. "How about you? Trev said you guys kissed and made up...and made love all over the house," she added with her tongue planted firmly in her cheek.

Jewel ducked her head a little with embarrassment. "Does Trevor tell you everything?" she challenged, trying hard to hide her grin.

"Not everything," she said sobering. "Only the things he finds most important in his life."

Not missing the intended compliment, Jewel lifted her eyes to meet Rae's. "I'm sorry, Rae. I don't know what I was thinking." She looked at Rae as if seeing her for the first time. "I gave Trevor way too much credit in all this."

The look on the other woman's face was making Rae uneasy. Maybe it wasn't going to be a pleasant discussion after all. "What do you mean?"

"I mean, I was pretty tough on him." Jewel took a sip of water before giving a small laugh. "I actually thought the man was proposing something underhanded when that wasn't the case at all."

Rae agreed. Trevor had gone along with the plan because he wanted a child, nothing more. "He wasn't trying to pull a fast one on you, if that's what you mean. I told you that."

"Yeah, you did." Jewel took a measured breath and continued looking at Rae with scrutiny. "The thing about Trevor is that he's really not complicated at all. I forgot that for a while. But you never did, did you, Rae?"

Rae felt sixteen years old again, being caught by her high school coach under the stands after a game with Todd Sunshine's hand in her shorts. "Listen, Jewel. I'm not trying to make trouble between you. I shouldn't have asked Trevor what I did…I dunno…I—"

"You love him," Jewel said simply.

"Yeah, I do," Rae admitted without apology. "He's always been there for me. I don't know what I would've done without him."

Jewel was watching her carefully. Rae suddenly felt as if her insides were hanging out. "What?" she asked in exasperation.

"I meant that you're in love with him," Jewel stated calmly.

"Naw, it's not like that between us, J., really." Rae's denials sounded hollow even to her own ears.

"You know what I think, Rae Angelique Paris?" Jewel asked with narrowed eyes as she sank back in the booth. "I think you've gone through so many men because you're looking for another Trevor."

"Have you lost your mind, girl?" Rae was growing uncomfortable. "Ain't a single man I've dated even come close to being like Trevor." With the exception of Sterling LeRoi, she thought. He'd come to her rescue the night she drove herself into a ditch, just as Trevor had. Still, she was making a point. "Remember Blue with his gold tooth and thieving hands? And Donald who could only make love when he was high? And Jerome—"

"I remember all of them, Rae." Jewel sat forward. "And that's my whole point. Why are you afraid of finding a decent man? Why are you spending all your time and energy on scrubs?"

"You seem to be the one with all the answers," Rae offered lamely, knowing she'd never intended to have anything more than short lustful trysts with each of her past boyfriends. In truth, she'd never entertained the idea of a lifelong relationship with anyone other than Trevor. But now she was over that. "Why do you think?"

"Because you like it when Trevor steps in to protect you. It's like he's your white knight. How close am I to the truth?"

Rae folded her arms and cleared her throat. "I dunno." She shrugged. "Maybe that's true."

"And maybe that's why you offered to have Trevor's baby."

Rae couldn't bring herself to meet Jewel's eyes. She still felt guilty hiding the truth of her pregnancy. "I only offered to help ease his pain, Jewel. It tore him up bad when you lost that baby," Rae defended, her voice unsteady. "But since we're being open and honest," she raised her eyes, "I really didn't think you would mind all that much. I don't think you wanted to be a mother. How close am I to the truth?"

"Yeah, you're right," Jewel had admitted as much to her husband. "I was afraid, Rae. Afraid that he wouldn't love me as much as his child. Afraid that I wouldn't come first in his life anymore. I couldn't bear the thought of it. All my negative thoughts poisoned my system, I think. I think I killed the baby with my jealousy," Jewel said with apology. "I've got to make it up to him."

Rae's heart went out to Jewel. They weren't so different. They'd both been jealous of Trevor, but Rae could never tell this woman how now all that had changed for her. "Jewel," she reached a hand across the table. "You make Trevor happy," Rae said. "That's all that matters to me now."

"For real?" Jewel asked skeptically.

Rae nodded. "Yeah. So, you want to make it up to him," she said with a smile. "How do you plan to do that?"

Their food arrived, forcing Jewel to wait before revealing her thoughts. After the waiter was assured that there was nothing more that they needed, he disappeared. Jewel leaned forward and spoke in a conspiratorial whisper. "I want to take you up on your offer."

Rae had taken a bite of her oriental salad. Because of the crunching of the noodles, she was sure she'd misunderstood what Jewel had said. "What?"

Jewel took a deep breath and repeated what she'd said, "I want to take you up on your offer. I want you to have Trevor's baby."

A piece of salad went down Rae's windpipe the wrong way and had her coughing to dislodge it. After a brief fit, she took a long swallow of soda and stared at Jewel as if she'd grown a second head. "You serious?"

"If you don't kill yourself first," Jewel said with a twisted grin. "Here's the deal," she continued. "You have the baby; it will be a part of Trevor that will always be yours. I'll have Trevor. He'll be mine, all mine, for the rest of our days. Got it?"

This was beautiful, Rae thought. She couldn't have planned a better resolution. Now Trevor had no more worries. Jewel had just let them both off the hook.

Rae had to give the woman props for fighting for what she wanted…and for putting a rival to the test. Jewel was waiting and Rae knew what she wanted—to see if she'd been serious about wanting a baby or if she'd just been trying to trap Trevor.

"Got it?" Jewel repeated.

"Yeah," Rae conceded. "It's really good thinking on your part, Jewel. Trevor gets the child he's always wanted from a friend who's only a friend, and he's got his incredibly understanding wife to thank for it. Yeah, I got it."

Jewel sat back with a satisfied grin.

Rae honestly found that she couldn't be mad at her. The woman had played this brilliantly. "I'll make the arrangements with the doctor and the clinic," she offered. She and Trevor had to plan a way to make this look legitimate.

"I'll break the good news to Trevor," Jewel said smugly.

Chapter Thirteen

Trevor sat on the lid of the toilet in his bathroom watching his hands tremble for the first time since he'd hit adulthood. Standing in front of the city council had been easy compared to the anxiety he was feeling at the moment.

But he had to go through with it. He had to tell Jewel tonight about what he and Rae had done—and that they were expecting in about eight months.

Standing, Trevor adjusted his jeans, then turned to the marble sink to splash water on his face. He towel-dried his beard then, with more care than necessary, took his manicure brush and ensured that every hair lay just right.

"Hey, Sir Trevor, you in there?" Jewel called out from the bedroom.

Even in the mirror, Trevor could see panic flashing in his eyes. He hadn't even heard the front door open and close. "Yeah," he acknowledged, trying to sound casual. "I'll be right out."

"Hurry. I can't wait to tell you who called me today while I was out showing the lake property."

Gripping the sink, Trevor dropped his head and took several deep breaths. Calm down, he repeated to himself. She'll understand.

"Trevor?"

Taking a final breath, he flushed the unused toilet. He checked his hands. Still trembling. What the hell, he'd shove them in his pockets.

He opened the door and greeted his wife with a forced smile. "Who called you today?"

Jewel, who was changing clothes, threw her suit on the bed and pulled on a pair of shorts and a T-shirt. "Get this," she beamed. "I got a call from one of the staff writers at Black Enterprise. They want to do an article about the SADI Initiative!" Her enthusiasm was infectious.

Trevor found his smile became real. "That's great, babe. When are you going to meet with them?"

"We are going to meet with them next week." She jumped up and down and threw her arms around her husband's neck. "We're going to be famous, Trevor."

He put his arms around her narrow waist, feeling them becoming steadier. "You're going to be famous, Jewel. This whole thing was your brainchild. I'll be the first one to tell them that."

"You're so sweet." She pressed her warm body against his and kissed him. "I don't deserve you."

Trevor pulled her tighter and laid his cheek against her hair. "No, it's me who doesn't deserve you," he said honestly, quietly. It was time for confession. "Listen, babe—"

"No, wait." Jewel pushed out of his arms. "That's not the only news I wanted to share with you." She held up her hands to stop him from speaking. "I met with Rae today," she began.

Trevor's mouth went dry. He forced his hands into his pockets and gripped the change he found tightly. "Really?"

"Yes. We had a nice lunch, and I told her I'd come to the conclusion that I wasn't going to be some selfish harlot of a wife."

Frowning, Trevor wasn't sure what she was about to say. "You're anything but selfish, Jewel," he countered. He already felt like a heel. This wasn't helping.

"Would you just listen?" she insisted.

He nodded and tried to swallow but found it difficult.

"I told Rae that I had reconsidered her offer and…and…would be grateful if she would give you the baby you've always wanted."

Stunned, Trevor couldn't move or speak.

Jewel smiled broadly. "That's the last thing you expected to hear, huh?"

Relief flooded Trevor, and he fell to his knees at his wife's feet. Grabbing her around her waist, he pressed his face into her stomach, wanting to cry. "Thank you, Jewel. Oh my God, I can't believe it." It was the answer to his prayers. Now there was no need to tell her about his indiscretion. No need. Everything was going to be all right.

Jewel laughed. "I expected you to be happy, but this is ridiculous. Get up, Trevor."

Trevor did as she instructed but took his time planting kisses on every inch of her body on his way up. "You don't know what you've done," he told her when he finally reached his feet. His feelings went beyond relief now as he realized the magnitude of what she'd just told him. "I know how hard this decision must've been for you, Jewel. I want you to know how absolutely unworthy I feel to have such a woman for a wife," he said sincerely. "I love you so much."

Her dark eyes filled as she gazed up at him longingly. "I did it because I love you, Trevor. More than you'll ever know."

Because his heart was full to bursting and his arms and body craved her, Trevor kissed his wife as if it were the first time. He backed her onto their bed, feeling his desire rising. This evening, he would make love to her the way he preferred—long and slow.

She stopped him just as he slipped his hands beneath her shirt. "Trevor?" Her voice was deep with lust.

"Yeah, babe?" Trevor only half-listened as he tried his best to kiss and suckle every inch of her neck and face.

"I want to renew our vows."

"All right, sweetheart. Whatever you want," he answered, never meaning anything more. She'd given him the world tonight. The least he could do was suffer through a small ceremony.

"This weekend," she added.

Trevor chuckled. "And just how are you going to make a wedding ceremony happen in two days?"

Jewel's eyes twinkled as she smiled. "We'll go to Vegas," she offered triumphantly. "They do weddings every night."

She could've asked him to take her to the moon, and Trevor

wouldn't have hesitated. He was in much too good a mood. "What the hell?" he laughed. "Let's do Vegas!"

"All right," she said, pulling him down on top of her. "Right after you do me."

Sterling knew something was up between Rae and Trevor. He'd known it that night he'd followed her home from the bar. When he'd gone to her house the next morning and caught them walking out together, the two of them had acted…awkward. Like they'd just been caught with their hands in the proverbial cookie jar.

He'd been jealous as hell, which was stupid. He had no claims on Rae Paris. Yet it had taken all his strength to keep from punching Trevor's cheatin' behind that day.

Even now, Sterling was bothered by the look on Rae's face whenever she stole a glance at Trevor. She wore a sort of half-smile and looked as if she was holding tight to the greatest secret ever.

Feeling Trevor's eyes on him, Sterling shifted his gaze. Trevor's unblinking glare was telling. But damned if Sterling knew what it was telling him. Don't touch? Don't ask? Don't start nothin', won't be nothin'? He responded by lifting his chin in acknowledgement—and to show Mr. St. John that he, as a single man, had every right to look at an eligible female.

Sterling turned his attention back to Jewel, who was discussing bids received by general contractors wanting to work on their project. He noted that she was in a better mood since the last meeting. The woman was back to making bedroom eyes at her husband instead of giving him looks that would cut diamonds. He had to give it to old, Trevor…Bro' had some serious mack goin' on with these women. But it was time for the man to share the wealth.

Fact was, the way Rae was looking in her melon-orange dress made Sterling want to eat her up like the fruit she resembled.

Just then, Rae looked his way. Sterling's heart flip-flopped in his chest, and it took a moment before he remembered to breathe.

Damn. He had it bad for her.

So bad that he couldn't look away when Rae twirled a corkscrew curl while listening to Jewel brag on her husband's ability to gain the city council's agreement to purchase the land and begin development.

Sterling thought it was the sexiest thing he'd ever seen. He was used to getting whatever he wanted, whenever he wanted, and not having Rae was beginning to make him irritable.

When Jewel finally adjourned the meeting, Sterling pushed out of his seat quickly. "Hey, Rae." He caught her just as she was leaving the conference room.

"Hey, Sterling." Her smile nearly stopped his heart again.

Act casual, he instructed himself. Ain't nothin' but a thang. "I'm takin' another trip out to Vegas this weekend. Wanna' tag along?"

Rae lifted an eyebrow. "Gonna try to beat me at poker again?"

"Naw. I've got to take a look at the blueprints for that property I'm investing in."

"Sounds boring." Rae shifted her weight to one leg and folded her arms. "What's in it for me?"

"I thought I'd get to know you some more. Find out what a brotha has to do to get with you."

Rae gave one of her throaty laughs. "I think you've forgotten that it was you who rejected me the last time we were together."

"Yeah, but I'd planned to make up for that when I came to your rescue that night a few weeks ago." He studied her carefully. "But your best pal, Trevor, got there before me. He didn't mess up my chances, did he?"

The smile left Rae's face. "That wasn't funny the first time you brought it up, Sterling. I'm tired of defending my and Trevor's friendship to you."

"I'm not trying to put you on the defensive, Rae," he insisted. "I'm just tryin' to tell you I'm here for you. That's all."

"It's a good thing you're only getting one room," she said, turning toward the door. "That way you won't feel lonely when you go without me."

Sterling took hold of her arm before she could leave. "Look at me, Rae. Please."

Slowly, she turned angry eyes in his direction.

"You deserve to have a man who's devoted only to you," Sterling said softly. "I'm willing to be that man. I just need you to know that."

Pulling her arm from his hand, Rae left the room in a rush.

Sterling fished in his pocket for his car keys and blew out a long breath. He'd taken a lot of risks in his life, but offering his heart to Rae Paris might just be the biggest gamble of all.

He smiled. Of course, if he won, that would make the payoff that much sweeter.

Whatever thoughts Eloise had about forgiving Charles Hunt while they were in London disappeared completely when they returned to America. She squeezed the handful of opened bills in her hand and continued to circle the kitchen island with Charles staying wisely on the opposite side. "How dare you meddle in my business?" She barely managed the words, her teeth were so tightly clenched.

"I was only trying to help, Elle. Silly me for thinking you'd be grateful," Charles argued.

"Grateful for what?" she screamed. Eloise never raised her voice—thought it was uncouth—but this was too much. Now he knew about her financial problems…knew she was about to lose her house…knew that she wasn't as successful as she'd claimed to be. Her career had been the one thing that had given her self-worth; now she didn't even have that. "What? I'm supposed to be grateful because you know I'm about to lose everything I've got? How's that supposed to make me feel better, Charles?"

"I took care of it." He flung his hands in the air, still careful to keep the island between them.

"What're you talking about?" Eloise was nearly shaking she was so angry.

"I paid up your mortgage, I paid up your bills. You don't owe anybody anything, Elle. Least not until next month."

Eloise shook her head. Obviously, she was hearing things.

"Where would you get money to pay my bills? You've never held a job for longer than a few months."

"I own my own motorcycle shop. I stayed in Los Angeles long enough to start one up. Turns out, there's lots of people interested in getting their motorcycles tricked out. Upgraded," he explained when she frowned in confusion. "I found someone to manage it, and I'm building another one here."

This couldn't be happening. Eloise had no idea what to say. "You have your own business…and you have money?"

Charles frowned. "Don't say it like it's so unbelievable, would you? But…yeah."

"Then why did you ask to stay here?" She was still trying to grasp what he was telling her. "I thought you were—"

"Freeloading," Charles stated flatly. "Well, I wasn't. I just wanted to be with you, Elle. That's all. I used the money I had in savings to bail you out. I was going to buy some property here in San Antonio if I had to…but I'm hoping I don't have to." His look said that he wanted her to let him back into her life.

Eloise was ambivalent. The Charles standing before her wasn't the same man she remembered, that much was evident. Even in London, she'd noticed the change. He'd been a tremendous support to her throughout her mother's funeral. He'd made decisions when she didn't have the strength, entertained her family when she was too tired. But mostly he'd been a strong shoulder to cry on. He'd paid so much attention to her without demanding a thing in return…not even sex.

Still, despite these visible differences, Eloise's paradigm was having a difficult time shifting. It was absolutely stuck in neutral. "I don't know, Charles—"

"Don't answer me today." He held up his hands to stop her. "I know it's going to take a lot more than paying a few of your bills to make up for the things I've done to you. All I'm asking is that you don't say no—not yet."

It was, perhaps, the kindest thing he'd ever said to her. How long had she wished he'd admit to his wrongdoing, to acknowledge that he'd had no right to put her through so much soul-stealing drama? Eloise squeezed her eyes shut to hold back the emotions threatening to burst through. "Are you saying that you're sorry, Charles?"

"No, honey." He came around the island then and placed warm, solid hands on her upper arms. "I'm saying that sorry's not enough. Not this time." He took her into his arms then and held her tight.

"Oh, Charles." She couldn't keep the sobs from catching in her throat. "I don't want to be your fool again," she whispered painfully. "I couldn't bear it if you hurt me again."

His lips were beside her ear when he whispered, "I won't hurt you, Elle. I promise. Just give me the rest of our lives to make myself worthy. That's all I'm asking."

Eloise felt herself weaken as his words wrapped themselves around her heart, drowning out reason. "All right, Charles. I'll give you today," she said, wiping away a tear. "But tomorrow's not promised to you." She tried to sound stern as she stared him straight in his dark, sexy eyes. "You've got to earn every tomorrow. Understand?"

The old Charles would've bolted out the door, spouting every cuss word and calling her every kind of ungrateful. The new Charles simply smiled and offered his agreement, "Whatever you want, darlin'. Let's seal the deal with a kiss, shall we?" he asked with a mock English accent.

The kiss itself, however, was decidedly French.

"Does this mean you and Daddy are back together?" Jewel clapped her Playtex-gloved hands and jumped up and down in the middle of Glendora's assisted-living apartment. Jewel had agreed to meet Eloise to help pack away her grandmother's personal things. The first few hours had been sad and solemn as Jewel and her mother worked in silence. Then, out of the blue, her mother had announced that she and her father would be living together again.

Eloise smirked at her daughter's reaction. "For the moment," she acknowledged. "I'm surprised you're so happy about it."

Jewel shrugged and went back to wrapping the pretty glass music boxes in newspaper and setting them neatly in the packing box. "I always wanted you and Daddy to get back together," she confessed. "I always knew it would make him happy…and…and I thought it might make you love me again." She looked at her mother sideways, trying to gauge her reaction.

"I'm so sorry, baby." Eloise looked terrible as she placed a hand on Jewel's cheek.

"Don't worry." Jewel held her mother's hand on her face a bit longer. "Now, I understand a lot more about how complicated relationships can be," she added to ease the guilt she read on Eloise's face. "Aren't they?"

Eloise blew a breath and laughed. "To put it mildly," she agreed. "I still can't stop wondering if I was foolish to trust Charles again." She headed for the kitchen and began taking down dishes.

"I dunno." Jewel went back to her packing. "Granny Glen always said that there wasn't any character flaw that time and old age couldn't correct."

"Hmph." Eloise's response was directed toward the cabinet. "I don't know how she formed her lips to say that. She was always so mule-headed, had to have her own way. Even on her way out, she arranged to have you and me together in hopes we would reconcile. You know that trip was just a setup, right?"

Jewel noted that her mother's tone held both admiration and faux irritation. "Yeah. It was a beauty," she admitted.

"Wouldn't surprise me at all if she'd planned her own departure just to bring us back together with our husbands," Eloise added with flair. "She was sure hell-bent on seeing it happen."

Jewel stared blankly at the newsprint in front of her eyes. "I'll bet she did," she acknowledged, thinking how delighted she'd been to see Trevor the day he'd arrived in London.

Trevor had been like her very own Prince Charming standing at the edge of the sweeping drive, dressed all in black, awaiting her at the palace that was her grandfather's estate. And that night...oh my, how they'd made love. "I'm not sorry I took Trevor back," Jewel said proudly. Maybe it was the apartment, the still lingering presence of her grandmother that made her want to chat. At any rate, now that the only person she had to talk to was her mother, she was finding conversation easier than she'd expected.

"I am having second...and third thoughts about allowing Rae

to have his baby, though." Jewel turned to Eloise. "Do you think that was stupid?"

"I….uh." Her mother struggled to voice her thoughts.

"Don't hurt yourself, Eloise. I know it was stupid." She sighed and hung her head.

"Maybe you can take it back," Eloise offered. "Tell Rae and Trevor you've changed your mind."

"I wish it were that easy." Jewel's heart fell. "You should've seen how happy Trevor was when I told him. The man fell to his knees thanking me. I can't keep jerking around his emotions. Besides, I proved something to myself with that gesture."

"That you're not as selfish and self-centered as you'd thought?" her mother guessed.

Jewel nodded.

"Then I guess you'll just have to go through with it," her mother said. "I'm finished in here," she announced, taping the box closed. "How about you?"

"Yeah. Just wrapping the last one," Jewel said. Her mother tossed her the tape.

"How about we get some lunch?" Eloise asked once all the boxes were secured and labeled. "I'm famished."

"Sounds good," Jewel agreed. She pushed a strand of hair back from her face and looked at the boxes that now contained the last part of Glendora's life. "What are we going to do with her stuff, Eloise?"

Her mother sighed and leaned against the counter. "I suppose we could sell it. Or put it back in her house."

"No need in doing that if we have to sell the house, too," Jewel said.

"I told you, that house belongs to you," Eloise chided. "Mama wanted you to have it."

Jewel shrugged. "I already have a house." She turned soft eyes on her mother. "I thought you might need the money…you know, to help out."

Eloise ducked her head. "I never expected to become a charity case," she sighed before meeting her daughter's gaze. "The last thing I want is you thinking you have to take care of me. So forget it."

"What about your bills, your house?"

"I'll get by." Eloise offered a crooked grin. "Turns out I found myself a sugar daddy."

"My daddy?" Jewel knew she looked skeptical, but her father hadn't been the kind to keep a job. In fact, Eloise had stopped expecting child support from the man after they'd been separated for a year.

"I know," Eloise shrugged. "Turns out Charles actually made something of himself while we weren't looking. He tricks out motorcycles."

Jewel laughed. "Do you even know what that means?"

"I do now," she stated as she lifted her chin high.

"Maybe he's redeemable after all, huh?" Jewel asked hopefully.

"Maybe." Eloise placed her arm around Jewel's shoulders. "Let's eat. The growling in my stomach is getting embarrassing."

Trevor and her father would be stopping by to move the boxes back to her grandmother's old house later that evening. Jewel took one last look around and decided that would be just fine. This place wasn't where Glendora's heart was—it was just where she was last.

"I miss you, Granny Glen," she said before tossing her gloves on top of a box and closing the door behind her.

Chapter Fourteen

Sterling knew he had it bad for Rae. Here he was in his favorite place—a four star hotel on the Vegas strip—and he couldn't manage even a tiny smile. He tossed his cell phone onto the leather couch as if it were to blame for his vicious mood. He'd hoped that Rae would be there with him, but she hadn't even returned his calls. Sterling knew exactly why. It was plain as the smile on Trevor St. John's face. Rae had only come on to him to make Trevor jealous. Now that she had him warming her bed on the regular, she didn't need old Sterling anymore.

And here he'd gone and told her, "I'm here for you." What an idiot.

Grabbing his wallet and the card key, Sterling stormed out of the room. He knew exactly how to get the woman out of his system—find a casino that was generous with their liquor and another woman who was generous with her body.

Lillian knew the moment she saw the good-looking Black man with the hard eyes and brooding expression that he'd be the best tipper of the night. He looked as if the world had just dealt him a low blow. Men like that tended to be free with their money if you helped to ease their pain.

Raising herself to her full five-feet-seven-inches, Lillian pushed out her size D cups that were barely contained in the scant waitress's outfit.

When the man took his seat at the poker table, she was

immediately at his side. "Would you like a drink?" She gave him her best seductive smile and an in-your-face view of her golden-brown cleavage as she leaned forward.

"Yeah," he said. "Whiskey sour." His eyes took the tour of her breasts before he offered a crooked smile. "If you make it a double, I'll make it worth your while," he added.

"You bet, sweetie. What's your name?"

"Sterling."

"I'm Lillian. But you can call me Lil." She winked at him before she left. A wink always led a man to believe that you were interested in him—and him alone. If only they knew. She blew a tired breath as she headed for the bar. He'd better make it worth her while. The rest of the boys at that table had been stiffing her all night. Some had only tipped her a couple of bucks in four hours. She couldn't wait to get promoted to the high roller room.

Jewel could barely contain herself as she looked at her trim figure in the gown she'd bought. The sales assistant at Neiman Marcus had called the color "blush." All Jewel knew was that its pinkish hue looked stunning against her dark skin.

Jewel was getting dressed in her mother and father's hotel room so that, when Trevor saw her that night, he'd be completely surprised… just like on their first wedding day.

"Don't you think you should stop all that primping and get your shoes on, honey?" Charles stepped up behind his daughter and kissed her cheek. "You couldn't look prettier if you tried."

Jewel twirled around to give him a big hug. "Thanks, Daddy. You think Trevor'll like it?" she asked.

"That boy would love you in a paper sack." Charles walked over to the bathroom door and tapped it lightly. "What's keeping you, princess?" he yelled to get Eloise's attention. "We keep Trevor any longer and the man'll turn into a damn frog."

"Why don't you go get Trevor, then," Eloise said, exiting the bathroom. "I've just got to put some earrings on and I'm good to go."

"Rae just went to get Trevor," Jewel said, pulling on strappy sandals. "They should be in the lobby by the time we get down there."

Charles was standing at the door now. "Then let's get this show on the road. I've been itchin' to get at the crap tables since we got here. Once this ceremony is over, I'm making a beeline for the closest one."

"Watch you don't gamble away Eloise's house payment for next month," Jewel teased as she walked past her father through the door he held open.

"Watch it," Eloise warned, following behind her daughter good-naturedly. "I'm still a little sensitive about being bailed out."

The trio continued joking and laughing down the hallway to the elevator.

Rae straightened her best friend's tie. Trevor had always looked his best in black and white suits. Tonight, he was gorgeous, as usual.

But something was different. For the first time ever, Rae didn't feel the desperate desire for him coursing through her veins. Tonight, she felt no jealousy or anger about Trevor and Jewel's relationship. Sterling's words were still resounding through her head. "You deserve a man who's devoted only to you. I'm willing to be that man," he'd told her. The look of sincerity in his eyes had nearly buckled her knees at the time, but Rae didn't know what to do about his declaration now that she was carrying Trevor's child.

And that was another thing. Jewel had somehow managed to see past her pride and allow her husband to have a child by another woman. It was the single most unselfish gesture Rae had ever witnessed, and she was truly humbled. Trevor really was a lucky man.

"So you ready for this?" she asked.

Trevor smoothed his neat facial hair and gave Rae a cocky smile. "I was born ready, my friend. Let's do this." He offered her the crook of his arm.

Rae accepted it and allowed him to usher her out of his hotel room. She adjusted the wispy material of her dress as they made their way to the elevators, wondering how women walked around in such fragile material all the time. "I don't know how I let your wife talk me into wearing a pink dress," she frowned.

"Stop complaining." Trevor looked her up and down appreciatively. "You look stunning."

"Better than prom?" she challenged.

Trevor sighed. "Hate to tell you this pal; you made that blue puffball prom dress look good. I know you don't like wearing them, but dresses are your thing."

"Liar." Rae slugged him in the shoulder playfully as they reached the elevator. "If that were true, you would've told me a long time ago."

"I would've," he admitted with a shrug. "But you were getting enough attention from the wrong kind of men without showing off your legs. I certainly didn't want to encourage more of the same."

"Whatever." Rae pressed the "Down" button.

"I mean it," Trevor argued. "You turn more heads than you think."

It was nice of him to say, but Rae knew better. She ran a hand through her wonderfully low-maintenance spiral twists and stood at attention when the elevator dinged and the doors opened.

Sterling LeRoi was standing there, albeit unsteadily, with his hands full of a buxomly waitress.

Rae's emotions ranged, in order, from excitement, to surprise, to pissed-off. "I see you had no trouble finding someone to get you through the weekend," she snapped. Surprisingly, she was very hurt to have been replaced so quickly.

Sterling blinked several times to make sure the liquor he'd consumed hadn't created an illusion before his eyes. "Rae? Trevor?"

"Yeah. Surprised?" Rae exaggerated the last word. "Is this your floor?" she asked, impatiently waiting for him to exit.

"I knew it." Sterling's eyes narrowed as he wobbled out of the elevator. He pointed at Rae and Trevor. "I knew it."

Trevor patted him on the back. "I don't know what you're thinking, man, but I would suggest you go sleep it off."

Rae didn't understand the looks passing between the two men, but she could see the warning in Trevor's hard expression.

A bit awkwardly, the two couples switched places until it was Rae and Trevor standing inside the elevator.

"You bet I'll sleep it off." Sterling pulled the waitress to his side so quickly she lost her balance and fell against him. "I will," he said a little less enthusiastically as the doors closed.

"What's he mean pointing at us and saying 'I knew it'?" Rae's crossed arms now reflected her mood.

Trevor looked at her as if she were dense. "He's in love with you. He thinks we're sleeping with one another."

"What?" Rae stared at Trevor. "How do you know?"

Dropping his head, Trevor sighed. "Women."

"If he loves me so much, what's up with the bar skank with overdone breasts?" Rae challenged.

"That…skank as you call her, is an act of desperation." Trevor waved an arm toward the door. "Seems you and Sterling have similar ideas about how to work a person out of your system."

Rae knew he didn't mean it to hurt her feelings, but it did. "I thought you and I were cool."

Trevor nodded and closed his eyes wearily. "We are, Rae. I'm sorry. It's just that this whole ordeal has me real uptight. At first, I was so relieved that Jewel agreed for us to have this baby. But now we have to pretend to go to the fertility doctor and pretend to give you shots and pretend, pretend, pretend…"

"You and your damned conscience." Rae shook her head. "Don't mess this up, Trevor. Sometimes the kindest thing is to spare a woman the truth. You don't want to hurt her again, do you?"

"No. Never."

"It'll be all right."

"So you keep telling me." He sounded far from convinced.

"Let's get through this ceremony, and then we'll take it one day at a time. All right?"

He agreed just as the elevator opened.

Jewel, her father and mother were standing just a few feet away near the casino entrance. Jewel turned to see her husband and beamed. She waved at them.

Trevor's hand went straight to his chest. "Lord have mercy," he whispered.

Rae laughed. "Go get her," she said as she pushed him forward. "I'll be right behind you, moppin' up your slobber."

Sterling's heart raced as if he'd run a marathon. He stabbed at the elevator buttons angrily. "Come on!"

"That's not going to help." Lillian the waitress was clearly irritated.

Sterling didn't care. "Do you need money for a cab or something?" he asked, pushing several bills into her palm impatiently.

The money quickly disappeared into the depths of her bra. "It'll do, I guess," she huffed.

An older couple also occupied the elevator. The woman clucked softly and looked at them with disapproving eyes.

Sterling didn't care about what they thought either. He just wanted this elevator to hurry up and get to the first floor.

Finally, it reached its destination and bounced gently before the door dinged open. Sterling pushed his way out and searched the area wildly. She had to be there. He had turned around and followed them down immediately.

He spotted her then, wrapped invitingly in a pink chiffon dress, being helped into an awaiting limousine by Trevor. Sterling really hated the man. "Rae!" he called.

She didn't hear him.

Of course, she couldn't. She was outside.

Sterling rushed outside. As the limo pulled away, he tapped the doorman on the shoulder, nearly throwing a hundred dollar bill at him. "I need a cab. Now!"

He was ushered into the next one in line.

"Follow that limousine," he ordered the cab driver. "Don't lose 'em," he insisted. To make sure, Sterling didn't let his own eyes wander from the black Hummer limo. He could only imagine what was going on inside those dark windows.

Visions of Trevor touching Rae, kissing her, laughing with her made Sterling angrier by the minute. But this was his own fault. He should've slept with her when he had the chance. He should've walked through the door when she'd opened it. Maybe she wouldn't be having this affair with Trevor if he'd stepped up and been a man instead of being afraid of how much he was feeling for her.

The driver interrupted his thoughts. "They're turning into the Chapel O' Love. Looks like someone's getting married."

"What the—?" Sterling watched as the limo pulled into the tiny parking lot as they went by. "Go back, go back," he insisted.

"It'll take too long to turn around. You want me to let you out at the corner?" The driver's questioning eyes were reflected in the rearview mirror.

"Yeah, fine." Sterling paid him and rushed back to the small chapel. The "Wedding March" was just beginning when he reached the doors. He'd pegged Trevor St. John for a player but not a bigamist. Sterling had to stop this mess.

He pushed through the doors and yelled at the sequined-jacketed minister. "This ain't right!" he shouted. Charging down the aisle, he tried his best to trample the pink flower petals on the floor as he narrowed his sights on Trevor St. John.

"You sorry sonofa—" Sterling sent a fist flying into Trevor's gut.

The man doubled over.

Sterling could feel someone trying to pull him back, but he fought out of that person's grasp. He sent another fist flying at Trevor's head.

"I'm gettin' sick and tired of people trying to beat the hell out of me," Trevor said, dodging the punch and countering with a solid blow to Sterling's jaw.

Sterling reeled back a few steps but wasn't down for the count. In fact, this was just what he needed to release some of his pent-up frustration. "Someone needs to beat some sense into your head, Trevor. You can't marry Rae. You're already married." His fist sank deep into the adulterer's ribs.

"I'm not marrying Rae, you idiot," Trevor gasped. He straightened with difficulty and swung at Sterling's head with both fists.

Dancing Mohammed Ali-like, if a little unsteadily, on his toes, Sterling evaded the other man's wildly thrown punches. "You're in a wedding chapel. Somebody's getting married."

"Jewel and I are renewing our vows," Trevor spat angrily, swinging again. This time, he caught Sterling square in the solar plexus.

Sterling gasped for breath. This time, someone successfully gripped him from behind.

"Don't let go, Charles," he heard Eloise Hunt say from somewhere behind him. Sterling looked around the small room, finally noticing Jewel's presence.

He also saw the minister and his staff cowering near the back of the chapel. One of his assistants asked if the police were on the way.

"Renewing your vows?" Sterling asked Trevor when he could speak and think clearly again. The irony was absolutely incredible. "Before you say 'I do' again, Jewel, you'd better find out if he's done sleeping with Rae."

For a moment all Sterling could hear was the pounding of his own heart. The room had grown absolutely silent.

"Sterling, you don't know what you're talking about." Rae finally stepped forward. She stood between him and Trevor, fury and panic in her eyes. "I thought you were giving your waitress friend a little pickle tickle. What're you doing here?"

"Hell if I know." Sterling could feel the anger seep right out of his bones as he looked at her—wanting her—loving her. The grip on his arms relaxed. "I guess I called myself saving you."

Rae looked amused. "From what?"

"Him." He pointed at Trevor. "Why would you settle for being his mistress when you could be my wife?"

Rae shook her head. Her voice softened. "I'm not his mistress."

"You're not?" Sterling didn't know whether or not to believe her. "But I saw you…the two of you…coming out of your house that morning."

"I can explain that," Rae spoke to Jewel who was looking hurt and confused. "It's not what he thinks," she said. Turning back to Sterling, she repeated, "It's not what you think."

"It is what he thinks," Trevor said, sighing and sinking onto one of the hard wooden pews. "Sort of," he added right before Jewel ran out of the building.

Sterling was sure she was crying.

"Look what you did, you big dope." Rae shoved at his chest before giving Sterling the longest, deepest, wettest, hottest kisses of his life. He was thoroughly aroused—and confused—by the time Las Vegas's Finest walked through the chapel doors.

Charles paced the living area of their hotel suite, anxious from having listened to his daughter's heart-wrenching cries for the past hour. Eloise left the bedroom and closed the door behind her.

Her weary face told him that Jewel wasn't feeling any better. "I'm going to call room service and have some tea brought up," Eloise said.

"You think that'll calm her down?" Charles asked hopefully.

"If not her, it'll help me." She dropped onto the sofa and tucked her feet beneath her. "Poor thing is distraught. I know just how she feels."

A pang of guilt gripped Charles. "It was that bad?" he asked quietly.

Eloise, realizing what she'd done, looked up at her husband with soft eyes. "I didn't meant to—"

"It's okay, Elle." He deserved it. If it had been a real dig, it wouldn't have hurt so bad. "What can we do?" he asked. He sat down next to her and ran a hand up and down the silk of her stockings. They hadn't bothered to change since they'd left the wedding chapel. "I can't stand to see my baby like this."

"I'm afraid the only one who can do anything about this is Trevor."

Charles bit his bottom lip and chewed on that for a moment before reaching a decision. "I'll go fetch him."

"She won't want to see him," Eloise warned.

"But he's the only one who can help?"

Eloise nodded. He could see weariness in her eyes.

"Well, then he'd better settle this tonight so we can all get some rest, hadn't he?"

It took every ounce of Trevor's strength to lift himself off the bed to answer the insistent knocking at the door. "Who is it?" he asked cautiously.

"Charles. Let me in."

Trevor cursed under his breath then reluctantly did as his father-in-law requested.

Charles studied him closely as he entered. "You look like hell," he said casually.

"Thanks." Trevor closed the door behind him. "Wanna beer?" He gestured toward what remained of the six-pack he'd bought at a liquor store, choosing to walk the several miles it took to reach the hotel.

"Don't mind if I do." Charles took the warm beer and downed half of it in one long swallow. "Listen, Trevor." He sought his son-in-law's eyes. "You need to see about Jewel."

Trevor scoffed. "I'm the last person she wants to see."

"You're right about that." Charles finished off the beer and crushed the can with a quick squeeze. "But if you don't go in there and talk to her, things'll only get worse."

"How can things possibly get any worse than this, Charles? My wife just found out I slept with my best friend." He pushed a hand against his forehead. "Of course, it'll be worse when I tell her Rae is pregnant because I slept with her."

Charles noted the wild-eyed desperation as he spoke and remembered a time when he'd been just as frenzied. He felt sorry for the man.

"Then there's the part where we were going to lie to her about having the baby artificially implanted in Rae's womb," Trevor continued, "that'll be about the time she kicks my behind to the curb for eternity."

"Is that the worst that could happen?" Charles asked him

pointedly.

Trevor looked at him as if he'd just grown horns. "Yeah. I guess that's about the worst it can get. What are you thinkin'? That's not bad enough?" he asked incredulously.

Charles shrugged. "I'm thinking that's not so bad. Let's have at it, boy."

"You're not serious?"

Charles fisted his right hand and warmed the knuckles with his left. "Serious as a heart attack, son."

Trevor touched his jaw and recalled the power of the man's fist. Not anxious for a repeat performance, he shook his head and slowly rose to his feet. "I'll be glad when this night is over."

When they reached the suite, Trevor felt his father-in-law's hand on his shoulder. "Switch keys with me," Charles offered his card.

Confused, Trevor fished his card from his pocket and swapped with Charles.

"Eloise and I will stay in your room while you work this out," he explained.

Trevor nodded his understanding.

Charles opened the door. Eloise was sitting there, pouring hot water over the tea bags in two cups.

Trevor could hear Jewel crying in the next room. Grief and guilt sat on his heart like a two-ton elephant as he realized he'd caused this.

"Go get your bags, Elle," Charles instructed his wife. "We'll take the kids' room tonight."

It took Eloise only a moment to realize his intention. "Let me take this tea in for Jewel first. I'll be right out." She shot Trevor a look of disapproval as she pushed inside the bedroom.

Trevor dropped his head and pushed his sore fists into the soft cushions of the sofa. "Damn, damn, damn," he chanted. Now he had Eloise angry with him. The situation was getting worse by the second.

"You know what Glendora told me before I came back to San Antonio?" Charles asked.

Trevor shook his head, noting that his wife's sobs didn't seem

191

to be getting any better since Eloise had gone in.

"She told me a real man fights for love, no matter how long or hard the battle," Charles continued. "She told me to stop sitting on the sidelines, to grab a weapon and get in the fight. I listened to her. I suggest you do the same."

Eloise exited the bedroom with her overnight bag, wearing a very concerned expression. "I'm not sure if she's up to this," she said to Charles as he wrapped his arm around her waist like a precious gift.

"Trevor is." Charles sent his son-in-law a steely glare. "Aren't you?"

Trevor nodded, knowing it wasn't true. "Say, Charles." He stopped the couple as they were walking out. "What weapon did you use?"

He looked at his wife as if her eyes held the answer. "First humility, then an act of kindness. They weakened her defenses, I think. But seems to me like the only thing that really brings down the walls is to show her you love her as much as she loves you," he answered.

The adoring smile Eloise offered her husband told Trevor she approved of her husband's answer.

Charles's eyes were glistening when he turned back to Trevor. "Unbreak her heart, son," he pleaded in a hoarse whisper.

When the door closed, an overwrought Trevor was left to deal with the mess he'd created.

Chapter Fifteen

Rae tossed the card key on the table and watched Sterling dive face first onto the sofa with a groan. "Well, you made a fine mess of things, Mr. LeRoi." She crossed her arms and leaned back against the door to his suite. "You kick Trevor's butt, you tell Jewel he and I are having an affair, and you nearly get arrested all in one night. What am I going to do with you?"

"Shoot me," came his surly reply.

Rae laughed. "If I do, then I can never find out if you really proposed to me or not." She walked over to the sofa. He made room for her.

She sat down and urged him to ease his head onto her lap. This was uncharted territory for Rae. She actually had feelings for Sterling that weren't born of lust, but she wasn't quite sure how to proceed. Of course, tact had never been one of her strong suits, so she just put herself out there. "You asked me not to settle for being Trevor's mistress when I could be your wife." She fingered the small scar along his jaw, trying to avoid looking into his eyes. "Did you mean that as a proposal? Or were you just throwin' out a hypothetical question?"

"Depends," he said, reaching a hand up to touch her face.

"On what?" She could feel her pulse rush under his touch.

"On if you'd say 'yes' to the proposal or not."

"Is that all it depends on?" she asked breathlessly, knowing there was more to be discussed between them.

Sterling sat up and brought her into his arms. "That, and you have to convince me you love me more than him."

"How do I do that?"

"You could start by kissing me."

That was easy. Rae pressed her mouth against his lips gently at first, offering brief, tender kisses against his soft mouth.

When Sterling groaned and pulled her closer, she gave him her all, opening her mouth to let their tongues explore and revel in the sensation. She did love him. It was evident by the way she felt in his arms, by the way her heart pounded in her chest, by the way she never wanted to leave this moment.

Pulling away slightly, Rae looked into his eyes, feeling a little drunk. "Convinced yet? Or should I keep going?"

"I could use a little more convincing." He pushed his mouth against hers hungrily. When his fingertips found their way to her breasts, Rae knew she was lost.

The thought sobered Rae. She pushed off Sterling as if he'd just caught fire.

"What is it?" He looked around in confusion. "What happened?"

"I can't do this," she said rising from the sofa. "It's not fair to you."

"What's not fair, Rae?" Sterling moved to her side. "You've got to stop running hot and cold on me," he scolded. "It's pissing me off."

Rae could see it was more frustration than anger, and she completely understood. "I know, Sterling. I'm sorry, but if we're going to have any kind of relationship, you've got to know exactly what's going on."

Sterling took a step back. "Something was going on with you and Trevor, wasn't there?"

She nodded. "But it was all me. He didn't have the same feelings," she explained. "I don't know how to explain this to you." Rae was wandering around the room aimlessly now.

"Try me," Sterling said. She couldn't tell what he was thinking now. His expression was unreadable.

She shrugged. "I've known Trevor all my life...well, since junior high," she began. "He was popular and good-looking, and all the girls were crazy over him. The only way I could get close to him was by becoming his friend. We both played on the same basketball court in the neighborhood, and we found out we liked the same things, had frustrations with our parents, but most of all, we just had a connection. It was like we had each other's backs all the time, you know? We made a pact to get out of high school and make something of ourselves."

She was simply talking out loud now, no longer knowing or caring if Sterling understood. "Anyway, I fell in love with him at some point...or at least I thought I had. I never told him because I thought it would push him away and mess up our friendship. I knew he didn't see me like he saw other girls. They were all sweet and sexy, and I was this tall, gangly tomboy." She could feel some of the old inadequacy of her younger years creep into her consciousness then. "He was all I had. The only bright spot in my whole dreary life.

"About the time he married Jewel, I figured I'd have to get over this longing for him, but I couldn't. He was my fantasy, and I wouldn't be satisfied until I lived out the fantasy of making love to him just once. I needed to get it out of my system so I would be free of him. At least that's how I rationalized it the night I made him sleep with me."

Rae now turned to Sterling to help him see what had really happened. "The next morning was a little awkward for us, especially when you showed up at my front door." She smiled.

He didn't respond.

"Trevor's been guilt-ridden ever since. He's madly in love with Jewel and wouldn't hurt her for the world. I honestly didn't want to hurt her either. I told him not to tell her what happened. I figured what she didn't know wouldn't hurt her."

"Same could be said for me, right?" Sterling looked peeved now. "So, why tell me?"

"Because...I like you, Sterling. Maybe I even love you. I didn't know until I saw you with your arm wrapped around that superskank waitress, but I know it now." She hoped he could read the sincerity in her eyes. "For the first time, I understand how Trevor feels. I don't want us to get into this relationship with secrets between us."

"So—"

"There's more," she interrupted him. "I got pregnant that night," she blurted out.

Sterling's expression grew hard. "On purpose?" he asked.

Rae looked upward and blew out a long breath. "Yeah." This was the only time she'd confessed that fact out loud to anyone. "Trevor doesn't know that part, though."

"But he knows you're pregnant?"

"Yeah."

"I don't get this." Sterling walked over to her. "If you and Trevor are about to have a child, what's this business about him renewing his wedding vows with his wife? Is this some big joke to the two of you?"

Shaking her head, Rae stood directly in front of the man she was certain she'd just lost forever. "You know when Jewel lost the baby earlier this year?"

He nodded.

"She can't ever have children now. Before any of this ever happened, I offered to have his baby for him. Of course, Jewel thought it would be through in vitro fertilization when she agreed to it. So you see, we didn't have to tell her about that night. Everything was going to be all right."

"Until I came in tonight and blew the roof off your house of lies, huh?"

"Right." Rae didn't follow him when he walked away from her.

"How can you say you love me when you did all this just to trap him?" he said with disgust.

"I didn't try to trap him, Sterling. I did all this so I could let him go. And I have. After all, I'm here with you, aren't I?" She figured that her presence in his room should be proof enough.

"You can't very well be with Trevor. I don't want to be the rebound man, Rae. I deserve better." He thumped his chest.

"You do. And so do I. That's what I learned by sleeping with

Trevor," she said, still surprised at the turn in her feelings. "Turns out the fantasy was just that."

Sterling looked back at her. "You're saying he wasn't any good in bed?"

Rae shrugged. "He was okay," she answered truthfully. "But the earth didn't move, and there were no fireworks. You know what I mean?"

"You're not in love with him," Sterling stated as his shoulders relaxed.

"That's about the size of it," she acknowledged. Taking advantage of the change in his demeanor, Rae walked over to where he stood. "Now when I kiss you," she ran her hands across his chest, "I can't even keep a clear thought in my head."

Encouraged by the beginnings of a smile, she placed her arms around his shoulders. "I can't wait to see what it's like to make love to you, Sterling LeRoi."

There was a slight hesitance in his response when she kissed him this time, but it was quickly replaced by the urgency of his probing tongue and quickly roving hands. His heat fired Rae's lust and sent her head spinning.

"You want to feel the earth move?" Sterling unzipped her dress expertly, freeing her from the pink wispy material that fell to her feet.

"I do." Rae felt lightheaded and euphoric as he kissed her breasts and fondled her behind.

"I've been known to create a few earthquakes in my time," he promised before leading her to the bedroom.

His lovemaking was frenzied and hungry. It hurt a little, but Rae could feel ecstasy coming just behind the pain.

Their bodies met like the force of two tornadoes colliding at a hundred miles per hour. When Rae pushed wildly against him, she found that the pain eased and her desire swirled madly.

Sterling cried out and spilled into her.

Rae felt an explosion of energy throughout her body. In the glow of the aftermath, Rae slowly rolled away from her new lover, convinced that no man in the world would ever make her feel this way again. "That was amazing."

"Good," he said tersely. He rose from the bed and went about pulling his clothes on. "Let's just say I needed to get that out of my system."

Rae was confused. She'd thought this was the beginning, but clearly Sterling was calling it quits. She felt helpless, sad. "So you are like all the others."

He picked up his jacket from the floor and looked at her. His shirt was unbuttoned, showing the hard muscles of his chest and a bold tattoo. He looked conflicted. His mouth shifted; his jaws clenched and unclenched as if he wanted to say something. "I've gotta go," he finally managed.

"Then go," Rae whispered.

He hesitated a moment, then was gone.

Rae pushed her face deep into the pillow, letting it soak up her tears.

Trevor stood at the door of the bedroom where his wife lay weeping. "Unbreak her heart," his father-in-law had told him.

How did he do that when he hadn't finished the job yet? Jewel wasn't aware that his night of indiscretion had led to Rae's pregnancy. What would that news do to her?

Trevor shook his head as he pushed the door open and saw her lying there. Sobs racked her body. She looked small and frail as she lay curled up on the bed. Her grief was king-sized, though, and it reached out and grabbed Trevor's heart with icy fingers.

"Jewel?" he asked entering the room, steeling himself against her reaction. "Honey?"

"Go away, Trevor. Go away," she said weakly.

"I have to talk to you." He moved forward, resolving to get through this. "I need you to listen to me."

"Why should I listen to you?" She rolled over to look up at him.

Trevor's heart nearly fell to the floor when he saw her ruined makeup, swollen, bloodshot eyes and downturned mouth. It was like the soul had been sucked right out of her.

"All you've done is tell me lies," she sniffed.

Technically, he hadn't told her anything, but there was no need in arguing the finer points of his deception. "I want to make this right." He sat on the bed and placed his hand on her hip.

She swatted it away immediately. "You no longer have the right to touch me."

"You're still my wife," he challenged, finding it difficult not to get angry.

"Not for long," she shot back. "Why are you here?"

The words were flung at him like sharp knives.

"Because I love you and I want to make this right," he repeated insistently. If he was going to war, he was going in with all the heart he could muster. "I'm not going to let you get rid of me."

"Give me one good reason why I shouldn't." Her voice was hoarse and rough from crying.

"Because you know me." He sought her eyes and held them. "You know what's inside me." Trevor took her hand, refusing to let go when she tried to pull away. He placed her palm on his chest so that she could feel how hard his heart was working. "The heart you feel pounding is yours, Jewel, and yours alone."

Her lips trembled and new tears formed in her eyes. "Then why did you do it, Trevor? Were you drunk?"

"No."

"Did she jump you? What? There's got to be some explanation."

"She begged me to make love to her just one time," Trevor explained. "Said she'd leave me alone forever if I just let her get me out of her system. She was drunk, so drunk she'd run herself into a ditch that night. She was hurt, she was crying." He took a hand and wiped a tear from his wife's eyes.

"I looked into her eyes, and all I wanted to do was help her, stop the hurt, heal the pain."

"It was wrong, Trevor," Jewel squeaked out between tears. "You betrayed me. Didn't you think about me at all?"

Trevor nodded. "I thought of you," he admitted as the thought of his loneliness resurfaced. "Thought of how badly I was missing you while you were in London. It tore me apart when you called and said you wanted a divorce. I honestly didn't know if I had much to lose when it happened."

She closed her eyes then. "So it's my fault you were lonely and needed her to warm your bed?"

"I'm not that weak, Jewel," he snapped. Why couldn't he get her to see what he was trying to tell her? "It was a favor, Jewel—a way to help out a friend. That's all it meant to me, nothing else.

"She got pregnant that night, Jewel," he finally confessed. It was time she knew everything.

Placing a hand over her eyes, Jewel rolled her head from side-to-side on the bed. "That's why you were so grateful. I blessed your screwing around when I so proudly announced that I would let her have your baby for you." Sobs nearly choked her as her face contorted with this revelation. "What do you want from me, Trevor?" She asked it so desperately, Trevor held tighter to her hand. "I can't say it's all right," she added. "It's not all right; it hurts too bad. It hurts so... bad."

"Then forgive me," he insisted, leaning over his wife and letting his own tears mingle with her own. "I didn't mean to hurt you. You know it, don't you, babe?"

"I don't know...I don't..."

"Yes, you do," he insisted. "Look at me." He pulled her arm away from her face and forced her to look into his eyes. "I love you. I would never intentionally hurt you. Can't you see how sorry I am?"

It happened then. Trevor saw a slight glimmer of light start in the soulless depths of her eyes. Encouraged, he kissed her cheek, tasting the salt of her tears.

"Just hold me for a while, Trevor," Jewel finally managed. "Just hold me."

Trevor kicked off his shoes and wrapped Jewel snugly in his arms. He kissed her hair softly. "Why don't you get some rest," he urged. "I'm not going anywhere."

He'd be crazy to move a muscle.

Epilogue

Rae stared at the baby girl in her arms with wonder. She couldn't believe how happy she was. "I sure didn't expect things to work out like this," she said to Sterling who sat on the hospital bed beside her.

Sterling kissed her cheek and ran a gentle finger along the baby's soft cheek. "It's a good thing you let me crawl back into your good graces, huh?"

Rae stroked his hand. "If you hadn't come back to that Vegas hotel room just five minutes after you left, I would've kicked you to the curb," she teased.

"I may be a lot of things, but I ain't stupid," he laughed. "I knew the second I left that I was walking out on the best thing that ever happened to me. So, I hightailed it back."

"Was it worth it?"

"Hell, yeah, Mrs. LeRoi," he acknowledged, kissing his wife's cheek. "It's been worth every damn moment."

They'd gotten married in a small ceremony in the backyard of their new home. Trevor and Jewel had shown up and most of her new WNBA basketball team. Rae had remembered it as the happiest day of her life…until today. "What about your stepdaughter here?" she asked tentatively. "What do you think about her?"

Sterling leaned back. "You worried about me? Didn't I ever tell you about my mamma?"

Rae shook her head.

"Well, she wasn't my birth mother."

"She wasn't?"

"Naw. My real mother, my dad's first wife, got thrown in jail when I was about three. My dad came and picked me up from Child Protective Services, took me home and dropped me in his second wife's lap."

"Nice," Rae chuckled.

"That woman never made a difference between me and her own children. I loved her 'til her dying day for that."

"So this is all right, then?" she tested.

Sterling ran a gentle finger along the baby's cheek. "Angelique Marie LeRoi is just perfect."

Rae sank back against the bed pillows, overwhelmed at how full of love she felt at that moment.

"Do you mind getting Trevor?" she asked.

"Naw." Sterling rose to his feet. "The man deserves to see his child. But I'm tellin' you now, Rae, we're gonna have to set some ground rules about how involved he gets…"

"I know, I know," Rae nodded her head. She knew Sterling and Trevor weren't exactly best friends yet, but they'd reached some sort of understanding. Trevor had been very respectful of Sterling of late. "Just go, would you?"

"Awright." Sterling walked out of the delivery room.

Jewel looked up from her magazine when Sterling walked into the waiting room. She appreciated how hard it must've been for Trevor not to jump out of his chair with excitement. She'd insisted on coming with him when Rae called to say she was in labor, but she wasn't sure now if she was ready to meet her husband's new daughter.

"She's gorgeous," Sterling said with a wide grin. "Come on in and see her."

"Coming, honey?" Trevor offered a hand to Jewel.

When she placed her hand in his, he squeezed tightly. She knew it was to reassure her, but Jewel couldn't help thinking that this was it.

This was the moment she would lose her husband forever. "I don't know, Trevor." She hesitated. "Maybe you should go in alone."

He pulled her into his arms and stared through her eyes straight to her soul. "I could, but it wouldn't be the same. Remember, we made a deal."

"What deal?"

"We wouldn't get married unless..." he prompted.

"Unless we promised to love each other forever," she completed.

"I've made mistakes, Jewel. Horrible ones. But have I ever broken my promise?" His voice was a hoarse whisper. "Have I, babe?"

His heartbeat was strong beneath her hand, and his eyes blazed with the intensity of his love. "No," she said as tears formed in her eyes. "You've never broken that promise, Trevor."

"Then trust that I will always love you. Come on in and share this with me."

Jewel nodded and let him lead her toward the delivery room. When they entered, they saw Rae beaming as she held the tiny bundle in her arms. She looked tired but happy as Sterling took a seat on the bed beside her. Somehow Jewel knew that she wouldn't be as happy if they were to switch places. She would've felt exactly as she did now—tense and jealous. She held her breath as Trevor took possession of the squealing little bundle.

There was no hiding his elation. His grin spread from one side of his face to the other as he simply gazed at the child with awe and wonder.

Jewel wanted to cry.

"Come over and see her, Jewel." Rae motioned her over.

She must've walked too slowly because Trevor met her halfway across the small room. "Wanna hold her?" he asked quietly.

Jewel waffled. "I don't know...she's so small."

"She didn't feel small when she was on her way out," Rae joked.

Trevor laid the baby in Jewel's reluctant arms.

To her surprise, she was warm and soft and light as a feather.

Just then, the child made a delightful little noise and opened her eyes. She seemed to stare straight into Jewel's heart and warm something inside.

Granny Glen had said it was easy to love a child. All it took was one look in their eyes, she'd said. It turned out she was right—just as she'd been about forgiving Trevor. He'd done nothing but fall all over himself for the past few months trying to make her happy. Lord knows she hadn't made it easy on him.

But here she was holding his child, the child she'd been dreading for years. "You're not so scary," she whispered to the cute impish face. "You're a miracle, Angelique Marie."

Jewel smiled. How hard would it be to be a good mother? Stepmother or otherwise? Even Eloise was managing to make a good show of it lately. She sought Trevor's eyes. "You do good work, Trevor St. John. She's beautiful."

He diverted the praise. "You're beautiful, Jewel."

When he put his arm around her and held her close, it was like the entire world had been set into place finally. And when he whispered, "I love you" in her ear, Jewel knew that she would never again worry about losing him. Never.

DISCUSSION QUESTIONS

1. What role did Glendora play in this story? Why did she feel the need to become involved in Eloise's and Jewel's personal lives?

2. Jewel is a successful businesswoman, but what was her fatal flaw?

3. What person in Jewel's life most influenced her views on love and relationships? Why?

4. What actions made Trevor's wife distrust him? Did he deserve Jewel's distrust? Why or Why not?

5. What feelings dictated Rae's actions in this story? What were her intentions when she pitched her proposal to Trevor?

6. What was the overriding theme in this story regarding trust in relationships?

NOTE FROM AUTHOR

This book was inspired by a conversation with an extraordinary woman who couldn't have a child but who supported her husband's desire to maintain a relationship with his child by another woman. I was intrigued that she'd made a conscious decision to accept and love the child, and her husband, through this difficult situation.

What became clear to me is that many of us have forgotten that we're all flawed and we need to forgive others for making mistakes—mistakes that are often made without bad intention. This book shows characters who've made mistakes, but who ultimately have to learn to get out of their own way in order to allow love to take hold and thrive.

ABOUT THE AUTHOR

T. T. Henderson was born and raised in Denver, Colorado. She currently resides in San Antonio, Texas. She became a fan of romance writing after attending a writer's conference in Colorado Springs in the early 90s. Her second year attending the conference, she won the Contemporary Romance category and was awarded the prize by the amazing best-selling author Nora Roberts. Ms. Henderson has written multiple romances (all with great reviews from readers and Romantic Times Magazine) while raising two children and a husband and maintaining a full time job at a Fortune 500 company.

Parker Publishing, LLC

Celebrating Black
Love Life Literature

Mail or fax orders to:

12523 Limonite Avenue Suite #440-438

Mira Loma, CA 91752

phone: (866) 205-7902 fax: (951) 685-8036 fax

or order from our Web site: www.parker-publishing.com

orders@parker-publishing.com

Ship to:

Name: _____

Address: _____

_____

City: _____

State: _____ Zip:_____

Phone: _____

Qty	Title	Price	Total

Shipping and handling is $3.50, Priority Mail shipping is $6.00 FREE standard shipping for orders over $30

Add S&H Alaska, Hawaii, and international orders – call for rates

CA residents add 7.75% sales tax

Payment methods: We accept Visa, MasterCard, Discovery, or money orders. NO PERSONAL CHECKS.

Payment Method: (circle one): VISA MC DISC Money Order

Name on Card: _____

Card Number: _____ ____

ExpDate: _____

Address: _____

_____

City: _____

State: _____ Zip:_____